The Replacement

BRENNA YOVANOFF

SIMON AND SCHUSTER

First published in Great Britain in 2010 by Simon and Schuster UK Ltd
A CBS COMPANY

First published in the USA in 2010 by Razorbill, an imprint of
the Penguin Group (USA) Inc.

Cover art by Nathália Suellen. Cover model: Pim Eissens.

www.brennayovanoff.com

Simon & Schuster UK Ltd
1st Floor
222 Gray's Inn Road
London WC1X 8HB

A CIP catalogue record for this book
is available from the British Library.

ISBN: 978-0-85707-505-5

1 3 5 7 9 10 8 6 4 2

Printed in the UK by CPI Cox & Wyman, Reading, Berkshire RG1 8EX.

www.simonandschuster.co.uk
www.simonpulse.co.uk

FOR DAVID
(The first one was always going to be for you)

PART ONE

SECRETS OF THE LIVING

CHAPTER 1

BLOOD

I don't remember any of the true, important parts, but there's this dream I have. Everything is cold and branches scrape the window screen. Giant trees, rattling, clattering with leaves. White rain gutter, the curtain flapping. Pansies, violets, sunflowers. I know the fabric pattern by heart. They're a list in my head, like a poem.

I dream about fields, dark tunnels, but nothing is clear. I dream that a dark shape puts me in the crib, puts a hand over my mouth, and whispers in my ear. *Shh*, it says. And, *Wait*. No one is there, no one is touching me, and when the wind comes in around the edges of the window frame, my skin is cold. I wake up feeling lonely, like the world is big and freezing and scary. Like I will never have anyone touch me again.

They were sticking students in the cafeteria, over by the trophy cases.

They'd hung a curtain to hide the blood-draw station, and it came down almost to the floor, but everyone knew what was behind it. Needles going in, tubes coming out. A butcher-paper banner was stretched over the west entrance, announcing the blood drive in giant Magic Marker letters.

We'd just come in from lunch. Me, the Corbett twins, and Roswell Reed.

Drew Corbett was digging through his pockets for a quarter to show me how he could fix a coin toss. It sounded complicated, but he had a way of taking any trick or sleight of hand and making it look easy.

When he tossed the quarter, it hung for a second and I was sure I could see it flip over, but when he showed me the back of his hand, it was still heads. He smiled a wide, slow smile, like we'd just exchanged a really good joke without either of us saying anything out loud. Behind us, his brother Danny-boy was in this ongoing argument with Roswell about whether or not the only local band that was any good could ever get radio play or score spots on late-night talk shows.

From far away, you could look at the twins and get the idea that they were the same person. They had the same long, brown hands, the same narrow eyes and dark hair. They were good at the same things, drawing and building and fixing stuff, but Drew was more relaxed. He listened better and moved slower. Danny was the one who talked.

"But look at what sells," Roswell said, raking a hand through his hair so it stood up in messy tufts, rust colored. "What makes you think that the same people who get all frantic for power chords would even appreciate a rarified talent like Rasputin Sings the Blues?"

Danny sighed and grabbed my arm. "Mackie, would anybody really take something that fundamentally sucks over something good?" He sounded impatient, like he already knew he was winning this one whether I backed him or not, so why were they still talking about it?

I didn't answer. I was looking at Alice Harms, which was a habitual behavior, kind of like a hobby.

Danny yanked harder. "Mackie, quit acting like a complete stoner and *listen*. Do you really think someone would pick the bad thing?"

"People don't always know what they should want," I said without looking away from Alice.

She had on a green shirt, cut low so it showed the tops of her breasts. There was a yellow blood-donor sticker stuck to the front of it. She tucked her hair behind one ear and the whole thing was sort of beautiful.

Except, I could smell the blood—sweet, metallic. I could taste it in the back of my mouth and my stomach was starting to feel iffy. I'd forgotten all about the blood drive until

I'd walked into school that morning and been greeted by the festival of hand-lettered signs.

Drew hit me hard on the shoulder. "Here comes your girlfriend."

Alice was crossing the cafeteria, flanked by two other members of the junior-class royalty, Jenna Porter and Zoe Beecham. I could hear the scuff of their sneakers on the linoleum. The sound was nice and reminded me of shuffling through dead leaves. I watched Alice but not in any really hopeful way.

Girls went for Roswell, not me. He was tall and knobby, with a wide, straight mouth. He was freckled in the summer, the hair on his arms was reddish, and he never got his sideburns even, but he was likable. Or maybe it was just that he was like them.

I was the weird one—pale, creepy. Blond hair might have been a strong point on someone else, but on me, it just made it harder to get away with how dark my eyes were. I didn't make jokes or start conversations. Sometimes, people got uneasy just looking at me. It was better to stay in the background. But now here I was, standing in the middle of the cafeteria, and Alice was coming closer. Her mouth was pink. Her eyes were very blue.

And then she was right in front of me.

"Hi, Mackie."

I smiled, but it felt more like wincing. It was one thing to look at her from across a room and think about maybe, possibly kissing her. It was another to have a conversation. I swallowed and tried to come up with any of the normal things people talk about. All I could think was how once I'd seen her in her tennis uniform last spring and her legs were so tan I thought my heart would stop.

"So, did you give blood?" she said, touching her yellow sticker. "You better tell me you gave blood." When she pushed her hair back from her face, I caught a flash of something silver in her mouth. She had her tongue pierced.

I shook my head. "I can't do needles."

That made her laugh. Suddenly, her hand was resting on my arm for no good reason. "Aw, that's so *cute*! Okay, fine, you're off the hook for being a huge pansy. So, are your parents all completely freaked out about the latest drama? I mean, you heard about Tate Stewart's sister, right?"

Behind me, Roswell took a sharp breath and let it back out. The twins had stopped smiling. I fumbled around for a way to change the subject but couldn't come up with anything on the spot.

The smell of blood was sweet and oozy, too thick to ignore.

I had to clear my throat before I answered. "Yeah. My dad's been pretty cut up about it."

Alice opened her eyes very wide. "Oh God, do you actually *know* them?"

"His dad's doing the service," Danny said in a flat voice. He and Drew had both turned away. When I followed their gaze, I saw they were watching Tate, who sat alone at one of the long tables, staring out the floor-to-ceiling windows at the sky.

I *didn't* know her. I mean, I'd gone to school with her my whole life, and she lived down the block from Drew and Danny, and I'd had at least one class with her every semester since junior high. But I didn't *know* her. I didn't know her sister either, but I'd seen them together in the parking lot at my dad's church. A chubby, smiling little kid named Natalie. Just this normal, healthy-looking kid.

Tate scraped back her chair and glanced in our direction. Her hair was dark brown and cut short, which made her face look strangely bare. From far away, she seemed small, but her shoulders were rigid as she stood up, like she was ready to take a punch. Until two days ago, she'd had friends. Maybe not the whispering, giggling, inseparable kind like Alice, but people had liked her.

Now there was an empty space around her that made me think of quarantine. It was unsettling to realize that it didn't take much to make you an outcast. All you needed was for something terrible to happen.

Alice didn't waste any time on Tate. She flipped her hair

over her shoulder and suddenly, she was standing much closer to me. "Just, you never think about little kids dying. I mean, that's so sad, right? My mom's kind of been going crazy with the saints medals and the Hail Marys since she heard. Hey, are you guys going to be around on Saturday? Zoe's having a party."

Roswell leaned in over my shoulder. "Cool. We might stop by. So you guys got suckered into the blood drive, huh?" He was looking at Zoe when he said it. "How was exsanguination? Did it hurt?"

Zoe and Jenna both started to nod, but Alice rolled her eyes. "Not really. Like, it hurt when she was putting the tube in—but it wasn't bad. It actually hurts more now. When she pulled the needle out, it kind of tore and now it won't quit bleeding. Look."

She held out her arm. There was a cotton wool ball taped to the inside of her elbow, covering the needle mark. In the middle, starting under the tape and spreading out through the cotton wool, there was a red splotch that grew and grew.

Iron is everywhere. It's in cars, kitchen appliances, and those big industrial machines they use to pack food, but most of it's mixed with other things, carbon and chromium and nickel. It hurts in a slow, exhausting way. I can take it.

The blood iron was different. It roared up through my mouth and nose, getting in my throat. Suddenly, it was hard to focus. My heart was beating very fast and then too, too slow.

"Mackie?" Alice's voice sounded thin and fuzzy, coming from far away.

"I have to go," I said. "My locker . . . I forgot this thing and I need to . . ."

For a second, I thought one or two or maybe all of them were going to follow me. Alice started to reach for me. Then Roswell put his hand on her arm and she stopped. His expression was tight, like he was pressing his lips together to keep from saying something. He jerked his head in the direction of the hall, just barely. *Just go.*

I made it through the maze of tables and out of the cafeteria without stumbling, but my vision was starting to tunnel and I could feel my heartbeat in my hands and in my ears. It was better once I got away from the sweet, suffocating smell of the blood drive. I took deep breaths and waited for the dizziness to ebb off.

The lockers in the junior hall all looked the same—five feet tall and painted a light, flaking beige. Mine was at the far end, past the hall to the math wing and the doors out to the courtyard. As soon as I came around the corner, I knew something was wrong with it.

On the locker door, at eye level, there was a red smear the size and shape of someone's palm. Even before I got close, I could smell the blood. It wasn't as bad as Alice's puncture wound. That had been warm, horribly metallic. This was cold and sticky, just starting to dry.

I looked around, but the hall was empty. The doors leading out to the courtyard were closed. It had been raining all day and there was no one on the grass.

The smear was a dark, gummy red, and I stood with my hands against my forehead. It was a joke, some kind of mean, stupid trick. It wouldn't be too much of a stretch to come up with it—you wouldn't have to guess. I am notorious for being the guy sitting on the ground with my head between my knees when someone gets a bloody nose.

It was a joke because it *had* to be. But even before I moved closer, I knew deep down that it wasn't. Someone had gotten creative with a paper clip or a key. They'd scratched the word *Freak* into the congealing mess.

I took my sleeve and scrubbed at it, feeling sick and out of breath. I got most of the blood off, but *Freak* stayed right there on the door. It was scratched into the paint and blood had settled into the letters so the word stood out dark against the beige enamel. Looking at it made the rush of static sweep in again. I backed away and almost fell. There was just my slow, stuttering heartbeat.

Then my hand on the wall, feeling for the door, the empty courtyard, the fresh air.

*

I was in kindergarten the first time my dad told me about Kellan Caury.

The story was short, and he told it over and over, like *Winnie-the-Pooh* or *Goodnight Moon*. When my dad told it, I could see the important parts like scenes from an old movie, flickering and grainy. Kellan Caury would be quiet and polite. A grown-up, maybe in his thirties.

He was like me. Mostly. Except that he had an extra set of joints in his fingers and I always pictured him in black and white.

He ran a music repair shop on Hanover Street and lived above it in a little kitchenette apartment. He couldn't tune pianos because he couldn't stand to touch the steel wires, but he was honest and fair and everyone liked him. His specialty was fixing violins.

When kids started to go missing, no one thought that much about it. It was the Depression, and no one had enough food or enough money, and kids were always disappearing. They got sick or ran away, or died from accidents or starvation, and that was too bad, but no one really got suspicious or asked that many questions.

Then the sheriff's daughter disappeared. This was in 1931, just before the end of October.

Kellan Caury had never hurt anyone, but it didn't matter. They came for him anyway.

They dragged him out of his little kitchenette apartment

and down into the street. They burned out his shop and beat on him with wrenches and pipes. Then they hung him from a tree in the churchyard with a bag over his head and his hands tied behind his back. They left his body there for a month.

The first time my dad told me this, I didn't get what he was trying to say, but by the time I was in first or second grade, I was already starting to understand.

The moral of the story is, don't attract attention. Don't have deformed fingers. Don't let anyone find out how amazing you are at tuning strings by ear. Don't show anyone the true, honest heart of yourself or else, when something goes wrong, you might wind up rotting in a tree.

Everyone has a point of origin. A place they come from.

Some people's places are just simpler than others'.

I don't remember any of this, but my sister, Emma, swears it's true and I believe her. This is the story she used to tell me at night, when I would climb out of bed and sneak down the hall to her room.

The baby in the crib: crying, in that anxious, fussy way. His face is shiny between the bars. The man comes in the window—bony, wearing a black coat—and grabs the baby up. He slips back out over the sill, slides the window down, pops the screen back in. Is gone. There's something else in the crib.

In the story, Emma's four years old. She gets out of bed and pads across the floor in her footie pajamas. When she reaches her hand between the bars, the thing in the crib moves closer. It tries to bite her and she takes her hand out again but doesn't back away. They spend all night looking at each other in the dark. In the morning, the thing is still crouched on the lamb-and-duckling mattress pad, staring at her. It isn't her brother.

It's me.

CHAPTER 2

NEVER TALK TO STRANGERS

Roswell found me in the courtyard. The two-minute bell had already rung and there was no one on the lawn to watch me. I was leaning against the building with my eyes closed, breathing in long gasps.

"Hey," he said, right next to me before I knew he was there.

I swallowed and opened my eyes. The sky was overcast, still raining that thin, dismal drizzle that was all wrong for October.

"Hey." I sounded hoarse and confused, like I'd been asleep.

"You don't look great. How are you feeling?"

I wanted to shrug and shake it off, but the dizziness rolled in and out in waves. "Pretty bad."

Roswell leaned against the wall and suddenly, I was sure that he was going to ask what happened or at least ask why I was hyperventilating alone in the courtyard. I wondered if he'd seen my locker.

I took a deep breath and cut him off before he could say anything. "Nothing like topping off a dead-baby story with some fresh blood."

He laughed and knocked his shoulder against mine. "Hey, she can't help that her brain is constantly misfiring. But I have to play nice with her if I'm ever going to have a shot at Zoe, and last names aside, she's mostly harmless. And I *know* you're not indifferent to those natural endowments, right?"

I laughed, but it sounded forced and kind of miserable. I still had a queasy feeling, like there was a chance I might throw up.

"Look," Roswell said, and his voice was unexpectedly low. "I know you don't talk to girls that much—I *know* that. But she would go out with you. I'm just saying, the opportunity is there if you want it, you know?"

I didn't answer. Alice was so incredibly, painfully hot, so perfect for watching from across the room, but the thought of actually going someplace with her made my chest feel tight.

The last bell rang, screeching out of the PA system on the roof, and Roswell stepped away from the wall. "Are you coming to history?"

I shook my head. "I think I'm just going to go home."

"You want a ride? I'll tell Crowley you had a family emergency or something."

"I'm fine."

The look he gave me was unconvinced. He ran a hand over his chin and stared out across the lawn. "I guess I'll catch up with you later, then. Are you going to be at the funeral?"

"Maybe. I don't know. Probably not."

He nodded. I nodded. We were both standing in the courtyard nodding but not really looking at each other. Sometimes Roswell asks very hard questions, but sometimes he has the decency not to. He didn't say anything else. He went back inside and I left through the outer gate.

I started feeling better once I got out of the parking lot, away from the school, the cafeteria full of needles, the clanging metal smell of blood. I put up my hood and stared at my feet, thinking, How are you ever going to get a girl-friend? And why would someone like Alice Harms even be interested in you anyway? And what a loser.

Still, she'd touched my arm.

The air was clean and damp, making my breath come easier. I felt cold, a little shaky, maybe, but I was okay. I felt okay. Still, I couldn't get rid of the nagging sense that things were about to get bad. At school. In the world. Alice's mom was saying Hail Marys and everyone was on edge, looking for the demon in their midst, looking for someone to blame. My whole body felt weak, like I was coming down with something.

One thing was clear: I needed to do whatever it took to avoid being noticed. The rain pattered steadily on the sidewalk, making me uneasy for no good reason. Maybe things were bad, but they were always bad. I was used to that. The real, fundamental problem was this feeling I had that they were about to get worse.

In another, earlier life, Gentry was a steel town, but over the span of four or five decades, it had turned into a sea of minivans and lawns and golden retrievers.

Almost everybody worked at one of the computer plants, assembling boards and packing chips, or else at the dairy farm or the junior college, depending on their level of education. There were plenty of other company towns in neighboring counties—suburbs with no city to spread out from, each with their own factory or tech plant to orbit around.

Gentry was just more self-contained than most. People were born and grew up and died without ever feeling compelled to leave. Everything you needed was already there.

The high school was built on the edge of what used to be the Gates refinery. For forty years, Gates had been the beating heart of Gentry, and a lot of local businesses and school mascots were still named after it. When Gates folded after World War II, first the machine shops and then the tech companies had come in with jobs, sponsored bridges and town squares, always deciding that Gentry was a better bet than the other eight or nine small towns in the immediate vicinity. They'd torn the refinery down before I was born.

Most people at school cut through the Gates property to get home. The residential areas were almost all on the other side of it, separated from the business district and the school by a narrow ravine. There was still all kinds of scrap and debris lying around in the grass, though, and the ground was saturated with iron. I always took a different route.

Now I walked along Benthaven, skirting the open field where the refinery had sat a lifetime ago, trying to figure out what had just happened. Someone had painted blood on my locker door. But the critical question was, *Why?* What had I done to make someone want to single me out? Why now?

Things always got tense around Gentry when kids died. Funerals were a bad subject, but I'd been careful. I'd been close to invisible. I'd done my part.

And Roswell and I had both known I wouldn't be at the service, but sometimes you have to play the game, even when there's no one else around. It puts you in the habit of pretending you believe what you're saying. When really it's just two people who know a secret, pretending that they don't.

Consecrated ground wasn't like stainless steel or blood iron. It wasn't something I could just deal with. If I went two feet inside the churchyard, my skin blistered the way other people get a bad sunburn.

There were parts of the property that weren't off-limits to me—storage sheds and the Sunday school addition and an unconsecrated section of the cemetery, reserved for suicides and unbaptized babies—but the idea of going into the churchyard just to stand in one corner of the cemetery and stare at the rest of it was depressing.

When I was younger, I'd gone to Sunday school. My dad had the classroom addition built on an adjoining lot when I was three or four. It was a reasonable expansion because they really did need the space, but he had an ulterior motive, too. He never consecrated the ground.

The new building had been a workable solution for a while, but now that I was too old for Bible classes, I had to settle for looking like that rebellious kid who didn't want anything to do with his pastor father.

I walked along Welsh Street until I came to the place where the road dead-ended. I stepped over the low concrete divider and started down the footpath toward the slag heap.

When the refinery was running, they'd just dump the gravel and quicklime into the ravine to get rid of it. It piled up for years, covered in skinny trees and clumps of weeds. It was the only part of Gates that still existed.

There were dump hills and slag heaps all over the county, but in Gentry, the elementary school kids never climbed the fences. Other towns' slag heaps were fenced for liability reasons. They were low and gray and not very interesting. Ours were so black they looked burned. They were fenced because it was better to stay away.

The stories people told were the campfire kind, possessions and hauntings. Grinning, rotting things that rose from the dead at night and walked around deserted streets. None of it was believable, but that was irrelevant. It didn't matter if the stories were just stories. You still didn't want to go there.

Partway down the side of the hill, the path split and followed a footbridge across to the other side of the ravine. A man was standing in the middle of the bridge, which was weird because it wasn't the kind of place grown-ups usually hung out. He was leaning on the railing, staring out with his chin in his hands. He looked familiar in a way I couldn't place.

I didn't really want to go any closer, but I had to walk past him to get home or else climb back up the hill and go all the way around to Breaker Street. I shoved my hands into the pockets of my jacket and stepped out onto the bridge.

"You look awful," he said as I came up next to him. It was a strange thing to say because it was rude and he was a stranger, but also because he wasn't looking at me.

He had on a long coat with frayed cuffs and military stripes sewed onto the sleeves. There was a row of holes down the front, like someone had cut the snaps out.

21

"Your eyes," he said suddenly, turning to stare at me. "Your eyes are black as stones."

I glanced back over my shoulder to make sure there was no one else on the path before I nodded. My eyes were always dark, but iron made it worse. The dizziness was nearly gone, although I still felt sweaty and pale.

The man leaned closer. The skin around his eyes was bruised, oily looking. His complexion was an unhealthy shade of yellow. "I could help you."

"I'm not an expert or anything, but you look like you need a little more help than I do."

That made him smile, which didn't improve his appearance. "My face is simply a result of my poor breeding, but you, my friend, are in bad shape. You need something to get you back on your feet." He pointed across the bridge to the other side of the ravine, my quiet suburban neighborhood and my house. "That way lies misery. It's what you're going home to, and I think you know it."

Rain pattered on the bridge. I glanced over the rail and down at the slag heap. It was so black that you could almost see other colors. My heart was beating harder than was comfortable.

"I'm not interested," I said. My mouth was dry.

He nodded gravely. "But you will be."

It didn't sound like a threat or a warning. His voice was flat. He took a watch out of his coat pocket and turned away from me, flipping the lid open but staring down at the slag heap.

After a minute, I edged past him, careful not to let our shoulders touch. I crossed to where the path climbed the other side of the ravine and came out at the intersection of Orchard and Concord. I kept going, trying hard to fight the panic in my chest. A small, fearful part of me was convinced he was following, he was coming up behind me, but when I turned back toward the bridge, there was nothing.

On Concord Street, all the houses were two stories high, with big wraparound front porches. Three houses down from ours, Mrs. Feely was out in her yard, nailing a horseshoe to the porch railing. Her hair was gray, arranged in tight poodle curls all over her head, and she was wearing a yellow rain slicker. She glanced over her shoulder and when she saw me, she smiled and gave me a wink.

Then she went back to nailing up the horseshoe, like the iron would protect her from something big and scary. I headed home, with the clang of her hammer following me down the street.

CHAPTER 3

HEARTBEAT

In the front hall, I dropped my book bag and yanked off my hoodie. There was blood all over the sleeve, and I debated just throwing it away, but I figured my dad would have something to say about that.

The laundry room was in a little alcove off the hall. I didn't like to go in there. The washer and dryer were both stainless steel and the room was so small that the air always had a dense, poisonous smell to it. For a minute, I considered running the washer anyway, but even just standing with the door open was making my pulse hammer in my ears. I wadded up the hoodie and made a mental note to ask Emma if she'd wash it for me. In scalding water. With bleach. Then I shoved it in the hamper and headed for the kitchen.

From the back of the house, I could hear the clack of the keyboard. My mom was in the office, tapping away at her computer.

"Mackie," she called, "is that you?"

"Yeah."

"Don't let your father catch you skipping class, okay?"

"Yeah, okay."

I got a glass of water and sat at the table, looking at the tablecloth and trying to figure out the plaid pattern. It went red, black, red, white, green, and then I lost track.

When Emma came in, I was so out of it that her hand on my shoulder made me jump. I started to ask about the laundry but stopped when I realized there was someone else with her. The second girl was tall and serious looking, with a long, bony face.

Emma got a jar of peanut butter from the pantry and took out a plastic picnic knife.

"Hey, ugly," she said, reaching to tousle my hair. "You're home early." She glanced across the hall at the office door, then said so quietly she was almost mouthing it, "Are you feeling okay?"

I wiggled my hand in a so-so gesture. "Aren't you supposed to be in botany?"

Emma was nineteen and not the kind of person who skipped class. She was taking every science course the junior college offered and her dedication was kind of scary.

"Professor Cranston gave us outside time to work on our group project." She waved her plastic knife at the other girl. "That's Janice."

Janice sat down across from me and folded her hands on the table. "Hi," she said. Her hair was muddy brown and hung in wild snarls on either side of her face.

I nodded at her but didn't say anything.

She was looking at me like I was a laboratory specimen, one of those bugs with the pins through it. Her eyes were huge and dark. "Why does she call you ugly?"

Other people could make pretty much any situation seem normal just by saying the right words. But I wasn't like that. I stared hard at the backs of my hands and waited for Emma to ride in and take over the conversation.

Emma, the master liar. Queen of my-brother-is-normal, my-brother-is-shy. My brother is sickly, has allergies, glandular fever, food poisoning, the flu, the biggest, messiest lie of all: *My brother.*

Reliably, she came up behind me and leaned her chin on the top of my head. Her hair was fine and limp. Stray pieces had come loose from the rubber band and hung down so they tickled my face. "When he was a baby, he was the ugliest thing you ever saw in your *life*. All yellow and wrinkly. And he had these *teeth*." She let me go and turned in the direction of the office. "A full set—right, Mom?"

"Just like Richard the Third," my mom called back.

Janice was still looking at me, crouched at the table like she was hungry. "Well, he's not ugly now."

"I'm going upstairs," I said, and pushed my chair back.

In my room, I lay on the bed but couldn't get comfortable. I felt restless, like little bugs were crawling around under my skin. The man on the bridge had been waiting for me—*me*, and not some random kid cutting across the bridge. He'd stared right into my face like he was looking for something. I was still cold and shaky from the blood, worse than I'd felt in a while and worse than I used to feel, ever.

Finally, I got up and went over to my closet. I got out my bass and my amp and plugged in the headphones.

The bass was strung with Black Beauties, and I'd pulled off the metal frets. If the song was fast, I used a pick, and when I didn't, the lacquer coating on the strings kept the steel from burning my fingers. But even if I had to play with bare strings, I'd probably do it anyway, just to get that low, humming sound, that feeling. Sometimes it's the only thing that helps. Anything that scares or worries you is suddenly a hundred miles away.

I played the lines to songs I knew and to songs I made up. I played progressions full of high, clear notes that hung forever and heavy tones that thumped and doubled back on themselves again and again and again.

After a long time, I started to get a strange feeling. Like someone was listening. Not the feeling of the house or even of Emma standing out in the hall. It was more like the warm, anxious rush of playing for a stranger. When I took the headphones off and went to the window, though, the backyard was empty. More time had passed than I'd realized and it was starting to get dark. I stared out at the lawn and the bushes, but it was ridiculous to think that someone had been listening. Completely ludicrous, when I was sitting there with the sound filtering through my headphones.

I sat back down on the edge of the bed with the Gibson propped across my knees and played a walking bass line that peaked and dropped and grew until I could feel it in my own heartbeat.

When I woke up a while later, someone was calling my name.

I rolled off the bed, untangling myself from cables and cords. I'd dozed off with my headphones on. From the floor, the amp hummed softly in the gloom and I felt hazy and numb. Outside, the sky was dark.

The house was very bright, which meant my dad was home. He has this thing for electric lights. If a switch can be flipped, he'll flip it. When I stepped out onto the landing, I had to shut my eyes against the glare.

"Malcolm," he called from the kitchen. "Come in here, please."

I went downstairs, blinking and shading my eyes with my hand.

He was at the table, and I could tell from his expression

and his necktie that he'd just gotten back from the church. From Natalie Stewart's funeral. His face was round and generally friendly, but right now it looked sort of raw. I wanted to ask about the service but didn't know what to say.

He was flipping through a pile of old sermons and making notes on them. His suit coat was slung over the back of a chair. He glanced up when I came in but didn't put his pen down. He looked tired and sort of exasperated, like he could hardly wait for the day to be over.

"Do you want to talk about why I got a call from the attendance office this afternoon?" he said.

"They had the blood drive at school . . ."

He watched my face, rolling the pen between his fingers. "Today wasn't a good day for doing things that could get you singled out. I'm assuming they announce something like that ahead of time?"

"I forgot," I said. "Anyway, it's not like it was some huge crisis."

"Malcolm," he said. "Your entire responsibility is not to *make* them see."

I stared down at the linoleum. "I didn't." After a second, I glanced back up at him. "I *don't*."

He arranged his sermons in a neat pile, lining up the edges. Then he got up and went to the counter. He got out a plastic knife and started using it to cut an apple into slices. I wanted to ask why he didn't just pick up the apple and eat it like a normal person, but everyone has their own private quirks.

After mangling the apple for a while, he threw the knife into the sink. It bounced like a pick-up-stick and snapped in half. "Why are there no paring knives in this house?"

"The good one's in the cupboard. Above the refrigerator," I said when he gave me a blank look.

My mother moves cutlery around like she's playing chess. Sometimes, she throws it out. Anything that can't be plastic or ceramic is aluminum. Anything that isn't aluminum, she hides.

He opened the cupboard, sorting through the pile of knives and stainless steel flatware, and took the paring knife back to the counter.

I watched his back as he sliced the apple. His shoulders were tight. He smelled like aftershave and this tense, sharp smell he gets when he's stressed out.

"I was thinking," he said without turning around. "Missy Brandt mentioned that it might be nice to have someone come in and help with the preschool class once in a while. Is that something you'd be interested in?"

I had a feeling that Missy *hadn't* mentioned it, that this was something he'd come up with on his own, and of course she'd said yes because what else can someone say when the minister asks you to babysit his sideshow of a son?

When I didn't answer, he glanced over his shoulder. "Is

something wrong? I thought it might be a good solution. This way, you have an official place in the congregation."

I dug my fingernails into my palms and tried to get my voice under control. "It's just so . . . *messed up*."

"Well, it might take you a few weeks to get used to being around little kids, but I think you'll do fine if you just give it a chance." He sighed, shaking his head. "That's the trouble with you and your mother. Both of you, you take a situation and start inventing obstacles right away. You never just give things a chance to get better."

So, we were back to the sticky politics of choosing sides. On one side, me and my mom—pessimistic realists, always. On the other side, my dad and Emma, glowing with all the ways the world could be good, and I couldn't just agree with them because I didn't really believe it. But I wanted to.

I picked at the tablecloth, then stopped because it was making me look uncertain, and that wasn't how I felt. I meant what I had to say to him. I just didn't want to say it. "Dad, this doesn't have anything to do with giving things a chance. This is just how it is and it's not going to magically get better. I'm not ever going to be able to just live my life like everyone else."

My dad turned toward the window so I couldn't see his face. "Don't say that again. None of this is because of you."

I leaned my head back and closed my eyes, feeling a deep, pulsing ache in the middle of my chest, like someone was hitting me. "It *is* because of me. You don't even treat me the same way you treat Emma."

That made him breathe out in a harsh gust, almost a laugh. "You're nothing like Emma. I try my best to figure out what *you* need, but it's hard. It's never been obvious with you, but that doesn't mean I don't try. That's all we can do, really—try to do the right thing."

I was about to tell him that the right thing was to go with what worked and not put me in charge of a bunch of little kids when Emma came in. She shuffled across the kitchen and opened the refrigerator. I stopped talking and my dad kept his back to both of us.

Emma rummaged through the vegetable drawer for a while, then looked at us. "You didn't have to be so rude to Janice," she said, and at first, I thought she meant me.

My dad set down the knife and turned to face her. "You know we have rules about unexpected guests."

We do have rules. We have a lot of rules. Roswell can come over, but only because my dad trusts him. A random acquaintance might be tipped off by our lack of canned food and metal kitchen utensils.

My dad raked his hands through his hair. "Both of you, *please*. This family is an extremely visible part of the community and we need to be conscientious about the image we're projecting."

Emma closed the refrigerator, hard. "What *image*? We

weren't embarrassing you. She was over so we could go through the seed experiment."

"Well, this isn't really the ideal place for a study session. Could you meet at the library, maybe?"

She put her hands on her hips. "Unfortunately, they have a policy about setting up germination trays at the library."

"Well, what about that nice little bookstore downtown? Or a coffee shop?"

"Dad!"

They glared at each other, but neither of them said anything.

They were the loud ones in the family, always shouting or laughing. I thought how strange it was that they were also the ones who'd perfected the art of a wordless argument. They could communicate just by the various ways they breathed in or out.

My dad made a huffing noise and Emma rolled her eyes and looked away.

She was standing against the refrigerator, staring at the floor. Suddenly, she leapt forward and hugged him around the waist like she was apologizing. They stood with their arms around each other and I knew that there'd never been any question about whether he'd hug her back.

She pressed her face against his shirt and said, "You better put that knife back when you're done. Mom hates it when the kitchen gets disarranged."

He laughed and turned to swat her with the dish towel. "Well, I certainly wouldn't want to disarrange her kitchen, would I?"

"Not if you know what's good for you."

She reached out to rumple my hair, but she was still looking at him. Then she turned and danced out of the room. He watched her go. They had an actual relationship—one I could never decipher or duplicate.

My dad left his mangled apple on the counter and sat down across from me. "I'm not trying to give you a hard time, but you know how important it is to keep a low profile."

"Some people pass out when there's blood. It's a known phenomenon."

He leaned down so that he was staring into my face. His eyes were pale green, like glass, and his hair was going from dishwater brown to gray. He had a way of seeming so good and so right when you didn't have to live with him, like anyone else could just go to him and find something warm and comforting there.

"*You* don't have the luxury of being like some people. You have to resemble the majority. I'm not saying they're bad, but this is a nervous, suspicious town, and it's going to be a lot worse for a while. A family buried their daughter today. You know that." Then his expression got softer. "*Did* you pass out?"

"No. I just had to go out and get some air."

"Did anyone see you?"

"Roswell."

My dad sat back in his chair, linking his hands behind his head, studying me. "Are you sure no one else saw you?"

"Just Roswell."

After a minute, he nodded. "Okay." He took a deep breath and said it again, like that decided something. "Okay. You're right—this isn't a crisis."

I nodded, looking at the floor and the shining granite counters. If you assessed our family dynamic based on just the kitchen, you would probably assume it was sitcom quality.

I leaned my elbows on the table like I was checking to see if it would take my weight. The smell of his aftershave was so strong that it kept getting in my mouth, making it hard to swallow. On the wall, the clock was ticking softly, inching toward eleven.

No. It wasn't a crisis. Except someone had scratched *Freak* on my locker door.

But there was no way to tell him about that. No way to make him understand that none of his rules and his safety measures mattered.

The word was still true.

CHAPTER 4

GENTRY AT NIGHT

Later, I lay facedown on the bed. The sounds of the house were familiar. Refrigerator, central air. The upstairs toilet that never quite stops running.

Downstairs, the front door opened and closed. Rustle of mail on the hall table, jingling keys. No scuffle of shoes. My mom wears white nurse's sneakers, rubber soled. Totally silent.

"Sharon," my dad called. It sounded like he was still in the kitchen. "Could you come here, please?"

My mom said something unintelligible. Must have been a *no* because a minute later, the shower came on. She always showers as soon as she gets home because her job is to splash around in blood. Because all day, she's been touching stainless steel.

I rolled onto my back and looked at the ceiling, the overhead light fixture. The way the fan spun, making shadows like dragonfly wings.

Finally, I pushed the window open and climbed out onto the roof.

From so high up, I had a view of the neighborhood and the backyard. I leaned forward and propped my elbows on the tops of my knees. The rain had stopped, but the sky was still spitting a fine, chilly mist.

Down in the street, there were motorcycles, fire hydrants, and parked cars. Trees lined up all the way along Wicker Street. The whole city reeked like iron, but under that, the green smell was alive and bright.

In the hall outside my room, someone was shuffling along, dragging their feet on the carpet. Then there was a knock, soft and cautious.

I rolled over and leaned in through the window. "Yeah?"

Emma opened the door. Her hair was twisted into a knot and she was dressed for bed, wearing her horrible fuzzy slippers. She climbed onto my bed and struggled out onto the roof. With her hands out for balance, she scooted down the slope on her butt so that she was sitting next to me on the wet shingles.

We looked out at the street and Emma leaned against me, resting her head on my shoulder.

I leaned my cheek against the top of her head. "So, you and Dad must've had a good one."

"Difference of opinion. His was that I was breaking a

cardinal rule, and in my opinion, he was acting like a crazy person. You kind of got the end of it. Sorry."

I shook my head. "He wasn't mad. He just wants me to be more inconspicuous. Because of that little kid today. Or because of Kellan Caury."

"Oh *God*, I wish he'd stop *talking* about that. Telling you antiquated horror stories is not helping anything."

I slid my fingers along the surface of the roof. The shingles were rough, full of galvanized nails. The burn was just painful enough to be distracting. "He didn't say it. It's just what he means. This girl at school—Tate. It was her sister."

Emma nodded and picked her head up off my shoulder. The air was cool. She shivered and hugged her elbows.

"It's hard for him." She wasn't touching me at all anymore, and her voice sounded strange. "It's hard for both of them. I guess that means it's supposed to be hard for me too, but I can't even feel it the right way, you know? You're the only brother I've ever had."

I stared at my socks. They were tarry from the shingles, stuck all over with little pieces of grit. "Could we please not talk about this?"

Emma took a deep breath and turned to face me. "I'm *tired* of not talking about it. Have you not noticed that everyone in this town is desperately committed to pretending that nothing is *wrong*?"

I nodded, but I had to resist an urge to point out that

sometimes it's just so much easier that way. I scraped at the shingles with my fingers and didn't say anything.

Emma crossed her arms over her chest. "You looked a lot like him."

I hunched my shoulders without meaning to. She was talking about the brother she should have had, and everything about him, even the little things, made me feel heavy and sort of numb.

She just went on in a soft, dreamy voice. "He was blond, I think, like you. I know that he had blue eyes because you did too, for a while. But then it was like the blue just wore out. Or trickled off or something. Maybe there was a spell or a charm, but it faded, and one day the blue was gone, and there you were."

"But you don't actually remember what he was like?"

Emma looked down at the backs of her hands, scowling like she was trying hard to picture something. "I was really young," she said finally. "I can't always tell the difference between before and after. I'll remember some detail and I can't even tell if I'm remembering him or you. The thing I remember best is a pair of scissors. Mom had a pair of scissors that she tied on a ribbon over the crib. They were pretty."

I thought about all the Old World superstitions. Tricks to guard the livestock and protect the house. It was obvious, more and more. They didn't work.

39

Emma sighed. "I guess I don't remember him at all," she said finally. "I just remember the things Mom did to keep him from being stolen."

She pulled one knee up so she could hook an arm around it. Her hair was starting to come down from the knot and she tugged at it, looking lonely and sad as a lighthouse. Sad as a nun.

I wanted to tell her that I loved her, and not in the complicated way I loved our parents, but in a simple way I never had to think about. I loved her like breathing.

She sighed and glanced over at me. "What? Why are you looking at me like that?"

I shrugged. The feeling was easy, but the words wouldn't come.

She looked at me a long time. Then she touched my cheek. "Good night, ugly."

She flopped headfirst through the window, landing on the bed with her feet sticking out over the sill. Her slippers were grimy from the shingles and I almost reached out and tweaked her ankle, but I didn't.

Below me, the neighborhood was sleepy and still. I leaned on my elbows and looked down into the street.

Gentry was two different things, and at night, I could always see that second thing better. The town was its green suburban lawns, sure, but it was also its secrets. The kind of place where people double-checked the locks at night or pulled their kids closer in the grocery store. They hung horseshoes over their front doors and put up bells instead of wind chimes. They wore crosses made from stainless steel instead of gold because gold couldn't protect them from people like me.

Maybe the brave ones buried quartz and agate in their gardens or left a saucer of milk out for luck—a little back-yard offering for whatever might be waiting in the shadows. If someone called them on it, they'd shrug or laugh, but they didn't stop doing it because hey, we lived in a place where people kept their porch lights on and didn't smile at strangers. Because when they set out a few pretty rocks with their marigolds, early snow never took the branches off their trees and their yards looked nicer than other people's. Because mostly, more than anything, night was about shadows and missing kids, and we lived in the kind of place where no one ever talked about it.

After a long time, I climbed back into my room and got into bed. I left the window open so I could breathe. The house wasn't bad, but still, it was hard to sleep with the air smelling like screws and brackets and nails.

When the breeze came in, I shivered and crawled deeper under the covers. Crickets were shrieking out in the yard, and the trees creaked against each other. Down by the road, in the tall stands of grass, there were mice rustling, night birds chirping away like spinning gears.

I put my pillow over my head to shut out the sound. The noises from the yard were muffled, and I wondered if this was what things sounded like to Roswell. To anyone who wasn't me. He could walk into class and not get distracted by the rustle of paper or the ventilation system. I had to remember not to flinch when someone closed a door or dropped a book, in case the sound hadn't been loud enough to startle anyone else.

This was life in Gentry—going to school every day, blending into a world where everyone was happier to ignore the things that didn't fit, always willing to look away as long as you did your part.

Otherwise, how could they go on living their neat suburban lives?

Maybe it wasn't that hard. Kids died. They got sick and then sicker, and no one could figure out what was wrong. Someone somewhere lost a son or daughter. Maybe they measured pollution or blamed it on the groundwater. Lead, maybe, or toxic seepage from the slag heap.

Natalie Stewart was just another casualty, buried in the Welsh Street graveyard with my dad standing over her, and that was a sad thing. I knew the script, the normal responses, but when I tried to feel some kind of sorrow or grief, even the polite kind, I just saw Tate sitting alone in the cafeteria. And when I thought of her there, the feeling I got wasn't sadness, it was loneliness. When I pictured the circle of empty seats around her, I wasn't mourning for her sister. It was just the same dull ache I felt every day.

The simple truth is that you can understand a town. You can know and love and hate it. You can blame it, resent it, and nothing changes. In the end, you're just another part of it.

CHAPTER 5

THE SCARLET LETTER

Friday was chilly and gray. The blood-draw station had been cleared away, but I was still feeling kind of rickety and made it a point not to go in the cafeteria. In the atrium at the main entrance, rain coursed down the windows so that the glass looked like it was melting.

I spent the morning avoiding things. Crowds and conversations and anyone who might ask me why I was wandering around like a zombie—so, mostly Roswell—but by fourth hour, I was running out of excuses for my lack of school supplies and had to go by my locker. It wasn't something I was looking forward to.

Freak was gone, though. Instead, there was a weird spiral pattern, covered in thin, snaking lines. The paint had been scraped away in a kind of spiderweb, leaving a network of bare metal that radiated out from what had been one accusatory word inlaid with blood. Some of the areas had been shaded in, black in places and a thick lumpy white in others.

"We fixed your locker," Danny said, coming up behind me.

Drew nodded and held up a marker and a bottle of Wite-Out.

I studied the tangle of spirals and circles. At the outer edge of the design, correction fluid had been carefully applied over the marker, then scratched away so the ink showed through in ghostly corkscrews. For a project limited by preexisting vandalism and involving only Sharpie and Wite-Out, it was nice work.

Danny leaned his elbow on my shoulder. "We weren't trying to squash your personal expression or anything. We just thought it might be a bad move to brand yourself too aggressively too early. It might, I don't know, set the wrong *tone*."

They both looked resolutely blank, like they were trying not to look too pleased with themselves. Drew was tossing the bottle of Wite-Out in the air and catching it again. They stood on either side of me and waited for my reaction.

I wanted to do something to show how relieved I was, how grateful, but all I said was, "Thanks."

Danny punched me. "Don't thank *us*. You're the one who owes the school sixty bucks to get it repainted."

If it hadn't been obvious yesterday, Tate Stewart was the new point of interest. She stalked through the halls, past clusters of people who whispered behind their hands. Their glances weren't the sideways glances of sympathy, but quick, furtive stares, full of curiosity.

They spent whole passing periods watching her and, at the same time, pretending not to. It didn't seem to matter. She moved through the crowd like she was alone. Like the gossip and the stares couldn't touch her. Her eyes were closed off, her expression was remote, but something about the set of her mouth made me feel sorry. She didn't look sad, which made everything a hundred times sadder.

The thing about Tate was, she didn't have any real interest in what people thought. She never tried to impress them or make them like her. Once, in seventh grade, she joined the boys' baseball team, even though the baseball team sucked, just to prove that the athletics department couldn't stop her.

As the morning went on, though, her mouth got thinner. There was a strange feeling coming off her, almost an electric charge. It hung in the air, like she was getting ready to explode, but things didn't really hit the fan until English.

We were finishing the unit on Romanticism and *The Scarlet Letter*. Mrs. Brummel was tall and thin, with bleached hair and a lot of different sweaters. She got very excited about the kind of literature that no reasonable person would ever read for fun.

She stood at the front of the room and clapped because

she was always clapping. "Okay, today we're going to talk about guilt and how Pearl's very existence condemns Hester more effectively than the *A*. This is most obvious in the fact that some of the villagers believe Pearl is the child of the devil."

Then she wrote it on the board: *Pearl as a concrete manifestation of guilt*.

"Does anyone want to expand on this?"

No one did. In front of me, Tom Ritchie and Jeremy Sayers were flicking a paper football back and forth, mock cheering each time one of them got it between the uprights of the other one's hands. Alice and Jenna were still watching Tate, whispering and then covering their mouths like they'd just said something so shocking it needed to be contained and giving each other significant looks.

Mrs. Brummel was making bullet points with her back to us, waiting for someone to start filling them in.

I watched Alice. When she'd taken her seat at the beginning of class, her skirt had slid up far enough to show the tops of her thighs, and I was enjoying the fact that she hadn't adjusted it yet. Her hair was loose down her back and looked almost like bronze in the fluorescent light.

She propped her elbows on her desk and leaned forward so she could whisper into Jenna's ear. "I heard that her mom won't get out of bed since it happened. Like, not even for the *funeral*. I can't believe she's acting like nothing's wrong. *I* just wouldn't even come to school."

Apparently, that one was loud enough for Tate to catch some or possibly all of it because she stood up fast enough to send her desk screeching along the floor. Her gaze was hard, sweeping over us, and I couldn't tell if I was dizzy from the screws and wires in the walls or from the way she was looking at me.

"Oh," she said, in a clear, challenging voice. "Was this what you wanted? Did you want a good look? Take a good look—*I* don't mind."

And maybe no one had really been excited about Hester Prynne and her illegitimate daughter, but they were paying attention now. I kept my head down, hunching over my desk, trying to get smaller. My heart was beating so fast that I could feel it in my throat and I kept telling myself that everything was fine, that I'd imagined she'd looked at me, because I had to believe that. I had to believe that no one in Gentry would ever hear the words *child of the devil* and then look at me.

No one said anything.

The room was so quiet that all I could hear was the buzz of the fluorescent light. I had the idea that it was buzzing right over me, like some kind of signal or alarm, but no one turned to stare accusingly. No one whispered or pointed.

Mrs. Brummel stood with her back against the white-board and the marker uncapped in her hand, staring at Tate. "Is there something you needed?"

Tate shook her head and kept standing. "Don't mind me. I'm just waiting for my big red *A*."

"This isn't funny," Mrs. Brummel said, putting the cap back on the marker.

"No," said Tate. "It's not. But we can all agree to smile anyway because it just makes things so much easier."

Mrs. Brummel retreated behind her desk and waved a box of tissues, even though Tate wasn't crying. "Do you need some time to pull yourself together?"

"No. Because I'm not unbalanced or grief stricken, okay? I'm pissed off."

"Would you like to go down to the counseling office?"

"No, I'd like someone to fucking listen to me!" Her voice was loud, unnaturally shrill. Suddenly, she hauled back and kicked the desk so hard that the whole room seemed to ring with the metallic clang of her work boot.

"You're excused," Mrs. Brummel said, but not in that wispy, understanding voice that teachers sometimes use. Her tone was no-argument, like if Tate didn't go, there was a chance that she would be escorted out by the school rent-a-cop. For a second, Tate looked like she might hold out for forcible removal. Then she grabbed the books off her desk and walked out without looking back.

The rest of the class sat in awkward silence. I held on to the corners of my desk to keep my hands from shaking, and Mrs. Brummel did her best to wrench us back to Nathaniel Hawthorne and Hester's big stupid dilemma until the bell rang.

Out in the hall, Roswell was just being dismissed from his math class and he swung into step beside me. "Ready for some conversational French?"

I shook my head and started in the direction of the back parking lot. "I need some air."

He looked at me like he was trying to figure out how to phrase something. "I think you should go to French," he said finally.

"I can't."

"You mean, you don't *feel* like it."

"I mean, I can't."

He folded his arms and suddenly looked a lot bigger. "No, you mean you just don't feel like it. Semantically, it's possible."

I pulled my sleeve down over my hand and reached for the door. "I have to go outside," I said, and my voice was low and unsteady. "Just for a little while. I really need some air."

"No, you need to tell me why you look like stone-cold death. Mackie, what is *wrong*?"

"I hate this," I said, and my voice sounded tight. "I hate

the way people are always fixating on things that aren't any of their business. I hate that no one can just leave it *alone*. And I *hate* Nathaniel Hawthorne."

Roswell shoved his hands in his pockets, looking down at me. "Okay. Not what I was expecting."

He didn't follow me.

I stood on the far side of the parking lot and leaned against one of the biggest white oaks, letting the rain filter down between the leaves and land on my face. The bell rang and I stayed where I was, numb and breathing too fast because I wasn't always the best student when it came to doing the reading, but I knew the book enough to know that maybe Hester goes around with a big red *A* pinned on her dress, but Dimmesdale's the one with it burned into his skin. He's the one who dies.

Behind me, there was the rough idle of a car and then a voice said, "Hey, Mackie."

Tate had pulled up next to the curb in this absolute monstrosity of a Buick and was leaning across the front seat. Apparently, she'd decided she was done with school for the day. Or, more likely, done being a public spectacle. She put her hand on the edge of the passenger window. "The rain isn't going to stop. Do you want a ride somewhere?"

The car sat idling against the curb, its wipers flicking back and forth. Long primer-gray body, poisonous fenders.

It made me think of a wicked metal shark. "That's okay. Thanks, though."

"Are you sure? It's not a problem."

I shook my head, watching the rain drip in a wavering curtain off the front bumper so I wouldn't have to look at her.

Her face was softer and younger looking than normal. I stood under the dripping oak and debated complimenting the way she'd faced down Mrs. Brummel, just to have something to say—tell her I was impressed by the way she could be sad and stared at and still tell everyone to go straight to hell.

After a minute, she killed the engine and got out of the car. "Listen. I need to talk to you."

When she came across the grass to me, she had this look on her face, like out in the parking lot, in the open, she wasn't so sure of herself after all. Like maybe I scared her. Her mouth had a bruised look. Her eyes were blue underneath, like you get from not sleeping.

When she came up next to me, she turned so we were standing side by side, staring out at the parking lot. The point of her elbow was inches from my sleeve.

"Do you have a minute?"

I didn't answer.

"Jesus, why don't you ever *say* anything?" She turned and stared up at me with her teeth working on her bottom lip.

It looked raw, like she'd been chewing it a lot. Even reeking like iron from the Buick, she still smelled crisp and kind of sweet. It made me think of flowering trees or something you want to put in your mouth. The kind of smell you shouldn't notice about girls who are covered in tragedy and Detroit steel.

"You weren't at the funeral yesterday," she said.

Between us, the current seemed to hum louder. I nodded.

"Why? I mean, your dad seems like he'd be all about 'pulling together as a community,' and considering he pretty much organized the whole thing . . . And, I mean, Roswell was there."

"Religion is my dad's business," I said, and my voice had a flat, mechanical sound that showed me for what I was—a bad liar reciting someone else's lie. "Anyway, a funeral isn't really an ideal social event. I mean, it's not like I would attend one for fun or anything."

Tate just watched me. Then she folded her arms tight across her chest, looking small and wet. Her hair was plastered against her forehead. "Whatever. It's not like it matters."

"You're taking it really well."

Tate took a deep breath and stared up at me. "It wasn't her."

For a second, I didn't say anything. Neither of us did. But we didn't look away from each other. I could see flecks of

53

green and gold in her eyes and tiny spots so deep and cool they looked purple. I realized that I hadn't really looked at her in years.

She closed her eyes and moved her lips before she spoke, like she was practicing the words. "It wasn't my sister in that box, it was something else. I know my sister, and whatever died in that crib, it wasn't her."

I nodded. I was cold suddenly, goose bumps coming up on my arms in a way that had nothing to do with the rain. My hands tingled and started to go numb.

"So, are you just going to stand there looking like a piece of furniture?"

"What do you want me to say?"

"I don't want you to *say* anything—I want someone to listen to me!"

"Maybe you should talk to a school counselor," I said, looking at my shoes. "I mean, that's what they're there for."

Tate stared up at me and her eyes were wide and hurt and, for the first time, full of tears. "You know what? Fuck you."

She crossed the lawn to her car and swung herself into the driver's seat. She slammed the door, wrenched the transmission into reverse, and backed out onto the road.

After she'd made it all the way down Benthaven and disappeared around the corner, I let myself slump against the oak tree, sinking to a crouch with my back against the trunk.

I barely felt the rain as it ran down my forehead and the back of my neck.

I hadn't given away my secret because I didn't even know how to say the secret out loud. No one did. Instead, they hung on to the lie that the kids who died were actually their kids and not just convincing replacements. That way, they never had to ask what had happened to the real ones. I had never asked what happened to the real ones.

That was the code of the town—you didn't talk about it, you didn't ask. But Tate had asked anyway. She'd had the guts to say what everyone else was thinking—that her true, real sister had been replaced by something eerie and wrong. Even my own family had never been honest enough to come right out and say that.

Tate had made herself a loner and an outcast when I was the one who was supposed to be the freak. I'd shied away like she might infect me, but she was just a girl trying to get a straight answer from the most obvious source.

And yes, I *was* obvious. When it came down to basic facts, I was weird and unnatural, and the game only worked as long as everyone else agreed not to see. If you took all the kids in school and lined them up, it was clear that I was the one who didn't belong. I was the disease. I crouched under the dripping tree and covered my head with my hands.

I'd treated her like shit because I'd had no choice. This was how the game went, and when you got down to it, what mattered most was staying out of sight. Everything else was secondary. There was no way to fix what I'd done, no way to take it back, because it was just me.

"I'm sorry," I said to the pale, drizzly sky and the dying grass and the tree. To the empty parking lot and my own shaking hands.

CHAPTER 6

FRIDAYS AT STARLIGHT

When Roswell picked me up after dinner for our weekly trip downtown to see the showcase of local bands, we didn't talk much. I stared out the passenger window while he messed around with the radio, trying to find something he liked.

Finally, he switched it off. "So, are you going to tell me what's wrong?" His voice sounded loud in the silence.

"What?"

He didn't look away from the road. "You're not too chipper tonight is all."

I shrugged and watched the strip malls go by. "Tate Stewart is . . . It's just, she freaked out in class today. She wanted to talk to me, and I don't know what to say. Her sister *died*—she needs a professional." And because those things were true but not the whole truth, I told him something else, so hoarse and low it was almost a whisper. "Roz, I don't feel good. I haven't felt good in a long time."

Roswell nodded, tapping his palms on the steering wheel in four-four time.

"What's it like?" he said suddenly. "Being—you know."

He made it sound so easy, like he was asking about hemophilia or having double-jointed thumbs. It took me a second to realize I'd stopped breathing. It was hard to describe something you weren't supposed to talk about. And yeah, maybe my dad liked to call it *uncommon*—this neutral, sanitary word—but I could tell sometimes, just by the look on his face, that what he really meant was *unnatural*.

Beside me, Roswell was still ticking his fingers against the steering wheel. Finally, he rolled his head to the side and looked at me.

He wasn't stupid. I knew that. He'd known me pretty much my whole life, so it wasn't like I thought I was fooling him. The thing that kept me mute was the chance that if I said it out loud, he'd look at me differently. Maybe it wouldn't be obvious—he'd try not to let it show—but the difference would be there.

And that was bad enough, but stranger, deeper was the fear that nothing would change at all. He might just shrug and carry on like always, which was somehow worse. The truth was an ugly thing, and I couldn't stand the possibility that he might be okay with it when it *wasn't* okay.

He was quiet, watching me in the pauses at stoplights, waiting for an answer.

I rolled down the window and stuck my head out, letting the rain splash against my face. I knew that if I opened my mouth, I'd tell him. The cold air was helping, a little, but under the car's fiberglass quarter panels, the frame was carbon steel and I was starting to feel sick. It was getting worse.

Roswell let out his breath in the long, pressurized sigh that meant he had something on his mind. "I've been thinking," he said after a minute. "This is totally not scientific, and maybe it's not even my business—but do you think you might be depressed?"

I looked down at my hands and then I made fists. "No."

I knew what it looked like. Lately, I was a mental-health pamphlet, answering questions in monosyllables, avoiding strenuous activities, sleeping too much. I wanted to tell him that it wasn't as bad as it seemed. I was just doing my part, playing invisible. That when you're tired all the time and you have to keep your sleeves pulled down over your hands so you don't accidentally touch a handle or a doorknob and a good day is defined by the fact that no one noticed you exist, that's pretty depressing. But it's not clinical.

The Starlight music hall had been a movie theater in the fifties and a regular theater before that. The building was three stories of chalky stucco, trimmed around the windows and the roof with spirals of wrought iron, but now it was rusting like everything else, leaving stains that ran down the front of the building like dried blood. We got in line and gave the bouncer two dollars apiece.

Inside, the crowd was pushed up close to the stage. The old curtain still hung over the stage in huge velvet swags. There were plaster columns along the walls, and the molding around the ceiling was carved with birds and flowers and leaves. Dollhouse of Mayhem was on, yelling about corporate incentives and the government. Their lead guitar sounded like what would happen if someone wedged a traffic accident into a blender. The whole place smelled like rusting iron and spilled beer, and the bad, shaky feeling that had been looming all day broke over me in an ugly wave.

Roswell was saying something very analytical about the music scene at any given time being a barometer for civil unrest, but his voice was fading in and out, and my mouth was full of too much saliva.

"And then you get these bands like Horton Hears," Roswell said. "I mean, no one would accuse them of being socially proactive, but—"

I knew suddenly that I was going to throw up and not in some distant, abstract future, but now, right now. I put up a hand to say *hold that thought* and went for the bathroom.

Crouched in a doorless stall, I tried to puke over the

toilet without actually kneeling on the floor, which was pretty disgusting.

Behind me, Roswell stood in the doorway. "Another day in the glamorous life of Mackie Doyle?"

His voice sounded easy and fake, and I got an idea that he was trying to counteract the moment. That he just didn't know what else to do. My whole life, I'd been able to count on him to just look the other way and pretend really hard that everything was normal.

Afterward, I stood at the sink, rinsing and spitting. There was a heavily graffitied mirror above the counter and I tried not to watch myself through the web of black marker. Behind the illegible scrawls, my face looked pale and shocked. I couldn't help thinking about Natalie. The fact that a body had been buried under her name when maybe it wasn't even the real body made me feel like I might pass out.

"You're shaking," Roswell said. He stood against the counter while I washed my face and avoided looking at my reflection.

I nodded and turned off the faucet.

"You're shaking really bad."

I wiped my mouth with a paper towel and didn't look at him. "It'll stop soon." My voice sounded hoarse, almost a whisper.

"This isn't funny," he said. "Do you think you should

maybe go home? If you went easier on yourself, maybe—"
Then he just stopped talking.

I jammed the paper towel in the trash and reached for
another.

He came up behind me. "Mackie—Mackie, look at me."

When I turned to face him, he was staring down at me.
His eyes were blue, which faded and changed in different
kinds of light. I wished that mine were any color but flat,
unnatural black.

"You don't have to go around acting like you're okay all
the time."

"I *do* have to." It came out too loud, echoing against the
tile walls. I leaned against the counter and closed my eyes.
"Please—I need to not talk about it."

After a second, he moved closer, and then I felt his hand
on my shoulder. It was unexpected, but the weight was reassuring, making me feel solid.

When I opened my eyes, Roswell was still standing next
to me, but he'd let his hand fall. After a minute, he took out
a pack of gum. He popped a square through the back foil
with the ball of his thumb, offered it to me, and I took it.

"Come on," he said, turning for the door. "Let's go find
Drew and Danny."

The twins were in the lounge by the bar, playing pool
with Tate. Roswell went over to them, but I hung back. Tate
was standing with her back to me and I needed to seem like

nothing had happened between us. Like I had never stonewalled her in the parking lot and then watched her walk away.

If I'd thought she would make a big show of being pissed at me, I was wrong. She glanced at us once, then went back to running the table. She made a straight shot. Not difficult, but she made it look impressive and tricky. Her hair was standing up all over the place like she'd just gotten out of bed. Mostly, she looked calm, not like a person who had just buried her sister and definitely not like a person who sought out the weirdest guy in school in order to discuss the theory that what they'd buried was not her sister at all.

The next shot was fancier, a corner shot, and she sank it like a rock. The ball clanged hard in the pocket, but her expression never changed.

"Nice," Roswell said as we came up to the table.

She jerked her head at Drew and Danny. "Yeah, well, these guys suck."

Drew just shrugged, but Danny snorted and flicked a crumpled piece of paper at the back of her head. "Get screwed, Stewart."

I stood slightly behind her and watched as she lined up the next shot. Compared to the others, it was nothing, but she jerked at the last second and the ball went spinning off in a crooked arc. It just kissed the bumper, then sat balanced at the edge of the pocket.

Danny punched her shoulder, but he was grinning. "Wait, *who* sucks again?"

She tossed the cue at him. "Yeah, yeah, yeah. I'm going to get a Coke."

Drew came up next to me, looking uncommonly cheerful. "We're getting close with the Red Scare. We just got a whole bunch of parts we bought off the Internet, and I think some of them are even the right ones this time. We almost stayed home to work on it."

Mrs. Corbett was an antiques dealer, which was a politically correct way of saying that she collected a lot of junk. The twins had been picking through her back stock since they were little, taking apart old toasters and radios, then putting them back together. The Red Scare had been their ongoing project for the last six months. It was a 1950s polygraph machine and didn't work. I didn't like to be a pessimist, but despite what Drew said, it was probably never going to work.

A low half wall ran around the outside of the lounge and I leaned against it and looked out over the crowd. On the floor, people were moshing. They slammed into each other, churning in circles, crashing together and pulling apart again. Watching it made me feel tired. I leaned forward so the top of my head rested on the wall and closed my eyes.

"Why did you even come out tonight?" Roswell said

from somewhere above me. His voice was almost buried under the music.

I took a long breath and tried to sound at least marginally energetic. "Because it was better than the alternative."

"Yeah," Roswell said, but he said it like it was the stupidest thing he'd ever heard.

When I straightened up and looked out over the crowd again, I saw Alice. She was standing with some girls from one of the newer subdivisions.

I leaned my elbows on the half wall and watched her. The light on her face was nice.

Onstage, Dollhouse of Mayhem finished their set, bowing off in a way that was probably supposed to be ironic. The silence when they unplugged their amps was so heavy that it made my teeth hurt. I just concentrated on Alice and the colored lights.

According to Roswell, I had a shot with her. But even if that was true, having a shot was different from knowing how to take it. She was a bright spot at the center of things, while I was destined to spend house parties and school dances standing against the wall with the guys from the Latin club. Except even that wasn't the right way to describe what I was.

Roswell was in the Latin club, and the debate club, and the honor society. He did things like collecting bottle caps and unusual pens. In his spare time, he built clocks out of various household materials, and it wasn't the big, defining core of him. He played soccer and rugby and ran in all the school elections. He smiled. He hugged everyone, all the time, and never acted like there was even a chance someone wouldn't like him. He could do what he wanted, hang out with anyone he wanted to and get away with it. When he talked to girls, even pretty, popular ones like Zoe Beecham, they smiled and giggled like they couldn't believe he was actually noticing them. He just took it for granted that everything would be okay, while I found a convenient wall and worked hard at disappearing.

Above us, the curtains opened again and Rasputin Sings the Blues came on.

The Starlight always had at least five bands on the bill, but everyone knew that Rasputin owned the stage. Everybody else just got to use it once in a while.

It wasn't only that other bands couldn't compete with the stage act and the magic tricks. When Rasputin played, the music was just *better*. When they covered a song, it was like their version of it was the only *real* version.

The lead singer, Carlina Carlyle, strutted onstage with her hair piled in a knot on top of her head. She was wearing a dark-colored dress with a high collar. It looked old-fashioned, except that the skirt was short enough to show her knees, along with about six inches of thigh.

She grabbed the microphone, striking a cool, superhero

pose. Her eyes were huge and too-light blue, black smeared around the lids, making her look crazy.

They were covering a Leonard Cohen song. The riff was hard and tight and the drums thumped like someone's aching heart.

Drew came up to the half wall and leaned next to me, looking out at the pit like it was the most boring thing. "I'm so freaking sick of Leonard Cohen," he said. "Man, do you have any idea how cool it would be if they did 'Head Like a Hole' or maybe some Saliva or Manson? Or the Gutter Twins."

Onstage, Carlina was singing *repent* over and over, not like the backup girls on the album track, but snarling it, screaming with her head thrown back. Down in the pit, the crowd was screaming back at her, pounding their fists at the ceiling in time to the beat. Leonard Cohen could be just as hard as Reznor or Manson if you did it right.

They launched into an original track called "Formula for Flight" and Carlina took a cigarette from behind her ear. The first lyric was *Burning towers down / Sleeping underground*. She stuck the filter in the corner of her mouth, sending the audience into a riot.

Over by the other end of the stage, Alice was laughing with Jenna and Zoe and some of the other hot girls. They were all wearing bright tank tops and tight jeans. When they danced, they seemed to move in unison, like they'd agreed on the steps ahead of time.

Onstage, the bassist stopped picking the line and stepped into the spotlight, reaching into his pocket for a handful of matches. The clips on his braces caught the light like mirrors.

"Light her up!" yelled someone from the crowd.

He saluted and stuck a match between his teeth, lighting it with an easy flick, then holding it out. Carlina put one hand against her collarbone and closed her eyes, bending to the match. He dropped it.

He lit the second one by striking it on his shirt cuff, but when Carlina leaned in, it went out by itself. The third, he didn't strike on anything, just snapped his fingers and it flared to life.

He held it to Carlina's cigarette and she breathed in, making the flame waver and gutter. She started to pace back and forth and the lead guitarist followed her, playing a solo that made me think of cracked glass and scrambled wires. He was wearing a black top hat and the shadow of the brim made his face look hard and hungry.

In back, the drummer still kept the tempo, but every time Carlina threw her hips to the side, he'd add a hard double beat on the bass drum. If she arched her back, that got the snare, a sharp rat-a-tat. I was utterly focused on her progress, and so was every other guy in the audience.

She stood in the spotlight while the guitar player circled around her, panting like a dog. She winked and put the cigarette out on his tongue. The whole time, he kept up that same complicated progression, and in the pit, the punk rock kids were slamming like it was the end of the world.

Carlina gripped the microphone and sang the bridge, *Going low, going down, going to burn the spires / No one in this sleepy town wants a race of monsters.*

Behind her, the guitarist spit out a mouthful of ash, making the solo climb. When the crowd stopped thrashing and started screaming for him, he raised his head, smiling up into the spotlight like he'd just found sunshine.

The chill started at the top of my head and poured down through my chest and arms. I knew him.

The angle of the stage made it hard to see his eyes, and the top hat shadowed his face, but even in the dark, I knew him. I'd seen him on the footbridge. He'd called me out on my dark eyes, sneered at my shaky hands and my blue mouth.

I stood in the crowd, looking up at a scary man with a scary smile.

I knew his secret and he knew mine.

After the Rasputin set, they tore their equipment down, and Concertina came on. The lead singer's voice was decent, but their arrangements were sloppy, with too much distortion, and without the expert stage presence of Carlina Carlyle, the Starlight was back to being dusty and run-down. Just rented space.

Alice still stood in a little herd with her friends, and I had an idea that I might feel better if I got a drink of water. It would be an excuse to go over to her. I could walk past. Maybe say something, or maybe she'd say something to me. I started for the bar.

The guitar player from Rasputin appeared without a sound. One minute, I was alone, edging my way along the wall toward the fire door. The next, he was right beside me, glowing weirdly under the green exit sign.

He nodded to where Alice stood, smiling like he knew something funny. "She's lovely. But you need to watch out for girls like that. She might ambush you in the parking lot. Kiss you with that cold iron tongue."

I took a step back and he grabbed me, catching me by the jaw, digging his fingers into the soft place under my chin. He pulled me close so that my neck was bent at an awkward angle. His breath was hot and smelled like burning leaves.

We stood in the green glow of the sign, staring at each other. His grip hurt, but I let him hold on. Maybe he was camouflaged onstage, but down on the floor, it wasn't smart to be so exposed. I could pass most of the time, but his eyes were too dark. His teeth were sharp and narrow, crammed close together. I kept still, ready to do whatever it took not to make a scene.

He leaned over me so the brim of the hat shadowed us both. "You're pale and you're cold, and you reek like steel." His voice sounded tight, like the words were getting stuck behind his teeth. "Don't pretend you're not infected or that it doesn't hurt. It's on your breath and in the whites of your eyes. It's in your blood."

I stood there, helpless to look away as he leaned in closer. He tightened his grip on my jaw and whispered hoarsely, "Do you really need a wretch like me to tell you that you're dying?"

CHAPTER 7

DYING YOUNG

My pulse hammered and I put out a hand to steady myself. The whole building seemed to surge in on me and then roll out again. I just kept my eyes on the guitar player and my hand on the wall. I didn't want to do anything that might suggest to him that he was right. *Dying?* The idea was so enormous it was disorienting. I might be sick, but *dying?*

Deep down, though, I knew the declaration had some truth to it. I thought about all the times I'd had a bad reaction to a car ride or the steel counters in the science wing, how it was always a little worse than the time before. When you got down to facts, I wasn't actually *supposed* to be alive. Under ordinary circumstances, I should have just worn out my welcome, buried years ago like Natalie Stewart.

No. Not like Natalie—like the thing that had been buried with her name.

The air was cold suddenly, and I started to shake. The

man hunched over me and smiled—almost kind. His nose was uncomfortably close to mine. "I could change your life," he whispered. "Come with me tonight and I'll save you."

But on the stage, Concertina was playing a song called "Kill All Cowards," and no one had saved Kellan Caury. It didn't matter that county justice was just murder with a different name or that he was harmless. You couldn't go around associating with strangers. If you did, you might wind up swinging.

I put my hand on the man's wrist and twisted away.

His eyes were just dark pockets of shadow, but suddenly they burned ferocious and hot under the brim of his hat.

I turned around fast, before he could grab me again, and went back the way I'd come.

My heart beat hard and panicky as I shoved my way through the crowd, back to where Roswell laughed too loud and waved his hands around when he talked and could almost always make me feel normal.

But I knew that this time, it was going to take more than pretending everything was fine. I could still hear the guitar player's voice. It reverberated in my head like a tinny echo, *You're dying*.

When I came up to the pool tables, Drew was terrorizing Roswell at nine ball, sinking numbers one after another, then starting another round and doing it all over again.

"So, what was going on over there?" Danny asked, jerking his head in the direction of the floor and leaning on his cue.

"Nothing," I said, clearing my throat. "Just a misunderstanding."

Danny gave me a hard look. When a situation started to get too weird or too bad, he could generally be counted on to turn it into some kind of joke, but he wasn't smiling now, not even close. "Kind of a strange place to have a misunderstanding, though. What did he want?"

You're dying. You're dying.

I glanced in the direction of the fire door without meaning to. The doorway was empty and the green exit sign still glowed over it, flickering a little.

Danny was watching me with a blank expression.

What did the guy want? He wanted to take me somewhere, or to tell me something or give me something. He said that he wanted to save me, and I wanted that too, only not in the middle of the Starlight where everyone could see, and not by someone with black, flashing eyes and yellow teeth. I couldn't shake the way Danny was looking at me, like he was waiting for me to show myself.

I was saved from answering by Tate. She came back to the tables breathing hard. Her face was shiny with sweat and there was a rip down the shoulder of her T-shirt where someone in the pit must have grabbed her by the collar.

She pushed herself up to sit on the half wall just as Alice came down the steps behind her. I figured they must be hanging out together, even though I never saw them talk in class, but Alice walked right past Tate and came over to me. "Hey, Mackie! I was looking for you. You seemed kind of rough yesterday. Roswell said you went home. Are you feeling better?"

I wasn't, really, but I shrugged. "It was no big deal."

She looked up at me, tucking her hair behind one ear. "So, I kind of wanted to ask you—Zoe's having that party tomorrow night. Do you think you'll go?"

I looked down at her and smiled. It felt good to smile. "Sure, maybe."

From somewhere to my right, I could feel Tate's eyes on my face. It made me want to look at her and also made me want to be someplace else.

Alice sighed and leaned against the wall so that her arm was touching mine. In the dim glow from the lamp above the pool table, her hair looked like bronze. "So, did you go up by the stage at all? It's *crazy* tonight. I mean, some guy actually pushed me into the soundboard—on *purpose*. I'm not some sweaty hard-core, okay? I'm a *girl*!"

Tate slid down off the ledge and gave us both an annoyed look. "Then don't go in the pit."

75

Alice opened her mouth like she was going to say something back, but Tate just stalked away and yanked Roswell's cue out of his hand.

Alice sighed, and when she turned to me, her eyes looked sad. "Wow. She is in so much denial about her sister. I mean, she just keeps acting like nothing happened."

I didn't answer, because that was not actually the case. It was just that the thing Tate thought had happened was different from the thing everyone else thought.

Tate was racking for eight ball, slamming balls into the plastic triangle. Suddenly, I wanted to apologize. I wanted to tell her that I was sorry for not being brave enough to listen to her, for letting her be the one to stand alone in front of the whole class when it should have been me.

Alice leaned against me, watching as Tate lifted the triangle. "So, do you know what the deal is with her family? I mean, she should be home right now, processing or grieving or something, right?"

I shrugged. The twins had been hanging out with Tate since junior high, but the thing was, you couldn't really know her unless she let you.

"Hey, Mackie, you want this one?" Drew said, jerking his head at the table.

I shook my head. Drew shrugged and tossed the cue to Danny, who chalked it and lined up his shot. The break was only okay, and he didn't sink anything.

Tate gave me a hard, clever smile and I got the impression that she was imagining how I'd look with a piece of reinforced steel through my chest. "Just so there's no confusion, I would have destroyed you," she said.

I nodded, but there was a nasty little whisper in my head. It went, *You wouldn't have to. I'm dying anyway.*

For a second, we just looked at each other. Then, without warning, she chucked the cue in Drew's general direction and stalked up to me, looking apocalyptic. Alice must have seen it too because she backed away.

Tate stood with her toes almost touching mine, staring up into my face. "Okay, I've had about enough. You need to start talking to me."

I wanted to sound assertive, but I had to look over her head to keep my voice from cracking. "We don't have anything to talk about."

She grabbed my wrist and yanked me closer. "Look, maybe you don't give a shit about any of this, but I'm not going to sit around and act like everything is normal and fine!"

"Tate, I don't know what you're talking about."

She shook her head and looked away. "You believed me today. You believed me and it scared you, and now you're just too much of a pussy to man up and say it." She was standing with her shoulders slumped and her eyes downcast, but her fingers were digging into my wrist. "Why won't you just *say* it?"

I stared down at her with my mouth open. Her jaw was hard, but I knew without a doubt that she wasn't nearly as mad as I was—not even close.

You don't get to tell me what I should do. That's what I should have said. You don't get to be self-righteous, because you have *no idea* what it's like to be me. People get beaten to death for being me. People have close, personal relationships with lynch mobs for being me. I am on the outside all the time, with no chance at a normal life, no way to be average or to fit in. Free weights in PE constitute a medical emergency, food poisoning means anything that comes in a can. Oh, and by the way, there's a really good chance I'm dying, so *that's* pretty awesome.

I just looked at her, and when she didn't say anything else, I jerked my arm out of her hand. Alice was standing against the half wall, watching us with a stunned look. I wanted to tell her I was sorry for the interruption, that my life was not usually this bizarre, but my throat was so tight I knew I'd never get the words out. I just walked out of the lounge and into the crowd to find Roswell.

He was over by the bar with Zoe and Jenna. I grabbed him by the back of his jacket and pulled him away from them. When he didn't shake me off or ask why I was acting like a lunatic, I thanked God and started for the door.

My getaway wasn't clean. It should have been a speedy, decisive exit, but I didn't have that kind of discipline. I glanced back—just once. But it was enough. Tate was standing in the lounge where I'd left her, with a pool cue in her hands and the most painful look on her face.

CHAPTER 8

IN NEED OF SAVING

When Roswell dropped me off at home, I waited until his taillights had disappeared around the corner. Then I sat down in the driveway and put my head between my knees. The air was cool and I sat there breathing it and listening to the rain.

My heartbeat was pounding in my ears and the look Tate had given me as I left the Starlight felt caustic, like it had left this huge raw spot in my chest. After a little while, I stumbled my way inside and tried to hang my jacket on a wall hook. It fell and I left it there because picking it up again seemed way too complicated. I had to stop halfway up the stairs to rest. The dark was lonely but familiar, and I fell into bed without pulling back the covers or taking my shoes off.

The dreams were worse than they'd been in a long time. Dreams of being left alone, leaves brushing the window screen. The curtains snapping on a sharp, dry breeze.

My joints ached, and even half asleep, I was uncomfortably aware of my heartbeat racing, lagging, stuttering. Slow, slow, fast. Nothing.

I dreamed about Kellan Caury. I dreamed that the Gentry lynch mob broke down the door to his little downtown apartment and dragged him out into the street. The picture was fuzzy and overexposed, like I was getting it confused with the windmill scene in *Frankenstein*. The townsfolk all had torches. I dreamed about the outline of his body, hanging from an oak tree at the end of Heath Road.

In the morning, I woke up late, feeling thirsty and worn out.

I dragged myself down the hall to the bathroom and got in the shower. After standing under the water for fifteen minutes without actually reaching for the soap or lifting my hands, I toweled off, got mostly dressed, and went downstairs.

In the kitchen, my mom was rattling a copper pan back and forth on the front burner. The sound made me want to climb out of my skull.

I watched her as she opened a drawer and dug for the spatula. Her hair was fine and blond, slipping out of its ponytail. Her expression was the same one she usually had, calm, patient. Completely unconcerned.

"Did you have breakfast yet?" she asked, looking at me

over her shoulder. "I'm frying potatoes, if you want some."

I shook my head and she sighed. "Eat something."

I ate dry cereal out of the box and my mom rolled her eyes but didn't say anything.

Outside, it was gray and rainy, but in my current state, the light seemed indecently bright, coming in the windows like a flash bomb. Fall leaves jittered and twitched, reflecting the slow, incessant rain.

I sat at the table, eating cereal in little handfuls. I wanted to put my head down on my arms or ask what time it was, but I couldn't think of how to phrase the question. My joints felt brittle.

"Where's Emma?" I said, staring into the open cereal box. It was dark inside.

"She said something about a lab project. She was going over to campus to meet a friend. Janet, I think it was."

"Janice."

"Maybe that was it." My mom turned to look at me. "Are you sure you're feeling all right? You're very pale this morning."

I nodded and closed the folding tabs on the cereal box. When I shut my eyes, I could still hear the gravelly voice of the guitar player. *You're dying. You're dying.*

"Mom," I said suddenly, feeling reckless and exhausted.

"Have you ever thought about what happens to the kids who get taken?"

At the stove, she stopped flipping the potatoes. "What do you mean?"

"Little kids. I mean, if they get replaced by . . . people like me, there's a reason, right? That can't be the end of it. They go somewhere. Right?"

"Not anyplace good."

Her voice sounded so quiet but so definite that for a minute, I almost couldn't bring myself to ask. "Are you saying that because you know I came from someplace really bad—because of how I am?"

"No, I know because it happened to me."

I sat at the table, feeling groggy and stupid. "Happened to you how?"

Her eyes were impossible, too wide and too clear. They fooled you into thinking she had no secrets, but she looked away before she answered my question, and I knew she was telling the truth. "They took me, that's all. It's not exciting or glamorous. It's just something that happens. That's all."

"But you're here now—you're here in Gentry, living a normal life. I mean, took you *where*?"

"This is not an appropriate topic of conversation," she said sharply. "I wish you wouldn't bring up ugly things at the table, and I don't want you to mention it again."

Then she got out an onion and started chopping it into

little cubes, humming softly under her breath. I shut my eyes. The information was awkward and unwieldy. I had no idea what to do with it.

My dad came in, completely oblivious to the way the two of us were managing a very uncomfortable silence. He clapped a hand on my shoulder and I tried not to wince. "Malcolm, any big plans for the day?"

"He isn't feeling well," my mom said with her back to him. She bent over the onion, chopping it smaller. Smaller. Microscopic.

My dad leaned down to look into my face. "Is that so?"

I nodded and didn't say anything. I *wasn't* feeling well, but from roughly two minutes ago, I had started feeling a whole lot worse.

My mom was humming again but louder now, faster. Her back was to both of us as she chopped, the knife flashing down, and then she gasped. The smell of blood rushed out into the room and she crossed to the sink, running her cut finger under the faucet.

I put both hands over my nose and mouth, feeling the room slosh in and out like the tide.

Without saying anything, my dad went to the cupboard above the refrigerator and took down a box of Band-Aids.

They stood facing each other at the sink, and then she offered him her hand. My dad dried the skin with a paper towel and applied the Band-Aid. She was always cutting her fingers or bumping her arms and legs. I'd never heard of her having any kind of accident when she was in surgery, but at home, she was constantly running into things, like she forgot that they took up space in the world and so did she.

When her finger was bandaged, my dad stepped back and let go of her wrist. On the stove, the potatoes had started to burn and they smelled like toast.

"Thank you," she said.

He kissed her on the forehead and then walked out. My mom just stood at the sink, gazing out the window. After a second, she reached over and turned off the burner.

I smeared my hand over my face and took a breath. The smell of blood drifted lazily, filling the kitchen. There was a dim, pulsing ache that came and went behind my left eye. "I think I'm going to go back to bed."

In my room, I yanked off my T-shirt and pulled the shades down. Then I lay down with my face to the wall and pulled the covers over my head.

I woke up with a bad jolt. It was dark. My phone was buzzing on my bedside table, and I rolled over. In the gloom, I could see the shapes of bass and amp and furniture. I wanted to go back to sleep. The phone just kept buzzing.

Finally, I reached over and answered it. "Yeah?"

"Whoa, don't sound so excited." It was Roswell.

"Sorry. I was sleeping."

"So, Zoe's having that party tonight, and there's maybe going to be one at Mason's. You want me to come get you?"

I rolled onto my back and squeezed my eyes shut. "I don't think so."

Roswell sighed. "Come on, you don't want to miss this. 'Tis the season for girls to dress like hookers. We'll catch up with the twins, get a little socially lubricated. I have this feeling that Alice is particularly looking forward to your company."

I scrubbed my hand over my eyes. "I'm not ditching out on you. Okay, I *am*. But not like that. Jesus, what *time* is it?"

"Almost nine."

On the other end of the line, a door opened and Roswell sighed. I could hear his mom in the background, telling him that someone needed to feed the dog and it had better be him. He said something back, but it was muffled, and I heard her laugh from somewhere far away.

The idea came to me that I'd gotten up for a little in the morning and that I'd had a really awful conversation with my mom. The whole thing was like a bad dream, though, and I couldn't pull all the threads together.

Then Roswell was back, talking into the receiver. "Is everything okay?"

"It's fine. I'm just not into going out right now. Not tonight."

After I hung up, I put the pillow over my head and was just starting to drift back into a pleasant state of oblivion when the phone rang again.

This time, I checked the caller ID but didn't recognize the number. I answered anyway, thinking it could be someone from school, calling about homework or something else just as improbable. I was thinking, but not admitting, that it could be Alice.

If I'd had any trouble recognizing Tate's voice, the lack of formal greeting would have tipped me off.

"Mackie," she said, "I need you to listen to me."

I took a deep breath and flopped back down on the bed. "How did you get my number?"

"If you didn't want me calling, you should have told Danny not to give it to me. Now, where can we meet, because I really need to talk to you."

"I can't," I said.

"Yes, you can. Okay, fine. I'm coming to your house. Are you at home? I'll be at your house in ten minutes, so you'd better be home."

"*No!*—I mean, I won't be here. I'm going to this party with Roswell and I'm just about to leave."

"Party," she said. Her voice sounded cold, and I could picture the look on her face suddenly—this weird mix of frustration and hurt. I had a miniature daydream, just a half second, where I imagined touching her, running the ball of my thumb over her cheek in an attempt to make her stop looking so sad, but it guttered out the next second when she said, "Something is disgustingly wrong, and you *know* it, and you're going to a party? You're unbelievable."

"I don't know *anything*, okay? I'm hanging up now."

"Mackie, you are such a—"

"Goodbye," I said, and hit *End*.

Then I called Roswell back.

He answered on the first ring, sounding easy and cheerful. "What's up? Are you calling to wish me luck in my quest to rescue Zoe from the tyranny of clothing?"

"Is it okay if I come with you?"

"Yeah, that's fine. Not with the clothing thing, though, right? I mean, that's kind of a one-man job."

I laughed and was relieved to find that I sounded almost normal.

Roswell went on in a fake-conversational voice. "So, you remember that I called you fifteen minutes ago, right? And during the course of that conversation, I asked if you wanted to go to a party and get chemically altered and possibly ravish Alice—I mean, I think I really sold the ravishing—but you said no? I mean, you do *remember* that, right?"

I cleared my throat. "I changed my mind."

He was quiet on the line for a long time. Then he said, "You sound like shit, though. Do you *feel* okay?"

"No, but it doesn't matter."

"Mackie. Are you sure you actually want to go to a party?"

I took a deep breath. "All I want right now is to get out of the house."

After I hung up, I closed my eyes and tried to get my head together. Then I rolled off the bed and stood up. If I was going to go with Roswell, I needed to do something about the rumpled state of my hair and also put on a shirt. I crossed the room and started going through my dresser. Usually, sleeping all day would be enough to get rid of the spins, but every time I turned my head, the room seemed to execute a lazy half turn, and I had to keep my hand on top of the dresser for balance.

"Mackie?"

When I glanced over my shoulder, Emma was standing in the doorway watching me. She was wearing sweats, and her hair was twisted into its customary knot. It looked soft and messy, like it had since we were kids. She didn't go out much, and it looked like she was all set for a night of reading.

I closed the drawer and turned to face her. "You can come in, you know."

She took a couple steps, then stopped again.

"Janice—my lab partner, Janice—she gave me something," she said. She was holding a paper bag. "She said it was a special kind of . . . holistic extract." The sound of her voice was weirdly shrill, like I was making her nervous. "She said—she just said it would be good for you." She crossed the room to my desk.

"Thanks," I said, watching as she set the bag down and backed away. "Emma—"

But she'd already turned and walked out of my room.

I picked up the bag and opened it. Inside, there was a tiny bottle made of brown glass. It had a paper label, and someone had written: *Most Beneficial Hawthorn. To drink.*

Instead of a cap or a cork, the bottle was sealed with wax. When I cracked the seal with my thumbnail, the odor of leaves was sharp, but it didn't smell spoiled or poisonous.

I trusted Emma. All my life, she'd made it her mission to take care of me, to make sure I was okay. But drinking something unidentified was a very sketchy thing, and while I trusted Emma, I wasn't at all sure that I trusted Janice.

But more insistent was the feeling that if something didn't change, if things just kept going on the same way they had been, I was going to wake up one day and not be able to get out of bed. Or, more likely, I was going to go to sleep and not wake up at all.

I touched the mouth of the bottle, then licked the residue off the tip of my finger and waited. After a few minutes of rummaging through old homework assignments and laundry, I figured Janice's hippie voodoo hadn't killed me yet, so I took a good-sized drink and then another. It wasn't bad. It wasn't *good*, but it wasn't bad. It kind of tasted like meths and dirt.

I put the empty bottle back in the bag and found a shirt with a collar and not too many wrinkles. I was pulling the shirt down over my head when I realized that I suddenly felt better—all-over better. I'd been exhausted for so long that I'd sort of forgotten I felt exhausted until I didn't anymore. I stretched and the muscles in my shoulders felt good, flexing restlessly.

In the bathroom, I stood in front of the mirror. My eyes were still dark but not freakish. They were just normal, black at the pupil and a deep, muddy brown in the iris. My skin was still pale, but it would be called "fair" instead of "terminal." I looked like a regular person, going out on a Saturday night. I looked normal.

I went back into my room and studied the bottle. The label was plain, heavy paper, with nothing else written on it besides the mysterious notation *Most Beneficial Hawthorn* and the instruction to drink it. I knew that hawthorn was a low, thorny tree that grew out along the country roads, but the label gave no other indication about what the drink actually was.

My head was cluttered with questions. What was it really, and how did it work? Was feeling better the same thing as a cure? Had Emma saved me? Even while my first instinct was to doubt it, I felt the grin spreading across my mouth.

Huge, relieved. I hadn't felt this good in weeks. *Months*, maybe.

I had a sudden, overwhelming urge to do something that took a lot of energy. I needed to jump around the room or laugh uncontrollably or find Emma and hug her until she started laughing too and we both couldn't breathe and had to sit down on the floor. I wanted to do handstands or backflips, but there wasn't enough space. I wanted to run. I turned off the light and went out into the hall.

"Emma." I leaned my forehead against her door, then when she didn't answer, I pushed it open. "Emma, what is this stuff? It's *amazing*."

But Emma wasn't in her room or anywhere I could find her.

For the first time since my encounter with the guitar player the night before, the voice in my head had faded. Maybe dying wasn't a foregone conclusion. Maybe there was a way to have a real, actual life, to be normal. Something in me didn't really believe it. That small piece of me stood apart and watched with deep suspicion as I studied a tiny bottle that was too good to be true. But the rest of me didn't care. There was too much pleasure in feeling free.

When I heard Roswell's car in the driveway, I bolted downstairs. On the front porch, I was hit by a barrage of smells: the raw vegetable reek of carved pumpkins, and the scorched smell of burning leaves, and faint but there, the swampy odor of the dry lake bed out on County Road 12. The night was deep and vibrant and ferociously alive.

Three blocks away, I heard Mrs. Carson-Scott calling her cat inside and that was normal. Then I heard the faint jangle of the bell on its collar and the rustle as it crept through the bushes. Even the cars on Benthaven sounded like they were right there in front of me.

Forget Tate. Forget dead kids and bloody lockers and the deep, pulsing ache I got whenever I thought about my family or my future. This was my life, right here.

And I wanted it.

PART TWO

THE LIES PEOPLE TELL

CHAPTER 9

ALL THAT GLITTERS

At Zoe Beecham's, the street was full of car doors slamming. The noise of voices was steady as people filed up to the house and around back. They were mostly in costumes, even though Halloween wasn't until Tuesday.

The whole neighborhood was decorated for the season. There were paper skeletons in the windows and jack-o'-lanterns on all the porches. The rain had settled down to a steady drizzle. In Zoe's front yard, someone had staked a burlap scarecrow of Gentry's own monster of legend, the Dirt Witch. Its hair was made of wire and twine, and someone had drawn a snarling face on the burlap in marker. It loomed off to the side of the porch looking huge and sinister.

Roswell and I walked up the driveway without talking. He didn't have a costume exactly, but he was wearing a pair of pointy plastic teeth that fitted over his real ones. He kept giving me strange sideways looks.

"What? Why are you looking at me like that?"

"You didn't—ow!" He touched his lip and then his new plastic teeth. "You didn't open the window. You know how long it's been since you didn't open the window in my car?"

And I realized that was true. I was fine, even after fifteen minutes in the car. "Is that a problem?"

"No. But it's weird."

I nodded and we stood at the top of the driveway, looking at each other. Behind us, someone was shouting the words to the school fight song, high and off-key.

We headed for the open side gate and started around to the back of the house.

The back door opened into a big, brightly lit kitchen, where too many things were shaped or painted like cows.

And there was Tate. Because she was everywhere, creeping in at the edges, getting all tangled up in my life, and she couldn't leave it alone. She smiled when she saw me, but it was a fierce, triumphant smile, like she'd just beaten me at some kind of game.

She was leaning against the counter between Drew and Danny. She wasn't wearing a costume either, but she had on this bizarre sort of headband. Two shining stars stuck up from it, swaying back and forth on long stalks. They were raining glitter everywhere.

I took a deep breath and tried to act normal, sliding past her on my way to the refrigerator. I got a can of Natty

Light off the shelf on the door and retreated across the kitchen.

Danny was at the sink, knocking around with measuring spoons and bottles, doctoring up some kind of mixed drink. He had on a store-bought skeleton costume with a gray zip-front hoodie over it, like the title character in the movie *Donnie Darko*. Drew was dressed like Frank the Rabbit of the same film, but his mask was off and lying on the counter.

When he was done adding sloe gin and grenadine, Danny shoved the glass across the counter at Drew. "Try that and tell me what it needs."

Drew took a sip, then coughed and set the glass down. "That's awful."

Danny scowled and tossed a dripping tablespoon at him. "*You're* awful. I'm looking for constructive feedback, asshole. What does it need?"

Drew threw the tablespoon back. "It needs to be taken out and shot."

"Make your own damn drink, Mr. Mixology."

They punched each other in a friendly way, then Danny slipped the bunny mask over Drew's head and they started for the living room. As they walked out, Drew reached over and yanked Danny's hood down over his face.

Roswell had already made a timely exit—probably to see where Zoe was. I was alone with Tate, not sure whether to start planning my escape because as unappealing as the idea of talking about her dead sister was, I was pretty sure she was just going to follow me, and it might be smarter to get the conversation over with while no one else was around.

I could see the shape of her, the curve of her body under the T-shirt. I knew I should stay back, but suddenly, all I wanted was to touch her. I crossed the kitchen and stood next to her so at least we wouldn't be shouting our secrets at each other across a room. Her mouth was set in a hard, cynical smile, and nothing good could come of it. Her hair smelled like grapefruit and something light and fluttery that seemed out of place on her, but it was nice.

"What are you supposed to be?" I asked, reaching over to flick one of her antennae.

"Oh, I don't know—I'm a robotic praying mantis. I'm a Martian. I'm aluminum foil. What are *you* supposed to be?"

I set down my beer and pressed my hands flat on the counter. I'm not me—I'm someone else.

I'm a normal, ordinary person, born to a normal, biological family, with brown eyes and fingernails that don't turn blue just because the cafeteria ladies used steel trays for the french fries instead of aluminum.

But I didn't say anything. Her eyes were hard and mysterious. She reached for Danny's failed drink without looking away from my face.

I dropped my chin and watched the floor. "Stop looking at me like that."

"Like what?"

Like I'm stupid and pathetic and you hate me?

I shrugged. "I don't know. Nothing." I glanced up and gave her a helpless look. "Just, what are you even *doing* here?"

There was a fast, pop-y track playing on the stereo—you know the one—how everything will be all right and you just have to be yourself and try your hardest and it'll work out and all that other bullshit. In the next room, girls were dancing together, singing along.

"The amazing thing about this song," Tate said, in a voice that sounded aggressively cheerful, like she wasn't changing the subject completely. "The amazing thing about this song is that it contains absolutely no irony."

Her gaze was direct, full of a sadness so raw and crystallized that I could see the shape of it. It ringed her pupils in rusty starbursts, but she was grinning—this terrible, ferocious grin. It made her look like she wanted to tear someone's throat out.

I leaned against the counter, trying to think of something to say that would end the discussion and not drag it out. I needed something definitive that would take care of the problem once and for all. She just finished Danny's drink in one long swallow, grinning up at me.

I couldn't work out what she actually wanted. Her sister was dead. Whether being dead happened in a pretty box on Welsh Street or someplace else, it didn't make a difference. Dead was irreversible. It was permanent. You couldn't do anything about it, and still, Tate seemed determined to take it back, like with the right answer, she could fix everything.

Her eyes were hard, and glitter showered from her headband, dusting the shoulders of her jacket. "Do you believe in fairy tales?"

"No."

"Not even the nice, grown-up kind where you follow all the rules and you work really hard and get a good job and a family and everything is happily ever after?"

I snorted and shook my head.

"Good. Then you should be just as righteously pissed off as *I* am that everyone around here loves a nice game of Let's Play Pretend."

"Look, you're taking this way out of context. I'm sorry about your sister, I really am. It's awful. But for the love of God, this is not exactly *my* problem."

Her smile looked frozen on suddenly, and she opened her eyes wide. Her voice was high and mocking and mean. "Oh, *let's* play pretend, Mackie! Let's play the part where you grow a pair and face basic facts and stop acting like everything is sunshine and unicorns! Let's play that you start treating the girl like she has half a brain and tell her all about how sometimes, nasty little monsters show up in the bed where her sister used to sleep. Why don't you tell her about *that*?"

My cheeks got hot, like I'd just been slapped in the face. "Why?" I said, and the question sounded very loud, coming out in a harsh bark. I brought my voice down to a whisper. "Why should I? What's in it for me?"

She looked up at me and shook her head, making silver sparkles dance all around her. "You really think that everyone is stupid, don't you?"

For a second I stopped breathing. Then I leaned close and made my voice as hard and as mean as possible. "So, now I'm supposed to be some kind of expert on why your family's all tragic? What did I ever do to make you think that any of this is *my* responsibility?"

Tate's laugh was short and scornful. "Believe me, if I'd had a choice, I would have picked someone with a little more backbone. You're kind of all I've got."

I threw the beer in the sink, where it foamed up in a white froth, and pushed myself away from the counter. Away from the kitchen and Tate's hard, merciless grin.

For the first time since Drew and Danny's art project, I thought about my locker and for a second, I got the idea that maybe Tate was the one who'd scratched *Freak* on the door. The idea died a quick death, though. The graffiti had happened the day of the funeral, which pretty much ruled her out, for the simple reason that I hadn't pissed her off yet.

In the living room, the sound system was louder, the crowd thicker. I made my way between superheroes and slutty witches, trying to find a place I could escape to.

"Mackie!" Alice was sitting on the sofa, smiling, waving at me. "Mackie, come over here." Everything about her was so effortless, a glossy island, normal, relieving. Just what I needed.

When I sat down next to her, she moved closer, so that her leg pressed against mine. She smelled like tequila and some kind of powdery perfume that made my eyes water.

She was dressed like a cat, which I thought was a very obvious costume. It was easier to think of her in a cotton tennis uniform, far away and spotless. But there was no avoiding the clip-on ears and the waxy black whiskers drawn on her cheeks. Every third girl was a cat.

"Hey," she said leaning closer. Her hair had come loose from one of the clips and it skimmed my arm in tangled waves. "We should go somewhere quiet."

Her lips were slick and shiny looking. In her mouth, the barbell still hummed at me—a mean, wicked little song. I wondered if the Most Beneficial Hawthorn was strong enough to protect me from the steel. Whether I even really wanted what I thought I wanted. I wanted to kiss her and not in the pure, longing way you want to kiss someone. I wanted it the way you sometimes want to jump into very cold water, even though you know it won't feel good. I wanted to go numb. To see what it felt like to be someone else.

She moved so that her chest was against my shoulder. "Do you want to go sit somewhere?"

"We are sitting." My hands were sweating.

She gave me an annoyed look and tipped her head to one side. "I bet there's someplace more private, though—upstairs? Bedrooms or something."

I didn't know how to answer. Yes and yes and no and yes.

I glanced in the direction of the stairs and then I almost stopped breathing.

Two girls were standing halfway up the stairs, leaning their elbows on the banister and whispering to each other.

One was pretty, wearing a huge, puffy dress, complete with a crown and a silver star wand. She looked soft and pinkish, the kind of girl who gets kissed awake at the end of a fairy tale, but she was short. Really short. Standing next to me, she wouldn't have come up to my elbow. Also, she had the biggest ears I'd ever seen on a real person.

She was standing up on the baseboard with her feet struck through the slats, holding on to the banister. She was talking up at the other girl, who wasn't small or pink or cute.

The second girl's face was shiny, like skin after a bad

burn. There was a jagged ring around her neck. No blood, just torn flesh and raw edges. Her grin was lunatic, almost as wide as the gash.

She was looking out over the crowded room, and when she smiled, she was smiling at me.

I turned to Alice. "We should go outside."

She shook her head. "It's cold out."

Across the room, the girl stepped away from the banister and started down the stairs. Even from the couch, I smelled the low stink of something dead. It wasn't a costume.

I grabbed Alice harder than I meant to, yanking her up off the couch. "Let's just go outside, okay? Let's go for a walk."

Out in the backyard, people were standing around in little clusters on the covered patio, laughing and smoking, drinking beer out of plastic cups. I tried to breathe slower, but my heart was beating hard and fast in my throat.

Next to me, Alice was wrestling with the cat costume. "God, this tail is so obnoxious."

It was, but not in the way she meant. Suddenly, she was right in front of me, pushing herself up on her toes.

In her mouth, the barbell twanged at me. Her hand on my arm was warm. Her lips were less than three inches away. I swallowed and tried to figure out why this wasn't the best moment of my whole life.

"What's wrong?" she said, breathing out another gust of tequila and stainless steel. She put a hand on her hip. "Look, are you gay or something?"

I stared at her. She was beautiful in the porch light and very far away. I shook my head.

"What's *wrong* with you, then? Seriously."

But she'd never really looked at me. She'd never seen me. Here she was, making up some complicated story, when Tate was right—the answer had always been dangerously obvious to anyone who felt like looking.

Tate, her face inches from mine as she stared up at me, telling me that thing in the box wasn't her sister, that something else had died in her sister's bed and all she wanted was for someone to listen when she talked.

Alice leaned closer. "Are you even *listening* to me?"

But I wasn't. I was standing under a rain-soaked tree with a girl whose sister was one more casualty of our shitty little town and who had the good sense to be angry about that instead of heartbroken. It was the only thing I could think of and Alice was so far away.

The screen door slammed behind us and I turned, bracing myself for the two strange girls, but it was Tate. She'd come out onto the back steps and was looking down at us with her elbows propped on the handrail, silver-glitter stars swaying back and forth.

The light from the kitchen was shining behind her. It lit

her hair around the edges, giving her a halo, like a neon supernatural being wearing deely boppers. I couldn't see her face, but her silhouette was going back and forth between us. Me. Alice. Me. Alice.

I stood in the yard and looked up, like she was a girl on a balcony. She stepped out from in front of the light and I could finally see her face. I don't know what I'd been expecting. Something remarkable, I guess. She looked like she always did. Completely unimpressed.

"Roswell's looking for you." Her mouth was thin and she was staring me right in the face.

I found him in the living room with a bunch of the student-council girls. He grinned and waved me over, then lunged to tickle Zoe, making her laugh every time he pretended to chew on her with his fangs.

I squeezed in next to Jenna Porter, who was looking bored and a little drunk. She was dressed in a toga, with leaves in her hair, but she was wearing her normal shoes. They were bright red, with little flowers die-cut on the toes, and didn't match her costume.

"Hey," I said.

She nodded and gave me a smile. Over by the coat closet, the two strange girls stood whispering behind their hands. I pretended not to see, but Jenna glanced at them, shaking her head.

"I can't wait to get out of here," she mumbled, touching

the little steel cross around her neck. "As soon as we graduate, I'm moving to New York."

"What's in New York?" I said, raising my eyebrows. My voice sounded easy, but the staring girls were making it hard to act normal. Suddenly, the last thing I was in the mood for was making conversation.

Jenna shrugged. "Chicago, then. Or Boston or L.A. or wherever." Her eyes slid out of focus, and she smiled without looking like she meant it. "Screw it—I'll go to Newark or Detroit if it means getting out of this godforsaken place."

She didn't have to say what she was really thinking—if it means getting away from these people.

I opened my mouth, trying to think of something generic and reassuring. Then I smelled rotting meat.

The girl with the torn throat had started toward me. She was pushing her way through the crowd with the little pink one scrambling after her, and my pulse was wildly out of control.

Jenna made a whining noise, somewhere between disgusted and scared. "That's the nastiest costume I've ever seen. Seriously. What are you supposed to be?"

The rotting girl didn't answer. She just turned on Jenna with her crazed smile, and Jenna backed away, looking glad to be going. I was on my own, with a girl who looked like she'd climbed out of a grave.

"Are you avoiding us?" she said, coming in close. Her

breath smelled cold and stale. "I'd have thought the hawthorn was good for a chat, anyway."

"Go away," I said in a whisper, looking past her, trying not to watch the way her neck gaped and squelched when she talked.

She smiled wider. Her teeth were sharp and yellow. "What's wrong? Are you worried we'll attract attention? Expose your little secret? This is our season, dear—the time when even the worst of us can go out on the town and look just like everyone else."

"Did you see the Orionid shower last night?" the little pink one asked, peering out at me from behind the other girl. "The Orionids are falling all the time now—astral bodies separating from the parent body. They originate from Halley's comet. Did you see them?"

I shook my head. Her cheeks were very pink.

"They won't peak until Monday. You have plenty of time."

The other girl turned on her. "Shut up, you ninny. No one cares about stars."

"He does," said the little pink one. "I saw him gazing in the kitchen. He was positively coveting them." She waved her toy wand at the other girl and tried to pat my arm. "It's quite all right, you know. Not everyone is as unmoved by beauty as *she* is."

I stared straight ahead, tasting rancid meat every time I breathed. "Look, what do you guys want?"

The other girl smiled wider. "You, of course. We've been hunting for you."

"Yes," said the little pink one, smiling so that her eyes squinted into crescents. "We're hunting." Then she tipped her head back and laughed like that was the funniest thing she'd ever heard.

The other girl leaned close, staring into my face with milky eyes. "Your foster sister accepted our services and now she owes us a favor. Come to the slag heap and be quick about it. If you don't, we'll find Emma and take the price out of her skin."

"Oh, don't be hateful," the pink one said, swatting the other girl with her wand. She turned to me. "Malcolm, please, if you're amiable and cooperative, everything is going to be fine."

Then they were gone and I was standing in Zoe Beecham's very floral living room, with a taste in my mouth that reminded me of roadkill. She had called me Malcolm.

Drew was next to me suddenly, smelling stoned and a little like papier-mâché. "Jesus," he said, taking off his rabbit mask. "What was *that* all about?"

I turned to face him. "What was what about?"

"Those girls just now." His expression seemed to narrow. "It looked like a pretty intense conversation is all."

I shrugged and looked down. "I never met them before."

Which, as we both knew, was not an answer to anything, no matter how factual the statement sounded.

He raised his eyebrows in a suggestive way. "Just as long as you weren't planning on hooking up with one of them. The tall one was ass ugly."

"That's not really a danger," I said, and reached for Roswell's arm. "Hey, you ready to get out of here?"

He didn't act surprised—he never did—just pinched Zoe's cheek and started for the door.

In the car, we sat looking ahead, not talking. My heart was skipping beats all over the place.

Roswell turned the key in the ignition. "So, are you up for going over to Mason's for a little?"

"Nah—" My voice sounded weird even to me and I started over. "I should get home. Stuff to do . . ."

Roswell nodded and put the car in gear. His profile was serious and younger looking than normal.

I didn't say anything else because I couldn't think of anything to say. There were too many things in my head. I told myself that Emma was at home, working on a botany project, maybe, or curled up with a book, already in bed. That she was safe. She had to be because I couldn't stand to consider the possibility that she wasn't.

Come to the slag heap, like some kind of invitation. But the slag heap was just a crumbling pile of rubble. It was weedy and abandoned, nothing to find if I went there.

Except if the girls were as unnatural as they seemed, there would have to be a secret that went along with it. There would be a way in because sometimes at night, the dead rose and walked around deserted streets. If you listened to the rumors and the dark murmurs of bedtime stories, something lived under the quicklime and the shale. I was no expert, but the girl at the party had been dead. The smell coming off her was the rank, clotted smell of decay, and nothing could live with its veins and arteries cut open. Her smile had been horrific, and I had a sneaking fear that she was just the beginning of what I'd find if I went there.

But only one thing really mattered as I stared out the passenger window on the drive home. Emma. She'd been trying to help—and the little bottle of hawthorn water *had* helped—but what was the payback, the price? When I thought about it that way, though, the answer didn't matter. I couldn't let anything happen to her. So I knew what I had to do.

CHAPTER 10

MONSTERS

When Roswell dropped me off, the neighborhood was quiet. No creatures, no dead things, nothing creeping in the shadows.

I walked along Concord to Orchard Circle, past the dead end and down the slope to the bridge.

It was lonesome walking so late at night and more lonesome navigating the deep ravine between my neighborhood and the center of town, not knowing what I was walking into. As I started down, I could smell a wet, mushy odor like garden compost and rot.

The guitarist from Rasputin Sings the Blues was standing on the footbridge, his silhouette barely visible in the dark and made unnaturally tall by his top hat. He was smoking a cigarette, and when he looked up, the cherry glowed a bright, violent red.

I stepped out onto the bridge. "Are you waiting for me?"

He nodded and waved toward the other end of the bridge. "Let's go for a walk."

My skin was prickling all over. "Who are you—what's your name?"

"Call me Luther, if you like."

"And if I don't like?"

"Then call me something else." After a fairly mysterious pause, he pointed to the other side of the ravine again, then jerked his head down at the slag heap.

"Where are we going?"

"Into the pit, of course."

The sound of his voice made shudders creep down my neck. A person would have to be crazy to go down into a lair of dead things. A person would have to be out of his mind. I knew that I should just tell him no deal, just walk away.

It was no good, though. There were all kinds of arguments for turning around, climbing the path, walking straight back home and locking the door. But when it came to Emma, my loyalty had never been in question. I would do pretty much anything.

I followed Luther across the bridge and along a tangled path that ran down to the bottom of the ravine, where the slag heap sat lumpy and black. As we moved deeper into the shadow of the ravine, it seemed to rise up, huge against the sky.

Luther smiled and touched the brim of his hat. "Home, sweet home."

"So, you live in the slag heap?"

He twitched his shoulders, almost a shrug. "Well, to be more accurate, underneath."

Then he reached inside his coat and brought out a knife. The blade was long and yellow, made of ivory or bone. I stepped back.

He laughed. "Don't be a fool. I'm not going to cut you."

Then he jammed the knife into the base of the hill, all the way to the handle.

When the blade sank into the slag, nothing happened for a second. Then a sheet of gravel slid away, exposing a narrow door.

He pocketed the knife and pushed the door open, waving me through. The entryway was dark and smelled like mildew. The opening was low and the air was wet and cold, but when he ushered me in, I didn't hesitate. I stepped inside and Luther followed me into a low tunnel. When I looked back, all I could see was the faded black of his coat as he guided me down.

We moved slowly, and I kept one hand on the wall. It was rough, crusted with loose debris, but the tunnel didn't seem to be in danger of collapsing. The floor sloped steadily downward as we went and I was increasingly aware that we were deep underground. Deeper than

116

cellars and basements and the water mains that ran in a complex network under the streets. The weight of earth above us was almost suffocating, but something about it was comforting, too. I felt surrounded, like I was being held in place.

As we kept going, the tunnel widened, and the air got wetter and colder. A long way down, there was light.

When we reached the end of the tunnel, Luther stopped, straightening his collar, adjusting his lapels. The light came from the narrow crack between a pair of heavy double doors. He caught hold of twin handles and dragged the doors open.

Then he swept off his hat and bowed low. "Welcome to the House of Mayhem."

I was standing in a kind of lobby, with a stone floor and a high ceiling. Torches burned in rows along the wall and the smoke had a black, oily smell like kerosene. The handles were mismatched, made from dead branches and baseball bats and one that looked like the handle of a garden shovel or an ax. The walls were lined with other doorways, lower and narrower than the one we'd just come through. On opposite sides of the room were two massive fireplaces, but neither of them was lit.

A group of girls stood around one of the fireplaces, watching us. All of them had on long, grimy dresses and stiff vests that laced up the back. The smell coming off them was worse than the girl at the party. It made me think of a morgue.

At the far end of the lobby, there was a big wooden desk. It was the kind that a librarian or a receptionist might sit behind, but no one was in the chair.

When Luther put his hand between my shoulders, the weight and suddenness of it made me jump.

"Come now," he said softly. "No need for alarm. She just wants an audience with you."

He pushed me closer and we leaned over the desk to look behind it.

A little girl was crouched on the floor. She had on a white party dress that looked like it was made of old surgical gauze and also like it might have been on fire at some point. She was sitting with her legs pulled up, drawing on the stone with a burned stick. All the pictures looked like eyes and giant mouths full of teeth.

Luther leaned against the desk and pressed a little brass bell. "Here's your boy."

The girl turned and looked up at me. When she smiled, I stepped back from the desk. Her face was young and kind of shy, but her mouth was crowded with small, jagged teeth. Not a nice, respectable thirty-two, but closer to fifty or sixty.

"Oh dear," she said, putting down her stick and reaching out a dirty hand. "I ought to have been more cautious." Her voice was soft, and her train wreck of a mouth made her lisp. "You think I'm ugly."

The truth was, yes. She *did* look ugly, maybe even horrifying, but her eyes were wide. She was going to be terrifying if she grew any bigger, but for now, she was cute the way even a turkey or a possum can be cute when it's a baby.

She patted the heavy, high-backed chair beside her. "Here, sit and talk with me. Tell me about yourself."

I didn't sit down right away. It was hard to know what to think of her. She was different from Luther and different from the girls at Zoe's party. Her jagged teeth and her tiny size made her seem more implausible, more impossible than all the rest of them.

When I took a seat on the edge of the chair, she went back to drawing on the floor.

"I've been curious about you," she said, scraping a new charcoal mouth with her stick. "We were so pleased that you survived childhood. Castoffs generally don't."

I nodded, staring down at the top of her head. "Who are you?"

She stood up and moved closer, staring into my face. Her eyes were dull black, like the feathers on a dead bird. "I'm the Morrigan."

The word sounded strange, like something in another language.

"I'm so pleased that you could find it in your heart to visit us," she whispered, reaching to touch my chin. "It's wonderful that you need us because we need you, you see, and business arrangements are so much more satisfying if they're reciprocal."

"What do you mean 'need you'? I don't need anything."

"Oh, darling," she said, smiling and reaching for my hand. "Don't be silly. Of *course* you need us. You're becoming *so* frail, and it's only going to get worse. This really is the best solution for all of us. You'll help me, and in return, I'll make sure you're supplied with all the remedies and analeptics you need and you won't have to live out the rest of your days in slow agony."

I watched her, trying to see the reason behind why I was even here. "What do you want?" I said, sounding more nervous than I would have liked.

"Don't look so alarmed. I won't ask you to do anything you don't already desire in your heart." She turned away and knelt on the floor again, picking at her hair. "While music is hardly the most powerful kind of worship, it's fine and adequate. We're always looking to bring new blood to our stage."

"What does that have to do with me, though? I'm just . . . no one."

"You have a good face," she said, crossing her legs and fidgeting with her dress. "An undamaged body. Your wholeness makes you immeasurably useful to me. If it's agreeable, I'll send you out onstage with the rest of my musical beauties to stand in front of the town and receive their admiration." Each time she pulled out a clump of hair, she set it carefully off to the side of her drawings, like she was starting a collection.

"Rasputin, you mean? When?"

"Tomorrow, at that estimable venue, the Starlight."

"But I just saw them. They played last night."

"We're in a bad time," she said. "Don't tell me you haven't seen the signs."

I thought of the rusting grates and brackets at the Starlight and nodded.

"The town is drawing away from us. The rains dishearten them, and their attentions are half felt at best. We need all the adulation we can get. If the season is bad enough, I'll send them up every night until the worst days have passed."

"What do you want *me* to do, though?"

The Morrigan smiled. "Now we come to it. Your sister has been a busy girl, as I'm sure you know. She appealed to us on your behalf, asking for medicines and cures, which we were only too happy to provide. It's easy enough to mix the medicines you need. All we ask is that you help us in our endeavor for applause."

I didn't ask what the point of applause was or how she even knew that I could play. Instead, what came out of my mouth was dazed and stupid sounding. "Why is it important to make them happy?"

The Morrigan ripped out another clump of hair. "They're better at loving us when they're happy."

I was beginning to get the feeling we were just going around in circles. "What does it mean, love us? How can they *love* you? They don't even believe you exist."

"They have to love because otherwise, they fear and they hate, and we'll all spiral down in one long decline. They'll hunt us—they've done it before. If we don't keep the peace, they kill us."

I knew that was the truth. All my daily concerns and everything that defined my life—it all came back to what had been done to Kellan Caury.

The Morrigan scowled and it made her look terrifying. "They can be very dangerous if they take it into their heads, so it's imperative that they remain placated. Their admiration sustains us, and our music makes them smile, even if they don't realize it's us they're smiling at."

"You live off groupies?"

She shrugged and drew a large, lumpy animal on the floor. "Off their attentions and their little favors." She added a pair of eyes, drew two slashes for pupils. "It's not the only form of tribute, but it's a good one."

"If it's not the only form, what else is there?"

"I have a sister who believes something else." She said it

122

lightly, but she was looking away and her voice sounded thin and high pitched. "She's a right vicious cow, though."

"That's not a very nice thing to say about your sister."

"Well, it's not a nice thing, snatching away children. It makes the town uneasy." She dropped the stick and crawled over to the corner of the desk, peering around it at the main doors. "And it means giving up our own precious babes to replace theirs."

The two girls from Zoe's party had come in from the long tunnel that led up to the slag heap. The one with the torn throat leaned in the doorway, while the little pink princess skipped around her, waving the star wand.

The Morrigan stood up and pointed to the rotting one. "The family knew her for what she was. They took her out into the hollow by Heath Road one night and cut her throat with a sickle."

I tried to breathe, but for a second, my lungs wouldn't cooperate. The girl was horrific, but the story was worse.

The Morrigan only nodded and patted my hand. "Terrible, isn't it? She was very young. Only a baby, really."

The girl stood by the double doors, tall and ragged. She was running her fingers over her torn throat, playing with the edges of the gash. When she caught me looking, she smiled.

I glanced away and turned back to the Morrigan. "How

could she have died when she was a baby, though? I mean, she's not little anymore—she grew up."

The Morrigan nodded. "And why shouldn't she?"

"Because when people are dead, they don't *do* that—they don't get older."

She waved me off, shaking her head. "That's ridiculous. How on earth could I keep a proper house if I had to spend all my time looking after infants who never learned to look after themselves?" The Morrigan smiled, sounding pleased with herself. "The dead mind me. It's not a hard trick to make them live again if you have the right tokens and charms and the right names to call them by."

"I don't know, but I think most people would say that's a pretty hard trick to pull off."

She looked up at me, shaking her head seriously. "Mostly, people just don't want to."

"People like your sister?"

She grabbed the stick and slammed it down on the floor. "My sister lives on blood and sacrifice. She cares nothing for what's already dead. But then, she has the distinct advantage of being born heartless."

"It's heartless to think dead things should stay dead?"

"No," said the Morrigan. "It's heartless to use children so callously, to toss them away simply because she'd rather have something else. But look at me, I'm going on. You've come for the hawthorn analeptic, and I intend to give it."

When she came around the front of the desk and reached for my hand, I followed her.

She led me out through a narrow door and down a short flight of stone steps. The air smelled damp and mineralized, but it was nice and I wanted to keep breathing it. I followed her through doorways and tunnels, amazed by how far the House of Mayhem seemed to sprawl.

We turned down a wide hallway and into a huge room, far bigger than the lobby. The floor of it was covered in patches of standing water, so much in places that there was no way to avoid it.

The Morrigan splashed happily, jumping into the smallest puddles and kicking at the surface so that water sprayed up around her. I followed more carefully, walking around it where I could.

"Mind the pools," she said, pulling me back from the edge of a wide puddle. "Some of them go quite deep and I would have to call Luther to fish you out."

I looked closer at the puddle I'd almost stepped in. The edges were steep, cut straight down into the stone, and the puddle was so deep that I couldn't see the bottom.

At the end of the room, we skirted around a pool that was even bigger than the others. A woman lay on her back, floating in the water. Her arms were crossed over her chest and buckled to her sides with canvas straps, but she drifted on the surface without going under. Her dress was stuck to her legs, sinking down so the hem of it disappeared into the murky water. Her eyes were open, staring blankly at the ceiling, and her hair fanned out around her head, tangled with leaves and twigs. There were deep scars running down her cheeks, crisscrossing and overlapping, like someone had carved a grid into her face.

The Morrigan barely glanced at her, but I stopped and leaned down to get a better look. "Is she dead too?"

The Morrigan scampered back and came up next to me. "Her? Oh, not remotely."

"What happened to her, then?"

The Morrigan took a deep breath, like she was trying to find the best way to explain something, and said carefully, "Some can go out and some can't, and some can only go out on nights when strangeness passes for merriment, and some used to go out but due to misfortune or accident cannot go out anymore." She slipped her arm through mine and whispered, "My sister's man did that to her—the Cutter. He laid iron rods against her face because it amused him, and now we have to fasten her arms down to keep her from clawing off her own skin."

In the pool at my feet, the woman opened her mouth but didn't make any noise. Her lips were a chilly blue and she stared up at me with wide, anguished eyes until I had to look away.

I turned to the Morrigan. "Why, though? What *good* does it do to hurt someone like that?"

"Not good. It's never a matter of good. But my sister does love to punish the innocent for our trespasses. She was displeased with me, so she took it out on someone else." The Morrigan fumbled for my hand. Hers was tiny and hot. "It wasn't my intention to make you sad. Here, don't let's dwell on misfortune. Come along and we'll fetch you something nice to take away with you."

When I looked over my shoulder, the woman was still floating, staring at the ceiling as the water slopped gently against her tattered cheeks.

The Morrigan glanced up at me. "It's not always so bad as that," she said. "My sister is only unduly cruel to those who cross her. She makes sure we know where we stand and who we answer to, but if you keep out of her way, there's nothing to fear."

We left through a door at the far end and went down another flight of steps to a little room off the end of a hall.

I stood in the doorway, staring into a room full of glass cabinets. A marble counter ran the length of the wall, with shelves and cupboards above it. The counter was covered with pipes and test tubes and glass containers in all different sizes.

Emma's friend Janice was sitting on a little hassock at the counter, picking through a heap of twigs and roots and leaves. I almost didn't recognize her. Instead of the wild tangle of curls, her hair had been scraped back hard from her face and twisted into a knot on top of her head, like Emma usually did before she went to bed. It made Emma look touchable and soft, but on Janice the effect was the opposite. It left her face completely unobscured, showing high, sharp cheekbones and a delicate jaw.

She was startlingly beautiful, but in a way that could never function in the world. The kind of thing so eerie that people can't even deal with it, and so they have to destroy it.

She had one leg stuck out behind her at an awkward angle, trailing her bare foot in the flooded place where water bubbled up from the stone.

"Hello, ugly boy who isn't ugly," she said without looking up. "Are you here for more of my restoratives and my analeptics?"

The Morrigan went skipping across to her through the puddles and hugged her around the neck. "He would like another dram of the hawthorn, please. Just a taste, to start with. If he does us proud tomorrow, we'll see about giving him a more practical amount."

Janice got up and went over to the row of cupboards. She was wearing a sort of romper suit. It buttoned down the front, with lace around the neck and armholes, and looked like it might be some kind of old-fashioned underwear. She opened a glass-fronted cabinet and started sorting through bottles.

When she found one she wanted, she took it back to the counter. With great concentration, she licked a paper label, running it carefully along her tongue, and pasted it to the bottle. Taking a pen from the knot on top of her head, she marked the label with what looked like a big floppy 3. Then she turned and looked up at me.

"A dram," she said, setting the bottle in my hand. "It isn't much, but it should be enough to hold you until you've earned your keep."

Behind her, the Morrigan was creeping toward the work-table, reaching for the pile of plant cuttings.

Janice spun around on her hassock and slapped the back of the Morrigan's hand. "Naughty!"

The Morrigan skipped back, looking guilty and sorry. Janice sorted through the leaves and stems until she found a small yellow flower and tucked it behind the Morrigan's ear.

The Morrigan ran her fingers over the flower, smiling and ducking her head. "She's very kind, our Janice. Isn't she kind?"

I held up the little bottle. "Is this why the dead girls and the people in the band seem okay?"

The Morrigan shook her head. She rolled her head so the side of her face was pressed against my arm. Her cheek was hot. "You are an entirely different class of people. Everyone has their own manner of survival. The blue girls are quite sturdy, only susceptible to true destruction by dismemberment and by fire. My players only need adulation if they're to thrive, and my lady-sister lives off the blood sacrifice of unfortunate creatures like Malcolm Doyle."

I stared down at her. "*Me*, you mean?"

She shook her head. "Oh, no, Malcolm Doyle was a little boy who was taken from his bed in order to feed the ravenous appetites of my sister. You are someone else."

It was the truth, but it still felt strange to hear someone say it. I am not Malcolm Doyle. I'm someone else. "So, they hurt him."

"She tore out his throat," the Morrigan said. "It was very quick. I suppose it may even have been painless, but I can't be sure. Yes," she said after a minute, winding a handful of hair around her wrist and then unwinding it again. "On second thought, I do imagine that it hurt."

"So, when you talk about feeding on the town, you mean murder."

"Oh, no, no. Not murder—sacrifice. And the cost is small. It hardly even qualifies as hardship, as it only comes in sevens, and the town grows strong on it for another handful of years, and when the town is well, so are we."

I remembered how bad I'd felt at the blood drive just smelling the iron. "Do you *drink* it?"

The Morrigan shook her head. "The Lady's methods are her own business and has barely anything to do with the House of Mayhem. Our job is only to stand in the churchyard and bear witness."

"What are you talking about? You can't go in the churchyard."

"Don't be dense. It has a plot saved just for us—you know, for the heretical and the unclean."

"For suicides and stillbirths and murderers, though. Not for people like you."

The Morrigan smiled up at me and squeezed my hand. "That ground *is* for us. Each seven years, we go down to the unholy ground and bear witness to the bloodletting."

I stared at her. "Bloodletting? But that means it doesn't even get *used* if they're just pouring it out."

"Intention is one of the most powerful forces there is. What you mean when you do a thing will always determine the outcome. The law creates the world."

"But you can't pour blood on the ground and have it make you strong because you think it *should*. The world is just . . . the world."

The Morrigan shook her head, smiling. "All great acts are ruled by intention. What you mean is what you get. In the House of Mayhem, we get what we need when they love us. That's why we need lovely creatures like you—there's a great deal of power in beauty, you know."

I thought about Alice, how she existed at the top of the social ladder for no reason except that the perfect symmetry of her face made people want to do whatever she said.

The Morrigan was hugging herself, rocking back and forth. She leaned against me suddenly, resting her cheek on my arm. "We love the town as best we can, and they love us back, although they don't always know they're doing it. But it isn't enough for my sister. She needs sacrifice."

She played with the flower behind her ear and said in a low, singsong voice, "She takes their pretty babies, and in exchange, she leaves them our own diseased flesh. Those are the ones who die, of course—almost always. It's nearly impossible to live outside the hill. So you see, we sacrifice our own too. But it's a small cost to give up the sick ones, the ones who are only going to die anyway. Except . . ."

"Except what?"

Her hand was small and hot when she reached for mine. She turned and smiled up at me, showing her jagged teeth. "Except you didn't. Isn't that the most wonderful thing?"

I didn't answer. I was too far into my own unsettling memory, thinking about the dark, flapping shadow and the screen. What it meant to be left somewhere and never found.

The Morrigan laced her fingers through mine, holding on tight. I looked down at her and she was shrunken and ugly, smiling like she knew something completely desolate.

Like she knew me. Her eyes were huge and dark, and I smiled back because she looked kind of pitiful standing there. She looked so sad.

"Promise," she said, hooking her little finger through mine and leading me toward the door. "Promise that you'll work for me and play glorious music, and in return, I'll make sure you never want for anything. Promise that you stay safe and out of the clutches of my sister, and in return, we'll cease to trouble your own sister."

"I promise," I said, because Emma was the most important person in my life and because it was nice to be able to breathe. "I promise."

CHAPTER 11

HUMAN LOVE

When I left the slag heap, the air was clammy, damp with autumn and the rain that never seemed to stop.

I climbed up the side of the ravine and crossed the footbridge, then started across Orchard Circle, headed for home. On Concord Street, porch lights glowed in a line all the way down the block.

Inside, I stood at the top of the stairs and leaned against the banister, making sure I was composed, before padding down the hall to Emma's room. I opened the door a crack, pressing my mouth to the gap so I could whisper without letting too much light in.

"Emma?"

There was a sigh, a rustle of blankets. "Yeah?"

Relief washed over me, making my chest relax. I stepped inside and closed the door and then there was just the splash of light shining in under it. I lay on the carpet beside her bed and looked up at the shadows on the ceiling. She didn't say anything, and I knew she was waiting for me to talk.

"I met some people tonight."

Above me, she rolled over but still didn't say anything. Then she took a deep breath. "What kind of people?"

The dead kind. The still-walking-around kind. The reeking, stinking, rotting-from-the-inside-out kind. Toothy and grinning, nasty with the dark and the dust of abandoned strip mines. But none of that was the whole truth. They were more than that. They were Carlina and Luther, electric on the stage, and the Morrigan with her hand on my arm like she knew me and had known me my whole life. And the Janice who showed up after school to work on botany homework with Emma was bony and weird looking, but the one who lived down in the House of Mayhem was beautiful, and the girl who liked stars was happy and pink and sort of cute.

"Why is Janice your lab partner?"

Emma answered in a tight, controlled voice. "Well, because group projects pretty much always involve a group."

"Are you lying to me?"

Emma was quiet a long time, and when she answered, she sounded defensive. "I saw her brush against a stainless steel table. She pulled away and then looked around to make sure no one was watching. I thought she might be . . . like you. I asked if she wanted to work together."

"You took something from them," I said, pressing my hands flat against the floor.

"To help you," she whispered. "Only to help you."

"This isn't *free*, Emma. I think they want something back."

"Then we'll pay them," she said, and I closed my eyes at the conviction in her voice. "We'll do what it takes."

"What if it's not that simple? What if they want something weird or impossible or . . . bad?"

Neither of us said anything after that. Sometimes things are so big and complicated that you can't actually talk about them.

"They make blood sacrifices," I said. "Just like in the books. I mean, it sounds crazy, like something someone made up. But it's the truth."

Emma didn't respond right away. When she did, her voice was unnaturally calm. "Maybe that's not surprising. A lot of cultures have a history of human sacrifice."

"It *is* surprising because it's *insane*. This isn't the Stone Age. We don't go around sacrificing people to the gods."

She laughed and it sounded shrill and breathless, almost like a sob. "We *do*, though. We take for granted that sometimes you lose a child. And sometimes everyone else gets hit by the recession. Everyone else's unemployment skyrockets, and their tech plants go bankrupt and their dairy farms fail, but not ours. Never ours because if you feed the ground, the ground feeds you back. You get food and prosperity and peace, and there are no disasters or plagues, and nothing bad happens."

"Except that every seven years, someone kills one of your kids."

"You have to understand, it wasn't always bad."

"So, some little kid gets murdered, but it's cool?"

For a second, Emma was so quiet it sounded like she was holding her breath. When she answered, she stayed very still. "I think it's complicated. It wasn't always a kid. Some of the Germanic tribes believed that volunteering to be sacrificed was a kind of magic by itself. Like a transformation. One of the old druidic texts in the Bevelry volume talks about going into a cave to be eaten by a goddess and coming out as the greatest poet of all time. They went into the dark and came out reborn."

I squeezed my eyes shut until I saw stars. "How can you be eaten and then become a poet?"

"Stop being so literal. It's a metaphor and you know it." Emma rolled over and her voice sounded farther away, like she was talking to the wall. "The prosperity rituals work on a trade-off. The cost is a way of showing that you're serious, that you'll give something up in order to gain favor."

I nodded, but it was more complicated than a straight trade. She wasn't just talking about what it cost to feed the Lady or look the other way while kids disappeared from their beds. I came from somewhere. I could have lived an ugly life in a world of tunnels and black, murky water and dead girls, with a little tattooed princess to watch over us. I would have belonged there. Instead, I was just a stranger in a strange house, with too many lights on. That was a cost too.

"It's been hard for you," she said finally. "All the time. How do you think that makes me feel, that everything is poisonous and everything hurts you and there's nothing I can do about it? And everything has to be a secret, everyone's always asking how we can be so different from each other. They all want to know how you turned out to be the delicate one, like it's my *fault* that my brother's prettier than me." Her voice was higher and softer than normal. "Girls are just *supposed* to be pretty."

"You're pretty," I said, and knew that if I could say it, that made it true.

Above me, Emma laughed like I'd just said I wanted to grow up to be a toaster oven or a giraffe. I got up and switched on her desk lamp.

She squinted at me, blinking in the light. "What? What's wrong?"

I sat on the edge of her bed, trying to get an idea of what other people saw.

"Stop it," she said. "What are you doing?"

"I'm looking at you."

Her face was soft, broader and flatter than mine, her hair limp, coming to just past her shoulders. It was brown, faded looking against her daisy-print pajamas. She was sitting up now, holding the blankets in a fierce double handful. Her cheeks were pink and shiny.

Around us, the bookshelves reached almost to the ceiling. Books about chemistry and physics and gardening, sure, but mythology and history too, all kinds of folklore and fairy tales. She read academic journals and ordered books online. She stockpiled literary criticism and essays. Her room was a private library of answers, trying to help me, save me, decode me. It was just another part of what made her beautiful.

She was looking off over my head. "They trade their sick children for healthy babies."

I nodded.

She hugged herself and still wouldn't look at me. "Sometimes, if the new mother loves it and takes really good care of it, the sick baby gets better. It stops being ugly and grows up strong and healthy and normal. Sometimes, if the mother just *loves* it enough, it becomes beautiful."

I knew that part too, but the way she said it was miserable, like she was trying to tell me something else. She was looking past me. Maybe thinking in the back of her mind that if our mother had just loved her more, she would have turned out looking like something in a magazine and not like the girl I'd known my whole life. I wanted to point out that *strong*, *healthy*, and *normal* were not words anyone would generally apply to me.

Anyway, the stories always missed one crucial thing. Mothers didn't love the hungry, scary things that replaced their kids. It wasn't their fault or anything. They just couldn't bring themselves to love something that awful. But maybe sisters could, if they were miraculously unselfish, if the trade happened when they were young enough.

My whole life, Emma had just been there. Cutting my hair with the aluminum kindergarten scissors just so I didn't have to go to the barbershop downtown, with its metal countertops and its stainless steel shears. Making me breakfast, making sure I ate and went out with my friends and did my homework. Making sure nothing bad happened. I wanted to hug her and say that everything was much better than she believed. It was just so strange that she couldn't see.

"Emma—" I got a tight feeling in my throat and started again. "Emma, Mom didn't make me like this. Keep me alive this long . . . You did."

CHAPTER 12

CONSECRATED

The next day was Sunday, and I woke up to rain coursing steadily down my window. I lay in bed watching it, waiting for my alarm to go off and feeling wide awake. In the daylight, everything looked gray and weak. The night before didn't seem so disturbing or so real.

I rolled onto my back, trying to decide whether I wanted to get up or just lie there awhile.

Finally, I pushed back the covers. Even overcast, the light was brighter than it had seemed in weeks, but it didn't hurt my eyes. Out in the yard, everything looked crisp around the edges.

I got out the bottle the Morrigan had given me, cracked the wax seal, and took a swallow. Right away, I felt good. My reflection in the mirror was shockingly, gloriously normal.

Downstairs, I could hear my dad humming to himself. His steps were quick and light and it was weird to think that Sundays made someone happy.

When I went down to the kitchen, Emma was already at the table. She was bent over a book, and when she looked up and saw me, she smiled. I stood in the doorway and watched her. She was small and destructible, with soft hands and fine, straight hair.

I wanted to be shocked. I wanted to be dumbstruck and appalled, but I couldn't do it. It was completely unshocking that there were monsters in the world, secret rituals and underground burrows filled with the dead, when in my own way, I was secret and sort of monstrous too. It just didn't show in the same way.

I was still standing in the doorway when my mom came wandering in, wearing her hospital sneakers and her scrubs. The outfit was radically inappropriate for church and I wondered if she knew what day it was. Her hair was pulled back in a ponytail and it looked very blond in the sunlight.

"Morning, sweetie." She poured herself a cup of coffee and put in more sugar than any reasonable person would need. "What are you doing up so early?"

I shrugged. "I thought maybe I'd come to church with you guys."

Emma set down her book. "The weather report said it's going to rain all day. Are you sure you don't want to stay home?"

"Nah, it's not that bad out. I'll hang around on the lawn or something."

We were late leaving the house. This was due entirely to the fact that my dad wouldn't start the car until my mom went back inside and changed out of her scrubs.

After they'd gone inside and the doors had closed, I sat on the lawn of the classroom addition and faced the church. It was large building, warm and buttery looking. Even under a gray sky, it made me think of sunlight, all vaulted roof and blond brick. The windows were pieced together with diamonds of colored glass.

Beyond it, the cemetery stretched back for almost two acres, graves planted in rows, neatly mowed. Along the north side, the unconsecrated area was less orderly. The headstones were grimy and ancient, the names worn off or else never chiseled on in the first place. They leaned drunkenly around a lone crypt, fourteen feet high and made of white marble. I didn't know how far back it dated, but it was one of the oldest fixtures in the cemetery. Everything else had sprung up around it.

I tipped my head back and looked up. The clouds were low, dark with the constant rain.

In the park across the street, the trees had already gone from green to red and yellow and orange. Now they were turning brown.

I lay on my back in the wet grass. The ground was cold through my jacket and I closed my eyes, trying to shut out the drizzle and the looming shape of the building. This was the place where everything in my life was clearly divided. My mom and dad and Emma disappeared through the double doors every Sunday, and I stayed outside.

It didn't matter how many David and Goliath coloring books I'd colored or how hard my dad tried to make everything seem normal and okay. The plain truth was, my family was there in the church, under the steeple, and that was someplace I couldn't go.

But maybe things were changing. It was hard to stop focusing on how good I felt. How completely different from my normal, awkward self.

"Good morning," said someone above me. The voice was raspy and familiar.

When I opened my eyes, I was looking up at Carlina Carlyle. She stood over me in scuffed boots and a long coat. She had on a bizarre kind of pilot's hat, with a leather strap that buckled under her chin. She looked exactly like she did when she took the stage at the Starlight. And at the same time, not like herself at all. Her features looked ordinary. Her fierce stage strut had turned awkward, the same way Janice could look weird and creepy in my kitchen and beautiful when she bent over her glass beakers and flowers. Above me, Carlina's eyes were pale like robin's eggs, without the devilish glow from the footlights.

When I didn't say anything, she flopped down next to me. "Don't you get cold out here?"

"Sometimes, I guess."

She looked like she was waiting for me to say something else. Her mouth was wide, but now it looked tight at the corners, like maybe she was the kind of person who could understand.

"Mostly, I just get lonely."

She nodded. "We like to think we're so solitary, so self-sufficient." When she smiled, it was tired and kind of ironic. Her hair was spilling out from under the hat, curling around her face. "What a stupid thing to be proud of, huh?"

"Who are we?" I said, and my mouth felt dry and sticky, like I didn't really want to know.

She hunched forward with her chin in her hands. With her face turned away from the overcast sky, her eyes were a darker blue.

"Do you *really* want to know where we come from?" she said. "In every century, in every country, they'll call us something different. They'll say we're ghosts, angels, demons, elemental spirits, and giving us a name doesn't help anybody. When did a name ever change what someone *is*?"

And that was something I understood. Because it didn't matter how often my dad called me Malcolm or introduced me as his son. It just made things worse. In fact, saying it once always seemed to make him say it again, like once it was out, he had to keep repeating it, so many times it just lost meaning.

"Does God hate us?" I asked, looking down at the ground.

Carlina didn't answer right away. She leaned forward, looking off at a glossy stand of barn-red maple trees, bright as blood.

"I don't know about God," she said finally. "But I know about tradition. We're literal people, you and me. Whatever the most obvious interpretation is, that's our truth. When the old churches made their laws, they set a precedent. They believe that hallowed ground rejects our souls, and because they believe it that much, our bodies hurt."

I nodded, but it was discouraging to know that an inanimate object could reject a person. That strangers could make a place hate me without ever having met me.

Carlina glanced over. "You'll be at the Starlight tonight, yeah?"

"I kind of have to be, don't I?"

"Yeah." She brushed wet leaves off her coat and stood up. "You do."

Then she sauntered out of the yard and down the street, looking proud and cool and about a century out of place.

I lay back, staring up through the rain. The lawn was dying in a soggy, golden way, cold against my neck, and the leaves shifted and slithered under me when I breathed.

When I thought about the church, I had a vivid, wordless impression of my dad, up there at the podium. His sermons on paper were quiet, but he wasn't a quiet man and I knew that when he read the words out loud, they must sound powerful and definite.

I stood up.

I wanted to watch the realest, truest part of him, how it showed in his face and his voice. I wanted to see what he saw. I'd never seen him in any way that mattered, and now I understood that I was probably never going to.

I crossed the lawn and was at the property line before I could change my mind. As soon as I stepped onto the property, though, the tight, cracking pain was there like always. My cheeks and forehead started to burn and I backed away fast.

I wanted so badly for the ground to have a different truth—*my* truth, but the church didn't waver. It wasn't changeable. It hurt like an electric shock because no special drink, no amount of conviction or belief could make me something I wasn't.

CHAPTER 13

APPLAUSE

That night, Roswell came to get me and didn't ask questions. I half wanted him to ask why I had my bass with me, but he didn't. We listened to the radio. All the songs were about true love and drug addiction.

When we pulled up at the Starlight, no one from Rasputin was there yet. Roswell and I stood in the middle of the floor and watched the crowd. A lot of people were in costumes, even though Halloween was still two days away. They moved easily through the Starlight, staring past me, and I wondered what they saw when they looked in my direction. Not a god or a monster. Maybe no one.

Then I heard a high, shrieking laugh and turned in time to see Alice. She was wearing her cat costume again, but this time she had a rhinestone collar around her neck and her whiskers were purple. She was walking with a guy named Levi Anderson, hanging on him as they came toward us. When they were almost even with me, she gave me a spiteful look, then plastered herself against Levi.

"Classy girl," Roswell said under his breath, but I didn't feel hurt or angry. My heart was starting to race and I didn't feel anything.

I found us an empty booth in the corner and sat staring at my hands while Roswell went up to the bar for something to drink.

"Are you okay?" he said when he slid into the seat across from me. He had a paper cup of Mountain Dew in his hand. "'Cause you kind of look like hell."

I nodded and stared down at the table. There were cigarette burns all over it.

"What's wrong?" he said.

"Do you ever think about the secret stuff in Gentry, the ugly things? Like, what it means when kids . . . when they die?"

He looked at me a long time before he answered, turning the cup so the ice clattered and cracked and the Mountain Dew splashed in circles, antifreeze colored. "I think that people are complicated and everybody's got their share of secrets."

I nodded and wondered why he wasn't pushing the conversation. Why he wasn't asking questions. I wanted him to make me say the things that wouldn't come out in words unless I couldn't avoid them. If he asked the right questions, I'd have to tell him. But he didn't say anything.

Across the dance floor, Carlina Carlyle was standing by the soundboard. When she saw me looking, she opened her eyes wide and waved me over.

Her hair was piled on top of her head. She looked strange and fantastical and startling and normal.

I stood up, reaching for my bass. "I have to go," I told Roswell.

"Go where?"

"Go work for them, play for them. Something. I'm in it now, and I don't think I can get out. I don't know what to do."

He just shrugged and nodded toward the stage. "So, go up there and do something amazing."

Carlina led me back through a narrow hall and into a tiny dressing room, more like a closet than a room. There was a gouged wooden dresser and a chair and nothing else. Everything smelled like dust.

I stood in the middle of the room with my heart racing. "Is this all you really need to survive? I mean, is there something I'm supposed to do to make the music work?"

Carlina was rifling through the dresser. She closed a drawer and turned to face me, shaking her head. "It's a living." Her voice sounded flat. "Gentry doesn't always remember that we're here, but they remember that they like a good performance. Everyone loves a good performance." She tossed a bundle of clothes at me. "Put these on."

I picked through them. Black wool slacks and a white button-down shirt, the blinding-black shoes, the braces. The fact remained, I wasn't really her bassist. I was quiet and skinny and sixteen years old and I got a tight, nervous feeling in my stomach if I was called on to answer in class.

Carlina sighed and turned her back. "Just hurry up and put them on."

I started stripping off my clothes. I yanked the slacks up, buttoned the shirt. I tried to figure out the clasps on the braces, but my hands were shaking.

"Here." Carlina took the clasp from me and opened it. "You need to relax."

When I was dressed, she sat me down at the little wooden dresser and reached for a comb. She started raking my hair back from my face, slicking it down with some kind of pomade that smelled like mint and honey and wax. Her hands felt cool on my forehead, like something was seeping over me.

I leaned sideways, trying to see myself in the dresser mirror. "Are you making me look like someone else?"

"No, you'll still look like you, but not so much that anyone down there would recognize you, if you know what I mean. To most people, even Luther doesn't look like Luther, and I don't look like myself." She touched the comb's teeth, greasing the tips of her fingers, twisting a lock of hair in front so it hung down over my forehead. "It's not a spell or a trick, nothing *changes*. They just see what they want to."

I looked down at my gleaming shoes and when I glanced in the mirror again, I recognized myself, and I didn't. I'd been getting used to how I could look like a whole new person when my eyes were dark brown and my color was good, but this was different. My expression was too far away, like I was looking into the mirror, but someone else was looking back. I was seeing what I wanted to see because what I wanted was to be someone besides myself. The visual wasn't comforting, though. The person in the mirror looked tired and hopeless.

Carlina put the comb down and turned me away from the mirror. She held my face between her hands, smiling her strange, sad smile.

"So we just give them some kind of distraction," I said. "Another lie."

She closed her eyes and pressed her forehead against mine. "No, what we're giving them is the unvarnished truth. They just don't know it. When you go out onstage, you'll be closer to yourself than you've ever been, and that's a beautiful thing. It's what they paid to see."

But that didn't make me feel better. My hands were shaking and my mouth felt dry. "I just feel nervous, though. I feel weird and freakish and pointless, and nobody wants to see that. I can't be what they paid for."

"Then you have to feel like that, then let it go and do your job." She whispered it, and I could feel her breath on the bridge of my nose. "We'll go out onto the stage in a minute, and when we do, you have to make them believe that whatever you show them is the real you because sometimes being believed in is just what it means not to die."

But I'd been waiting to die my whole life. I'd spent years expecting it any day because that was just what happened. Going onstage was different. Out onstage, the Starlight would be dark, with the spotlight shining down and no place else to look, and that was something I couldn't just live with and couldn't wish away. Being seen was the worst thing that could happen to someone like me.

"I just—I've never played in front of anyone before."

Carlina nodded against my forehead. "They'll love you, though, just like they love us. Do you want me to announce you as a special guest?"

"No, just let me come on with you guys like I belong there."

She let me go, then stood looking down at me. "You do."

*

153

As soon as the curtain came up, the noise of the crowd was deafening. The footlights glared in my face, and beyond that, there was nothing but a sea of voices and long, shrill whistles.

The drummer and I were supposed to set the tempo, but Luther was the one who stepped into the intro like he owned it, like it was *his* song—fast and frantic and I knew it in my fingers, even when I didn't know it by ear or from memory. Earlier, Luther had laughed when I asked to see the set list, but now I understood that set lists were meaningless. They just played whatever they felt like playing.

Luther grinned, watching my face, leading me through each verse and chorus, making me race him. I listened to his changes and found the counterpoint, making every note rumble and screech because the song was about mayhem and being totally, arrogantly out of control.

Adrenaline was coursing through my fingers, tingling in my blood. This was what it felt like to be a rock star.

As soon as I came to the end of the song, though, the feeling stuttered, then disappeared. I let the guitar hang heavy against the strap and my hands felt cold and shaky again. Suddenly, I was very aware that I was standing on a stage in front of two hundred people, and all I had was a cherry-red Gibson reissue and someone else's shoes.

Luther just swung his guitar around in an arc, sneering down at everyone in the audience. Then he went straight into "Common People," not caring that it was supposed to have a synthesizer or that it was about thirty years old and most of the kids in the Starlight had never even heard of Pulp. He just picked it and played it, making the guitar sing in his hands, while Carlina acted both sides of a conversation between a rich girl and a working-class guy and screamed herself hoarse about all the ways that being poor sucked.

Every now and then, Luther cut his eyes at me and I tried to read the cues in his glances. He picked the tune faster, showing me how *every* song was a conversation, a debate between rhythms and tones. I just had to listen and then respond.

We played in tandem, working off each other, until he switched into an old Pearl Jam song. It was "Yellow Ledbetter."

The bass line was low and inevitable. I hit the first note and the whole building seemed to creak and shudder.

It was a song about loss, but the melody was sweet, and if Eddie Vedder sounded kind of like a stumbling wino in his version, Carlina sounded husky but clear.

Her voice was like loneliness. It was regret. She sang about a past you couldn't get out of and didn't want, and standing alone in the cool blue light, she was beautiful— more beautiful than the shows where she wailed and pranced, strutting back and forth across the stage, far more beautiful than she'd been standing over me on the church lawn. With her hands cupped around the microphone, she was the realest part of the Starlight, the realest voice in Gentry. Luther and I supplied the melody, but all the notes were leading up to her. She was the purest, biggest truth, while all the audience were just kids wearing their costumes.

She wailed the first chorus with her chin up and her back straight. Then she brought the mike close, smiling over at Luther. "Now, make me cry."

Luther smiled back. Not his sly, toothy grin, but a real one, open and honest. He bent over the guitar and played a solo that was just for her—a slow progression of notes, running hard and sharp and up.

I followed it, making my own melody thump and buzz underneath his like a heartbeat, letting each note hang for minutes or years. And then something happened.

It wasn't like the other songs. There was no story, no conversation. This was just the feeling, without words or pictures, and it had nothing to do with Luther or his clean, stinging guitar.

It was the sound of being outside, of being alien. It was the pulse that ran under everything and never let you forget that you were strange, that the world hurt just to touch. Feelings too complicated to ever say in words, but they spilled out of the amplifiers, seeping into the air and filling up the room.

Out in the crowd, everyone had stopped moving. They stood in the pit, staring up at me, and when I stopped playing, they started to clap.

"Mackie," Carlina said, coming close to whisper in my ear. "You can't *do* that."

"They liked it, though."

She nodded, touching the collar of her dress. "It's just—it's not good for them to feel it for very long. It's exhausting, feeling like that."

Down in the pit, the clapping had already started to die. People were staring up at the stage and the colored lights. Luther went into a frantic version of "Here Comes Your Man" that sounded like a three-day coke bender, and they stood around like dairy cows.

When the Pixies didn't get a reaction, he pulled out Nick Cave and then Nine Inch Nails, but nothing seemed to get them moving again. He played one last hard, flashy change, then quit torturing "Mr. Self-Destruct" in the middle of the riff.

Behind us, the drummer gave the snare a few more half-hearted beats, and then he stopped too and got up. The four of us stood motionless on the stage and I had just fucked up the special surprise Halloween show, and royally.

Luther shot Carlina a desperate look and jerked his head toward the wings. "We have to bring out the piano."

She shook her head.

"Do it—play them one of those sad-bastard ballads and finish us up. It's all they'll want now anyway."

"Fine," she said in the long silence. "Fine, bring it out."

Luther and the drummer dragged an old upright piano out of the wings and pushed it into the center of the stage. The finish was wearing off the wood in pale stripes.

Carlina tossed her hair back over one shoulder and settled onto the bench. She raised her hands and spread her fingers over the keys. Then she found the first chord.

It was a Leonard Cohen song. I knew it but had never known it like this. It wasn't bitter or cynical. It was broken.

The piano wasn't miked, but it didn't matter. The notes scaled up, shrill, cracking. The whole place was absolutely silent as Carlina ran through the intro and into the first verse. The sound of her voice was painful. She screamed, sobbed, whispered *hallelujah*, but she never sang it.

Down in the audience, people were reaching for each other, hugging, holding hands. Near the front, a girl with crazy chopped-up hair and too many piercings was crying so hard that her nose was running. Her eye makeup looked mysterious and scary, but her mouth was crumpled like a little kid's.

Carlina slammed down on the chords, plodded over the keys, but her voice was high and clear, talking about more than being used, being rejected. How when you love someone, sometimes it means that they strip you down, peel you open, and you have to *let* them and not worry about how much it's going to hurt.

I was holding the neck of the Gibson too, too tightly as she came to the end. My fingers felt cramped and sticky.

"Hallelujah." She said it flatly, coming down hard on the last note, and then she let it fade.

There was nothing.

Luther and the drummer were already breaking things down, but I stood at the edge of the stage, staring out at the crowd. No one was dressed like themselves, but they were all suddenly illuminated, lit with something real, their own private versions of the song. It had gotten inside them. I stood above the packed floor, looking down at all of them, shining like lanterns with their love stories and their tragedies.

I just stood looking until Carlina caught me by the arm and dragged me back into the little dressing room. She was breathless and smiling, but her face was pale and she looked tired. "Did you have fun?"

I nodded and unhooked my braces. The room was cold and the rush was already starting to trickle away. I yanked off the button-down shirt and reached for my T-shirt and my hoodie.

Carlina stood by the door, politely keeping her back to me. "There's going to be some festivities down in the pit tonight. Kind of like . . . an after party. You should come."

I laughed and shook my head. "Thanks, but I think I'll skip it."

"Are you sure? You haven't had a chance to see us when we're wild. It's called Mayhem for a reason, you know."

I knew that she was just being friendly, and when it came to my survival, being friendly with people like Carlina was probably my best option. Still, that didn't mean I was a fan of the Morrigan's house or of anyplace where dead girls huddled and whispered behind their hands and mutilated women floated in pools. I wasn't sure I wanted to see their version of wild.

"I'll pass this time."

Carlina shrugged. "Suit yourself, but don't be a stranger. Our house is yours."

And in a bizarre way, I didn't doubt that.

When I was back in my own clothes, I sat at the dresser, staring at the strange reflection that was just starting to look like me again. "That was magic, right, what just happened out there?"

Carlina smiled and shrugged. "I guess. As much as music is ever magic. Or always, I mean. Music is our best language. It's just what we do."

"You could take over the world with what you do."

She laughed, much softer, much shyer than I ever would have pictured her a week ago. "Gentry's enough."

CHAPTER 14

CRASHING

When I went back out into the crowd, no one really noticed me. I was carrying my bass, and my hair was sticky with pomade, but everything else was ordinary.

I realized I was smiling, which was strange, and stranger to realize that I meant it. Usually, I only smiled when other people were there to see. When it was what they expected from me.

Someone touched my arm and when I turned, Tate Stewart was standing very close.

"It *is* you." Her voice was low. "I wasn't sure."

My heart was beating hard but steady. A good beat, and not a faltering one. I felt different and new, like I could be someone else.

Over the top of her head, I could see Drew and Danny at the farthest pool table. Drew glanced up and grinned at me. Then he waved me over.

I didn't go right away. Instead, I stood in the middle of

the floor, looking down at Tate. She stared so hard that I got an idea she was seeing through layers of pointless, ordinary things, all the way down to how I felt about her—whatever I was feeling—like it was there in my eyes if I forgot to blink.

Her face was close to mine. "I don't get you," she said. "You spend every day at school trying to disappear and now you're dancing around onstage like a fucking rock star, like you don't have anything holding you down? I mean, who *are* you?"

There was nothing to say to that. I didn't know what performance she'd been watching, but I hadn't felt carefree up there—not anywhere close.

She shook her head and turned away, and even with the ferocious scowl, even looking disgusted with me, I kind of wanted to follow her.

In an unprecedented display of good judgment, I made my way over to where Danny was bent over the table, lining up a combo.

"You did good," he said without looking up. The shot was eight ball to two ball to corner pocket. He made an open bridge on the top of his hand and sank it.

I stared down at his bent head and smiled wider. "You recognized me?"

Danny straightened up and gave me a bored, incredulous look. "Well, *yeah*."

162

"Jesus," Drew said. "We just saw you at that party last night. We're not *senile*."

"I don't look different?"

Danny butted his cue on the floor. "You do, but it's a good kind of different. You're *happy*, Mackie. I can't even remember the last time you were happy."

"I just—I feel better lately."

Drew was fidgeting with the chalk, making blue slashes on the back of one hand with his fingertip. "That's good," he said, but he said it without looking at me.

"What? What's wrong?"

Danny shook his head. "Nothing. Just be careful. You know?"

I nodded and waited for him to tell me what I was being careful of or why, but he didn't say anything else and they both went back to studying the table.

After a minute, Drew looked up again. He glanced in the direction of Tate and the arcade, then raised his eyebrows. "What the hell is up with you two? I keep expecting someone to break out the grenades."

I didn't answer. There wasn't really a word for what we were doing, except that it was stupid and confusing, and Tate had a way of sticking her chin out that made me want to stand much closer than necessary.

Out on the floor, I pushed through the crowd, avoiding the kids from school and the strangers.

163

Tate was in the arcade, playing Earthshaker pinball, dropping quarters in with icy precision.

"Hey," I said when I came up beside her.

She pulled back the spring-loaded plunger and shot the first ball out into a sea of flashing lights and bright plastic sirens.

I leaned on the top of the machine. "So, did you like the show?"

She was hunched over the game, watching the ball as it clanged through a minefield of bumpers and bells. "It was pretty good, if you're into that kind of thing."

"What kind of music do you like?"

"Whatever. A lot of stuff. Would you please get off the glass?"

The sound of her voice made shivers race up the back of my neck and it was hard to tell if it was all from nerves, because I kind of liked it. I stood next to the pinball machine and watched the ball careen through obstacles and pitfalls.

The Morrigan's tonic was just starting to wear off, and the feeling was disorienting but not unpleasant. It felt leisurely and free, like being just a little drunk. I was at that perfect point where the world is manageable and nothing seems too overwhelming or too bad. I stood in the arcade, watching Tate. She worked the flippers like it was serious business. She didn't say anything else.

When the last ball had disappeared down into the

machine, she sighed and turned to face me. "*What?* What do you *want*?"

"Will you give me a ride home?" The words were out before I'd had time to consider them.

Her face was unreadable, turned up to stare at me, and her chin was so obstinate I wanted to grab her by the shoulders just so she would stop looking at me like that.

After a long pause, filled with pinball sirens and flashing lights, she nodded.

We were only a block from the Starlight when it occurred to me that I might have made a bad decision. The hawthorn was wearing off much faster than it had the night before and so was the euphoria of playing for a crowd. Every uneven section of the road, every pothole rattled the car and jolted through my bones.

Tate didn't seem to notice. She stared straight ahead, peering through the rain on the windshield, talking about school and various independent movies. Her voice was light, like she was in no hurry, waiting for the perfect time. That moment when she would spring some critical question and I would have no choice but to answer her. The air was thick with the smell of iron. I swallowed it down and cracked the window.

We were six blocks from my house when regret hit, sickening and official. I closed my eyes and counted backward, trying to get the shaking under control, get the bad air out of my lungs. Something lurched in my stomach and I tried to ignore it, taking slow, deep breaths. I was sweating.

When the warm, squirming thing lurched again, I cleared my throat. "Tate, could you pull over?"

"Hey—hey, what's wrong?"

"I feel pretty sick." Which was a massive understatement. The feeling I had wasn't like any reaction I'd ever had, even to blood iron or stainless steel, even on my worst days.

The dizziness came in waves, making everything slide. It was radio static in my ears, a rain of black dots that swept in and covered everything. The smell of metal filled my mouth and nose. It was under my skin, in my blood, pounding away in my joints, my bones.

Tate pulled onto the shoulder and slammed the transmission into park. "Is this—"

But I was already yanking at the door.

I made it out but could barely stand. In the dark, the ground pitched up at me. I got down on my knees and held very still until the worst of it passed and I was steady enough to lie down. I needed to be someplace quiet and alone. I needed to curl up in a dark room, with no movement and no sound.

I pressed my face into the grass and breathed the green smells of leaves and stems and roots. The rain felt light and cool against my face. I needed the Morrigan.

"Mackie, are you okay?"

Tate was kneeling over me, reaching like she wanted to put her hand on my shoulder but was scared to touch me. I was shaking in huge wrenching spasms.

I squeezed my eyes shut and tried to stay very still. Every time I took a breath, it touched off a storm of throbbing in my chest.

"Mackie, tell me if you're okay." Her voice sounded tight.

The pain in my knees and elbows was getting worse, going from low and throbbing to something more like being hit with a hammer. I looked up at her and tried to find something to say that would make her stop talking. I was afraid of what my voice would sound like.

She reached for my hand, her fingers sliding over my knuckles, my palm. Her touch wasn't rough, but the pressure made pain shoot up my arm and I jerked away, biting down on the inside of my lip.

"Your hands are cold," she said.

The concern in her voice made my throat hurt worse. I squeezed my eyes shut and prayed for her to go away, to leave me so I could get myself together and figure out what to do. Her worry made me too aware of how bad the reaction was. It knocked the breath out of me. I needed her to leave, but nothing would make her do that. Even if I hurt her feelings, called her the worst things I could think of, she wouldn't just go because I told her to. Her face was a white

167

oval floating above me. The only place for help was the House of Mayhem.

"You have to go," I said, making my voice as steady as I could.

"Excuse me? I can't just leave you on the side of the road. Jesus, I think you're going into *shock*. If you're hurt or sick, you need someone to stay with you."

"Tate, listen to me. I need you to find Roswell and bring him here, okay?"

"Mackie, you're scaring me."

"Please, just go get Roswell."

She didn't like it, but she stood up, looking more frightened than I'd ever seen her, and started for her car.

When the Buick pulled away from the curb, I closed my eyes. I breathed out, this miserable, rattling sigh that sounded nothing like relief. It was thin, which made it easier to pretend that it was coming from someplace else than that I'd made it myself. Easier to pretend that everything was coming from someplace else and I was asleep, maybe at home, dreaming the way my chest seemed to tighten and seize. The air was too thick to breathe, almost like water, and the ground had stopped feeling cold.

I turned my face into the grass and wondered if this was how people felt when they knew they were going to die.

PART THREE

THE RESTLESS DEAD

CHAPTER 15

THE AFTER PARTY

I lay on the ground for way too long, with my face against the wet grass and the rain soaking into my clothes. I knew if I stayed, Tate would come back with Roswell, and then they'd want to take me home or worse, to the emergency room.

I had to get up and get moving. It was a painful and multi-step process, but I did it. The street was empty and the rain made everything disorienting. I was wandering through patches of light and deep shadow. The streetlights hummed so loud that my joints ached each time I passed one. I was on Welsh Street, then Orchard, then down the slope of the ravine and crossing the footbridge. My knees felt weak, and all the times I'd thought about my condition or the chance that I might die, I hadn't understood what it meant. I hadn't understood how much I wanted to live.

The ground was slick and muddy, but I made it, sliding on the steep path down to the bottom of the ravine. The slag heap was a vague, looming shape. It had never looked so welcoming.

I slumped against the base of the hill, resting my head on the loose gravel. There was nothing to show me where the door had been, nothing for me to catch hold of or grab onto.

I lay in the shale and the fill, trying to think what to do. I was starting to lose feeling in my hands when I heard the crunch of footsteps, not in the ravine but from inside the hill. The gravel slid away and the door swung open, showing a yellow rectangle of light.

It was Carlina.

"Decided to come after all?" she said, holding a lantern up so that it cast a circle of light over both of us. "You look a little out of sorts."

I nodded and struggled into a sitting position, trying to catch my breath. "Please, do you think I could get paid now?"

Carlina stood in the doorway. The lantern was so bright that it was hard to see her face. "What have you been doing to yourself? No, never mind. You'd better come in."

I got unsteadily to my feet and followed her inside.

She closed the door behind us, then turned to face me. "What's the matter with you? Don't you keep anything on hand for first aid?"

I shook my head.

With a sigh, she took a tiny bottle out of her pocket and uncorked it. "Okay, deep breath."

She held the bottle in front of my face and I breathed in, feeling my lungs expand. It wasn't the analeptic, but the green smell of leaves rushed over me and then the huge, shuddering relief of finally getting enough air.

When I'd gotten my breath back and was standing upright without using the wall, Carlina took me by the elbow and started to lead me down toward the lobby. "Is that better?"

I nodded, still a little stupefied over the difference between breathing and suffocating.

Carlina led me down, talking under her breath, shaking her head. "What is it about boys? Why do you always have to push things as far they can go? Just because you're not completely ragged anymore doesn't make you invincible."

I nodded again and followed her along the tunnel and through the main lobby into the huge, high-ceilinged room where the floor was covered in puddles and water welled up from the ground.

The entire room was full of people, talking and laughing. Some of them were playing cellos and violins, and over in a corner, a girl with long, stringy hair was tuning an upright harp, but mostly they just stood around in little groups, looking happy. The floor was covered with intermittent puddles and drifts of bright autumn leaves.

The Morrigan was sitting by one of the dark pools. She'd taken off her shoes and socks and was trailing her feet in the water. She was playing with a folded paper boat, pushing it back and forth across the surface with a stick.

Carlina put her hand on my shoulder. "Here, sit down. I'll have Janice grab you some more of the hawthorn and we'll get you sorted out."

I sank onto the floor, careful to pick a dry spot, and leaned my back against the wall. It was nice to be able to breathe again, but I was exhausted.

The Morrigan glanced over her shoulder and saw me. She jumped up and ran across the room, clambering over my legs and scrubbing her wet feet against the cuffs of my jeans.

She gave me a huge smacking kiss on the cheek and settled down on my lap to watch the milling crowd. I leaned back against the wall and let her hug me around the neck. I was still wet and cold, and she was very warm.

Some of the dead girls were splashing around over by the Morrigan's pool, laughing and trying to push each other in. The little pink girl from the Halloween party scampered between them, still wearing her princess dress and waving her star wand.

In another pool, farther along the room, a blue-faced girl surfaced slowly, rising out of the water in ghostly silence. Her hair was the powdery-green color of mold and her nose had started to rot away in places.

The Morrigan squeezed my face between her hands. "Aren't you pleased with yourself? *You* did this—you and the other players—you've made everyone so pleased."

I didn't know how to respond to that. There was something disturbing about being responsible for partially decayed girls going swimming.

The Morrigan rested her head on my shoulder. "They're happy," she said. "The performance was a success, and everyone feels quite merry right now."

Out in the crowd, a girl with a ragged hoop skirt and no skin on the ridges of her collarbone raised a glass above her head. Her hair was arranged in a braided crown around her head and the hoops showed through the frayed fabric of the skirt like bones. "A curse on the House of Misery! May God strike down the harridan and let her rot!"

That made the other girls laugh and shriek, tossing handfuls of red and orange leaves, splashing each other. "Let her rot," they sang. "Let her rot in the House of Misery!"

I smiled uneasily at the way the girls howled and danced, but the Morrigan just sighed and fidgeted with her stick.

"The what?" I asked. "What are they talking about?"

"It's properly called Mystery," the Morrigan said. "My sister's venerable house, which they ought to speak of with reverence. Instead, they mock and make jests at her, but it's only because she frightens them."

"Why are they scared of her?"

"Because she earns it." The Morrigan's head was heavy against my shoulder and she was talking around her thumb. "She frightens me too, come to that."

Janice wound her way through the crowd and over to us. She was still barefoot but had changed out of her romper suit, or at least put a dress on over it. Her hair was up, and she was carrying a wide, painted fan. She looked rumpled and sleepy. The bottle she held was much bigger than the tiny vials they'd given me before.

"Here's to wild nights and the maddening crowd," she said, handing me the bottle. "May you continue to put that bass to good use. And you," she said to the Morrigan, "you leave him alone until he's had a chance to get his breath back."

The Morrigan gave me a quick pat on the cheek. Then she jumped up and went skipping back to her pool and her boat. "Feel better," she called over her shoulder, waving the stick.

I cracked the seal on the analeptic and took a long drink.

My obvious relief made Janice laugh. "If you lived here like a proper ugly boy, this wouldn't happen to you."

Luther and Carlina came over together. They were holding hands, leaning against each other as they walked.

Janice shook her head at them. "Have you talked to this one? He lives up in the town like a local."

Luther rolled his eyes. "*Why*, I have no idea. It can't be pleasant or easy. You're as bad as that lunatic, Caury."

I stared up at him. "Kellan Caury? The guy from Hanover Music?"

Luther nodded. "He was a strange one. Thought he could live topside if he just drank his restoratives and played nice with the locals. And look where that got him."

I looked at the bottle. There was no denying that whatever Caury had believed, it had gotten him someplace messy.

Over by her pool, the Morrigan and the star girl had dropped their toys and were hopping around in a circle, holding on to each other's hands.

Janice watched as they spun and then fell down. "She's a sweet little thing. Petulant to try the devil sometimes, but she never misuses us or asks for more than we can give. She cares for us."

"Why does she use us for music?" I asked. "I mean, does the town really need it?"

It was Carlina who answered. "When we play for them, we give them something rare and wonderful, and in return, they give us their admiration. I know you felt it tonight. You must know you that belong here, with us, playing for their admiration and helping to keep the peace."

Luther slipped his arm around her waist and pulled her against him, leaning down to kiss her.

I looked away because it seemed impolite to watch them. When they kissed, it was completely unselfconscious, holding on like they loved each other. It bothered me to realize that in my own experience, loving anyone, even my own family, just made me feel sort of awkward and shameful.

In the House of Mayhem, it was different. It wasn't shameful to be strange or unnatural because everyone else was too.

When I felt better, I got up and crossed the room to sit at the edge of the Morrigan's pool, watching the paper boat. It was painted with wax to make it waterproof, but it couldn't last forever, and the bottom was starting to get soggy.

The after party wound down and people began trailing out, leaving the room in twos and threes. Others lay tangled together on the floor or pinned each other against the walls.

The blue girls didn't seem to be included in the fun, though. Even in the House of Mayhem, the dead ones weren't popular at parties.

Over in a corner, Carlina still had her arms around Luther's neck. She kissed him hungrily, pulling his mouth down to hers, and his bony face and jagged teeth didn't matter because she was beautiful enough for both of them.

The initial wave of euphoria from the analeptic was wearing off and I started to wonder about Tate. What she'd thought when she'd gotten back to the side of the road with Roswell and found me gone. I hadn't had a choice. It was get myself someplace where someone could help me or stay on the side of the road until I passed out. Even now, I remembered the pain, the terrible weight in my chest, like I was never going to be able to breathe again.

I didn't want to be so invested in what happened to her, but her eyes were hard to forget. Her grief seemed almost like a solid thing, and I couldn't stop thinking about it.

I looked down into the water, trying to see the bottom. The pool was too dark to see much, but there was a series of shallow steps cut into one wall, leading down.

"Why are there steps?"

The Morrigan gave me a puzzled look. "For going up and down."

"Why would you want to climb up and down in the water, though?"

The Morrigan turned her paper boat with the stick, making it wobble and spin. "The water wasn't always there. My noble sister has been punishing me with a flood. The lower floors are unusable now, except by the restless dead because they aren't troubled with the inconvenience of breathing."

"Where does it come from?" I said, watching the boat as it wavered and spun.

"From everywhere. It falls from the sky and seeps up from the ground."

"Aren't you worried that she's going to flood you out?"

"She'll relent soon and tire of abusing us. Perhaps she'll

even regret her fit of pique. Until then, we're quite adaptable." The Morrigan smiled and kicked her legs, slapping the soles of her feet against the surface of the pool. "My sister makes the mistake of assuming that because we live one way, we're bound to it, but that just isn't so. Give us the corpses of children and we raise them. Give us water and we learn to swim."

"It's a lot of water, though. I mean, what will you do if it doesn't stop?"

"She'll be kinder after All Souls' Day. Once she gets her libation, we might even prevail upon her to be more sparing with the rain."

"I don't know All Souls' Day. Is that the same thing as Halloween?"

The Morrigan laughed and tapped me on the head with her stick. "Don't be silly. Halloween is just another name for All Hallows' Eve, when the locals burn their lanterns and throw the bones of their livestock on the fire to keep the devils away. Next comes All Saints', for the pious to be revered and sanctified and have their fingers cut off and kept as relics. And very last, there's All Souls' Day, and that's for the rest of us."

"The rest?"

The Morrigan nodded. "The creatures in the ground. All Souls' is when my sister renews her hold on the town and sacrifices an offering to herself. It's when we gather in the churchyard and burn sage and rue. And then, just before the sun comes up, we bear witness to the bloodletting, and the world is better again."

She said it like she was reciting a poem or telling me some kind of story instead of discussing something that happened in an aging steel town on a regular basis.

I gave her a hard look. "And you don't see anything wrong with that? The Lady takes kids so that she can slaughter them, and you're fine with it. You act like what she's doing is normal. You keep *saying* that she's so bad, that she's so out of line—then why doesn't someone do something about it?"

I watched her face, the way she kept touching her mouth, like she was trying to cover her teeth without meaning to. "Do yourself a service and keep out of her way. She's a hard, cruel mistress and she'll punish you as easily as breathing. She has the child in her house and will keep it safe until the night of ritual and blood."

"So, you're saying you're all just going to stand around and let her kill a little kid?" I thought of Tate's hard eyes, her desperate insistence that the girl who'd died wasn't her sister. My mom hadn't wanted to discuss the subject, but the kids who were replaced went somewhere. They didn't just vanish. If there was any purpose or reason to the substitutions, then Natalie was alive right now, waiting for someone to collect her blood.

The Morrigan stood up, raising the stick like a sword or

a scepter. "There is nothing you can do for that child. My sister is a wicked beast of a woman, and you'll only come to harm if you cross her."

"You're talking about killing a kid. Someone's daughter." I took a deep breath and closed my eyes. "Someone's sister."

"And it's only a small thing in the grand design of the world. One very small thing, every seven years. What a trivial cost to pay for health and prosperity."

Janice had come wandering over and she sat down next to me, sticking her feet in the pool. "The town needs this, Mackie. We *all* need this."

"So, you all line up in the graveyard and burn your sage and kill kids? That's great. That's just really amazing."

"It's not us doing it."

I could feel my throat get tight, almost like I was going to laugh, but not in a way where everything is so cheerful and humorous. "You're *letting* it happen."

Janice sighed, putting her hand on my arm. "You aren't thinking about this in a rational way. *Every*one benefits. Us, the House of Misery, the locals and the town."

"No," I said. "It doesn't benefit the town. It hurts and it terrorizes them. How can they be happy when someone's taking their kids?"

The Morrigan nodded eagerly. "That's why we have music. The Lady punishes the town, but we make them happy again."

"And it never occurred to you not to make them miserable in the first place?"

Janice shook her head. "You don't understand, this is just what we do."

"Yeah?" I said. "Well, it's not what *I* do."

The Morrigan reached for me, clutching at my wrist. Her hand was wet from splashing around in the water, but it was still warm. "Oh, don't be hateful. You know the course of events as well as we do. You know the way this has to end."

"Yeah, I do." I peeled her fingers off my arm and stood up. "I leave."

CHAPTER 16

NORMAL ENOUGH

I climbed out of the ravine onto Orchard and started toward home. I felt angry and disgusted or else disgusting. I wasn't about to be involved with something so ugly—I couldn't be. But the House of Mayhem was still where I came from and how I'd wound up in Gentry in the first place. If I wanted to be healthy, I had to work for the Morrigan, but the thought gave me a sick feeling.

I wanted to talk to Emma, but I didn't want to talk about any of the things that were actually bothering me, and anyway, she wouldn't be up. When I checked my phone, it was two forty-five. It was still raining, but what else was new.

A car was coming down the street toward me, the yellow beam of its headlights glowing out of the rain. It pulled over so abruptly the front passenger tire skimmed the curb and ricocheted off.

Tate got out and crossed the street, leaving the Buick parked crookedly in the bike lane.

"Hey," she called, splashing through the gutter and onto the sidewalk.

I stopped and waited.

When she reached me, she stood with her hands on her hips. She'd put the hazards on and they pulsed behind her in the drizzle, flashing on and off like a flat orange heartbeat. "I have your guitar."

I wanted to ask what she was doing out so late, driving around by herself. "Do you know what time it is?"

She squinted up at me. "Yes, as a matter of fact. It's the middle of the goddamn night. What the hell happened to you?"

I shrugged and tried to look unreadable.

"You didn't fake that," she said. "That, what happened in the car, that was real."

I nodded.

She scraped her wet hair away from her forehead. "Well, are you *okay*?"

"I'm fine. Don't worry about it."

She turned and looked off over the subdivision and the road, shaking her head. "Look, what's wrong with you?"

I didn't answer right away. I had a feeling that even if I managed to answer without using specifics, she'd just rephrase the question and ask me again, so I skipped to the most basic part of it. "Has there ever been something about yourself—or about your life—that you just really hate?"

She laughed, a sharp little bark of a laugh. "God, where do I start?" She was still looking up at me, sort of smiling, and then her face changed.

"What?"

"Nothing. Just, your eyes are really dark." Her expression was thoughtful and a little worried, like she wasn't condemning or judging me, just looking.

I took a deep breath and put my hand on her arm. "I want to talk to you about Natalie." I steered her toward the edge of Mrs. Feely's lawn. "Here, sit down."

She looked unconvinced, but she settled herself on the ground and I sat next to her.

"Can I ask you something first?" I said.

She nodded and yanked up a handful of dead grass, watching me sideways. She'd stopped smiling.

"What would you do if I told you that someone took your sister—that you're right, and this is a shitty town that lets terrible, screwed-up things happen? Would that make any difference? Would it help?"

The rain was striking up from the road in tiny splatters, catching the glare from Tate's hazards. Down at the intersection, the traffic light turned red and the pavement suddenly looked bloody. I had an idea that it had been raining my whole life.

Tate didn't answer, just pulled up another handful of grass. Her expression was stony.

"What are you thinking?" I sounded like I was whispering, even though I didn't want to be.

"Nothing." She said it in a really miserable way, looking tough and helpless at the same time. "I just thought, you're right. It doesn't matter. Whether you know something or not—it wouldn't matter because it already happened. No one could have saved her."

Two days ago, I would have paid money to hear her say that, to have her drop it and just start accepting the situation for what it was so she could let it go and move on. Now, everything had changed. If the Morrigan was right, then Natalie was still alive, at least until Friday at dawn, and I was a world away from knowing what to do about it.

When I reached for Tate's hand, she let me take it.

"I just want to know how it happened. How something like that could happen."

I didn't know what to say, so I just held on, smoothing my thumb over the back of her hand. "It isn't personal or malicious. It's just something that happens. Other people have hurricanes and earthquakes."

She nodded, staring at the street. She had an expression I recognized, like she was holding her breath. With my free hand, I reached across and touched her hair. It was softer than it looked. I brushed her bangs away from her face and she closed her eyes.

"This whole place is so full of hypocrites, it's unbelievable. They're so good at the charitable casseroles and the funerals, but they never do anything to stop it. They just say, 'How sad.'"

I let go of her hand and put my arm around her. I wondered if she was going to start crying. Emma cried at everything, even animated movies and greeting card commercials, but Tate wasn't like that. She felt smaller than I'd expected and softer. I pulled her against me, running my hand up and down her arm.

"I did believe you. Right from the beginning."

"Why didn't you just *say* that, then? I mean, you could have just said that."

She rested her head on my shoulder, and for a second it was pretty much all I'd ever wanted out of life. Then I felt a sharp, burning pain through my shirt. I held my breath and tried not to ruin the moment by pulling away.

She leaned against me and her voice was very soft. "I wasn't trying to blame you. I just thought you might know what happened was all. It's not because of you. I know that."

I nodded, clenching my teeth against the stabbing pain in my collarbone. She *should* be blaming me. Now was when she should be throwing a fit, demanding to know everything I knew because I finally knew something definitive and damning. And she had no idea.

She moved and the pain jolted along my shoulder and down my chest like an electric shock, those paddles, how the EMT yells *clear*. I gasped and let her go.

She leaned away from me fast, looking at the ground. There was a metal ball chain around her neck, tucked down inside her shirt. I wanted to explain, but the words were pretty much nonexistent. I stood up.

"Where are you going?" Her voice sounded hoarse.

"Nowhere. Let's go for a walk." I reached down, offering my hand. "I don't think I can get back in your car. Feel like walking me home?"

Once she got to her feet, she tried to pull away, but I held on. For a second, we were standing by the side of the road, holding hands. Then she yanked her hand away in a hard jerk, like she couldn't stand still long enough to let me touch her.

We walked down Welsh Street, toward the church, not talking much. At the churchyard, we stopped, standing out on the sidewalk.

Tate nodded toward the little cemetery. "They put the body in there. I can show you if you want."

I shook my head. "That's okay."

"I promise I'm not going to do anything all girly and emotional-baggage-y."

"I can't go in the cemetery."

The look she gave me was spectacularly unimpressed.

"What are you talking about? Your dad is the *minister*. You can go wherever you want."

"It's complicated," I said. "It's just . . . this thing."

She looked at me for a long time, like she was considering all the different things she could say.

Then she started for the edge of the property line. "Okay, we'll go around and look from the side."

She led me around the building and up to the fence, where a bed of orange flowers were turning brown.

"There," she said, pointing over the fence. "They just put the headstone up. The little white one, back against the wall."

She was pointing past the anonymous headstones and the crypt to the unconsecrated section, where early parishioners used to put anyone they thought was unclean. In the dark, only the marble markers showed with any clarity. They glowed palely from the shadows, while the granite ones were only faint outlines. The stone Tate was pointing to sat square and straight, but most of the others were starting to lean.

There were other plots in other places in the cemetery. Consecrated places. But the thing that wasn't Natalie had been buried with the outcasts because it belonged there, which meant the unholy ground was exactly what the Morrigan had said it was—just another way for the town to play along, to be involved. Something they all agreed to, without having to say it.

Tate stood looking up at me and I knew suddenly that she wasn't the kind of girl who ever looked away. She could take your skin off if you let her look long enough.

I closed my eyes. "I wish I could do something. I don't know how to help you."

Tate moved closer, and her voice was low and breathless, like she was telling me an awful secret. "You know what did it? What made me absolutely sure? It wasn't how big her teeth seemed suddenly or the way her eyes got strange. I mean yeah, those things mattered, but they didn't prove anything. It was her pajamas. These pink footie ones with bears on them—she used to wear them all the time, and then, a couple months before she died, I couldn't find them anymore, but you know what? It didn't matter because she never *asked* for them anymore, and she didn't like picture books and she didn't like toys. And I'd tell myself it was just because she was sick, but that's not the real truth because at night, when you think all those things you can't stand to think about during the day? At night, the real truth was, she wasn't my sister."

I stood in the wilted border, leaning on the fence. Beside me, Tate looked small and sad. Her mouth was meaner than I'd seen it in a while. For the first time since that afternoon under the oak tree, she wasn't looking at me like she expected something.

I wanted to hold on to her, but everything was wrong—

191

the time and the place and the way she jerked and fidgeted, like she couldn't stand to be touched, so I settled for pressing my forehead against the top of the fence. "There's something else I need to tell you."

"So, tell me."

"I like you." When I said it out loud, the admission felt hopeless—inescapable, like I'd hit on something that until now, I just hadn't had the words for. But it felt that way because it was true.

Her laugh was incredulous. "You *what*?"

I looked at the ground and the dark, drizzling sky and pretty much anyplace that wasn't her. "I like you. A lot." When I finally glanced at her, my face was hot and it was hard to keep looking.

She squinted up at me. Then she crossed her arms. "This is a really inappropriate place to be having this conversation."

"I know. I like you anyway."

Saying it a third time was like breaking some kind of spell. Her face went soft and far away. "Don't say that unless you mean it."

"I don't say anything I don't mean." I leaned closer, smelling the metallic smell again. "Take your necklace off."

"Why?"

"Because if you don't, I can't kiss you."

She stood looking up at me. Then she reached back and

192

undid the clasp. Her mouth was open a little. She shoved the necklace into her pocket and I put my hand on her cheek. Then I leaned in before I could think about it long enough to chicken out.

I'd never expected much from Tate. Long, bored looks, maybe. A couple rounds of vicious-clever ball breaking that I had no comebacks to. Maybe get my ass handed to me a few times at pool or darts or cards. Instead, here I was, kissing her behind the church. Her mouth was warm and I was surprised by how good it felt not to breathe.

She had her arms around my neck, then she was grabbing at the back of my shirt, fumbling behind her for the sloping ground, and we sat down. She was holding on to me, pushing me flat on the grass. Above her, the sky was wide and full of water. Against the fence, a huge oak tree spread its branches over the corner of the churchyard. The leaves that were left were wet, covered in tiny drops, and each one caught the light from the street in a collection of little starbursts.

Tate brushed my cheek with her fingers, like maybe she was brushing off the bright spots of light. But it was just the rain.

She glanced over her shoulder at the glittering tree, then turned back, smiling a smile that was sly and sort of tender. She was on top of me, straddling me. It's strange when you're not happy for a long, long time and then suddenly, you are.

She leaned down and I could taste ChapStick, smell iron and shampoo and under it, that crisp, clean smell.

We lay in the grass beside the cemetery fence, kissing and shivering. Her teeth started to chatter and I pulled her against me, which made me feel like a superhero for no apparent reason. She was clinging to the collar of my jacket like I'd just done something outstanding.

She put her hand on my chest, moving her fingers so that I got chills all over.

I pulled her closer, holding her so her head was tucked under my chin. "I'm not normal, Tate."

"I know." Her hand was working its way under my shirt, then touching my skin, sliding over my chest and my stomach, down into my jeans. "Does this feel good?"

I closed my eyes and nodded.

"You're normal enough."

CHAPTER 17

CONFESSION

I got through school in a daze the next day. I was running on very little sleep, but the analeptic made things manageable. Roswell wanted to know what had made Tate so upset, and I told him a completely worthless story about feeling carsick, which he didn't believe, but he left me alone after that.

I'd spent the morning preparing myself for another encounter with Tate, but she wasn't at school. It was the first day she'd missed since before the funeral, and on the surface, it was way overdue. Even so, I couldn't help thinking that after telling me all that stuff about her sister, or maybe because I'd kissed her, she was avoiding me.

The idea was more relieving than I would have expected. In the last few days, my life had gotten kind of unmanageable and Tate was a complication I didn't know how to handle. Still, throughout the day, during lectures and homework reviews, I caught myself going back to kissing her.

By the time I got home, all I wanted to do was sit down in front of the TV and turn off my brain.

When I walked in the front door, Emma was laughing. She came out of the living room as I was scraping my shoes and peeling off my wet jacket. She smiled in that wide, helpless way, like even if she wanted to, she couldn't stop—it was just that funny. She was wearing a floppy black rain hat.

"It's Janice's," she said, yanking the hat off and trying to flatten down her hair. "We were just messing around." She reached for me with a worried expression, catching my face between her hands and pulling me down to look at her. "You look exhausted. Are you sure you're okay?"

I nodded and was a little surprised to realize that I was telling the truth. The only reason I was exhausted was because I'd been out all night. "Just tired."

Emma gave me a doubtful look and walked out again. I got an apple from the kitchen, then went into the family room to see what the deal with Janice was.

She was on the couch, leafing through a textbook. Her hair was down around her face and she was back to looking kind of plain and unfortunate.

"What are you doing here?" I said. "I gave you what you wanted, so quit harassing Emma."

Janice flipped to the index, then back through the chapters. "I'm not harassing Emma. We're doing homework. And not to be pedantic, but she came to *me*. I wasn't out looking for pretty musicians, I was just attending classes."

I sat down across from her and watched as she made notes in a little leather-bound book. "Why is someone like you even going to school? I mean, what's the point?"

She ran her finger along the caption under a color diagram of a cell, then looked up. "The point is to learn everything I can about my field."

I raised my eyebrows. "Your *field*?"

"Pharmacology, they're calling it now." She closed the book and leaned back. "Scientific knowledge changes so fast that it's hard to keep up, but Emma's been really nice. She explains a lot of the horticulture. I've never actually grown things before and it's nice to understand things like seed propagation. She's been giving me lessons."

I nodded, reflecting that in a place like the House of Mayhem, keeping houseplants was likely to be tricky.

"Emma," my mom called from out in the hall. "Are you going to use all that peat moss, or should I put it away?"

At the sound of her voice, Janice got a strange, awkward look. She turned toward the door.

"Emma," my mom said, coming into the family room, and then she stopped.

Janice stood up, offering her hand. "Hello, I'm—"

"Get out," my mom said. "I know what you are. Get out of my house."

197

"Please . . ." Janice trailed off, taking her hand back, picking at the inside of her elbow.

My mom stood with her chin up and her shoulders back, like if she looked away for even a second, that might be all the time Janice needed to do something terrible.

Emma came in behind her with an armful of books and then just stood there. Janice was already edging toward the door, looking sad but like this was about what she'd expected.

Emma watched her. Then she turned and stared at our mother. "What's going on? What did you say to her?"

My mom breathed in like she was making herself taller. "Tell her to get out," she said, and the look on her face was one I'd never seen. "Tell her she's not wanted here."

Emma raised her eyebrows and made her mouth very small. Her cheeks got pink, which was a sure sign she was about to say something regrettable. It was normal for her to get pissed at our dad, but she never yelled at our mom. I couldn't figure out if she didn't because it would be too easy or because something about our mom's flat silences could be scary.

Finally, she closed her eyes and took a deep breath, like she was trying to sound patient. "She's helping me with botany class."

It sounded almost convincing, but my mom wasn't deterred for a second. "She's unnatural."

I dug my fingernails into my palms, while Janice just stood there.

Emma kept her temper for roughly three seconds. Then she threw down the stack of books. "So, you're determined to hate her just because she's not exactly like *you*? Does it matter that she's nice or that ever since I met her, she hasn't done anything but *help*?"

"You have no idea what you're talking about. She's the worst kind of creature."

"You don't even know her! They're not automatically *bad*. What about Mackie?"

"Don't you *dare* bring him into this. Mackie is *fine*. He grew up in a decent household, with decent principles. He's like *us*."

Emma stood over her scattered books and said, very quietly, "Well, maybe *they're* like us too."

My mom didn't answer right away. When she smiled, it was hard and bitter. "Like us. Tell me, do any of our friends and neighbors have a fanatical devotion to a demon? Do they steal children? Do the parishioners at United Methodist kidnap babies and farm them like cattle and sacrifice them to a lost cause? Mackie is a sweet, normal boy, and they are *monsters*."

All of us got very still. The dropped books shifted and slid over each other, coming to rest on the carpet. My mom looked like she wanted to cover her mouth with her hands, take it back before she went too far.

Suddenly, I was sure this was it. We were going to talk

199

about all the nasty, screwed-up things in Gentry, like how nice, normal babies got switched out for freaks. Maybe even how I wasn't really her son and a kid named Malcolm Doyle was dead because a bunch of people who lived underground got off on collecting blood.

We were going to get into the dirty stuff.

My mom took a deep breath and said with her hands clasped tight, "They always come back. It was just a matter of time. They watch and they wait, and then, when you let your guard down, they come in and take everything."

"Stop calling her *they*. She's a person!"

My mom just went on in the same deadly voice. "I knew they'd take my children if I gave them the chance. I did everything I could to prevent it, every trick and charm. I filled the house with bells and coins and embroidery scissors, and in the end, it didn't matter. Someone took down the scissors, and they came in and got him anyway."

She and Emma stood looking at each other. I pictured the house, full of her charms and tricks. How later, she must have had to throw all of it away just so I'd stop screaming in the crib.

Emma took a deep breath. "Yes," she said. "Yes, I took them—I took the scissors down and didn't put them back— *I* did it. Is that what you want? Is that the big revelation you were waiting for? That I was four years old and a stupid little kid?"

The room felt too small for the four of us, even with me trying to make myself inconspicuous and Janice backing up against the bookcase. My hands were shaking and Emma looked furious.

I realized numbly that she *did* blame herself.

There were the simple reasons—because she took the scissors down, because she didn't scream or call out when someone came in the window and took her brother. Because she didn't even go for help after he was gone but stayed with me all night, sticking her hands through the bars. But those were the simple reasons. More than that, I was here because she'd spent years smiling and listening and protecting me. Because she loved me. I was everything because of her.

"Fine!" Emma yelled, and her voice spiked up, weird and shrill. "Fine, it's my fault, okay?"

Our mom stood alone in the middle of the room, shoulders slumped, arms limp at her sides. "No," she said. "It's mine."

Her tone was defiant, though, like when people really mean that it's someone else's fault.

Janice was still standing against the bookshelf, still touching the inside of her arm. When I cut my eyes toward the hall, she just ducked her head and slipped out. A few seconds later, I heard the front door open and then close, and we were alone with fifteen years of silence and the sad, patient ghost of Malcolm Doyle.

None of us said anything and the room seemed to buzz with a low charge that had nothing to do with the lights or the wiring.

Then Emma sighed and threw up her hands. She gave me a hopeless look and walked out. My mother stood alone in the middle of the room with her back to me and her hands pressed against her face.

"Mom?" I reached out and turned her by the shoulders. "Mom, don't."

"What have you been doing?" she said, and her voice was high, bordering on hysterical. "Have you gone underground? What in God's name did you *do*?"

I jerked away. The panic in her voice was alarming and I couldn't close my mouth.

"Sit down," she said. "We need to talk."

I sat on the edge of the sofa and when she sat across from me, she didn't say anything for a long time. Against the wall, the upright clock ticked steadily on and on. I had a scary picture of the two of us, sitting across from each other for the rest of my life and never knowing what to say.

After a long time, she reached across the coffee table, taking me by the wrist.

I held still and waited.

She rubbed her thumb across the back of my hand. "When I met your father, I thought it would be my chance at forgetting. A fresh start, but I was so naive. They're never really gone when there's still a chance they could gain something."

I closed my eyes, trying to think of something they'd want to gain—something I could *give* them. They had the whole House of Mayhem, full of laughing monsters and flooded tunnels. "I already gave them what they wanted. It wasn't even bad or dangerous. They just want to be loved."

She laughed and it was an unpleasant sound, hard and bitter. "*Love?* Don't you believe it. They're looking for a warm body. They have a tax to pay, just like everyone at United Methodist tithes to the bank box each year and the same way everyone lines up in April to give money to the government. It's like that, except their account only comes due every seven years and the coin of the realm happens to be blood."

I nodded and didn't think about Malcolm Doyle. I didn't think about his blond hair or his true-blue eyes or his bad, bloody death. If I let myself picture it, I'd be dreaming about him for years.

My mom sat with her head bent, looking at her hands. "They guard the town and keep it safe and they make us lucky. It takes certain sacrifices to do that. And because they're not completely immune to sentimentality, they prefer to use someone else's children."

"You, you mean?" But what I meant was Malcolm Doyle, Natalie Stewart, anyone who was stolen away so they could donate their blood.

"I was a special case. Not intended for general use." Her eyes were vague and downcast, like I was supposed to see how ironic the whole thing was. "The Lady liked me. She called me precious and kept me like a pet and told me about all the offerings they'd made to her. Little kids who cried and screamed. How six hundred years ago, they used warriors who came to her offering their victories and defeats. How she would never let anything happen to me. She kept me for so long it was like being kept in a jar."

"But if the Lady didn't want you to go home, why didn't she just stop you from leaving?"

"She would have. She would have kept me, but someone came and took me back. A strange creature—a monster—took me out of the hill one night and led me out through the park. Then she left me on my parents' doorstep, the way you'd leave a lost dog."

I stared at her, trying to understand the hurt in her voice. It made no sense. "But that should be a good thing, right? You went home."

"You can't," she said. "Not really. They find ways to stop missing you after a while. They *move on*. And what do you do with a girl who can't stand the smell of car exhaust? Who goes blind in the sunlight? Listen," she said. "I *know* them. I know how they think, and it's always in terms of what they can gain."

"But what *can* they gain?"

She shrugged, loose and jerky. "I don't know, but you can be sure it's something. They'll use you, manipulate you, and then they'll throw you away when they don't need you anymore." She smiled suddenly, a scary, helpless smile. "I sat on a cushion at her feet and played with a clockwork bird. I sang little songs and she sang them back. You can't go back to them. Not for any reason."

I took a deep breath. "They told me if I didn't help them, they'd hurt Emma. I can't just sit around and let that happen."

My mom raised herself up and leaned close. "Emma is almost twenty years old. She can look after herself. You are rare—maybe valuable—and they want something from you. When someone underground wants something, it's never harmless. Do *not* go back."

"What if they do something awful to her to punish me?"

"They'll *always* punish you," she said, "because they hate to lose. When they stole Malcolm, it was to punish me for leaving."

"But you weren't the one who decided to leave. You were just a kid—a *victim*."

"But I *did* leave, and the Lady can't forgive that because it's all that matters." She took her hands away from her face and looked up at me. "They're just going to use you, Mackie. What will it take to make you see how dangerous they are?"

205

But when I tried to picture *dangerous*, there was just the look on Janice's face, this mix of loss and confusion. Having Emma explain seed propagation wasn't using, it was just sharing a common interest. It was what you did when you wanted to be friends.

"I'm better," I said finally. "This is maybe the first time in my life I've ever felt okay, and it's because of them."

"Don't you understand? They *bought* you. They found your price."

But in the grand scheme of things, my price wasn't unreasonable. They'd given me more than I'd ever hoped for, but the tipping point hadn't been relief from pain or exhaustion or even the promise of being normal. *Emma* was a thought so big and clear suddenly that there was no room in my head for anything else. "I didn't have a choice."

My mom sat on the edge of the high-backed chair with her arms around herself. Her eyes were clear and hard. "Everything in life involves choice."

CHAPTER 18

BEAUTY AND TRUTH

Emma and my mom were already gone by the time I went down for breakfast on Tuesday, and I ate cold cereal alone, standing over the sink.

I closed my eyes and tried to hear the roar of the crowd at the Starlight, taste what it was like to kiss Tate, feel her hand in mine. But there was just the conversation with my mom the day before, like a scrape I could test with my finger. Something about the rawness made me want to reach for it and just keep digging.

In the living room, my dad stood at the window with his hands clasped behind his back, staring out at the empty street.

I sat down on the floor and leaned against the couch. The sound of the rain was giving me a dull, hazy feeling, like I might be sleeping but wasn't sure.

I leaned against the couch, thinking how hard it was to ever communicate with anyone. How I couldn't ever figure out how to say all the things I meant. Because it was more complicated. More complicated than kissing Tate and more complicated than the terrible secret I knew about her sister. It was the claustrophobic idea of someone getting that close, of knowing that much about you. How, for her, I'd have to turn into something real.

I kept thinking about her mouth. How she'd slid her hands under my shirt. How I was so excellent at picking things that weren't right that it was hard to know if anything was what I should actually want.

I couldn't help thinking that maybe making out by the churchyard had been some kind of reward, a prize for believing her or a bribe so I'd tell the rest of what I knew. That Natalie was still alive. But I'd only just discovered that interesting fact myself, and there was no way she could have known, so the thing in the grass had to have been real. It had to mean that she'd wanted to kiss me. At least a little?

"You're in a brown study this morning," my dad said, turning from the window.

I shrugged and didn't correct him. What I was was completely out of my depth.

I left for school earlier than usual, trudging along Orchard and cutting across the footbridge. It was foggy down in the ravine and mist hung around my feet as I crossed the bridge, thinking about my mom's warning, which was in

208

complete agreement with what the Morrigan had said about keeping out of the Lady's way.

I crossed Welsh Street with my hands in my pockets. The neighborhood was deserted and I was starting to feel lost again, the same way I did at night sometimes, like maybe I didn't exist, when I saw someone ahead of me. Someone in a gray jacket, with short, messy hair, and I hurried to catch up.

"Tate, hey."

She looked over her shoulder and made a face that wasn't even close to a smile. Waved one hand, dropped it again.

I came up next to her. "How are things?"

She shrugged and didn't answer.

I turned so I was in front of her, walking backward. "Did you do that worksheet for English?"

"Don't," she said. "Don't pretend this is a normal conversation, okay? Don't keep acting like everything's fine."

"What do you want me to say?"

Tate sighed. "Why do you keep asking that? I don't want you to say anything. I want it to matter that she's gone."

I felt hot and awkward suddenly but didn't look away. "Nobody's saying it doesn't *matter*. It's just not something we can help, you know? It's not like we can do anything about it."

And that was true. It was the indisputable truth, but I felt like a liar saying it. Natalie was alive until Friday. Right now, I should be figuring out a way to save her because that's what brave, honorable people did and I had a weird feeling that Tate could see the guilt on me, this big dishonest smear, splashed across my face.

Everything about her seemed to have locked down since our fifteen or twenty minutes by the graveyard. It was disconcerting to think that I had kissed her and now I could barely look at her.

"How come you don't have your car?"

She pushed past me. "It wouldn't start."

I stepped in front of her again. "What's wrong with it?"

"If I knew that, don't you think I'd have *fixed* it?" She gave me an exasperated look. "Look, I'm in kind of a hurry. Could you maybe let me keep walking?"

By the time I got to English, I was feeling pretty agitated, but I couldn't tell if it was with myself or with Tate. The idea that she'd only made out with me to thank me for finally admitting I believed her or else to make some kind of point was just low, but on another level, I didn't really care. I still wanted to kiss her.

A few rows in front of me, Alice sat staring at the whiteboard and playing with her hair. She kept winding it around her finger, then unwinding it again. Her face was smooth and regular, like something you already know is going to be imperfection free.

"Tate," Mrs. Brummel said, with a sugary smile, like she was trying really hard to prove that nothing uncomfortable had happened on Friday. "Would you hand back the tests, please?"

Tate slid out of her desk and she was more like something by Van Gogh, all color and texture and light. Her hair was standing up in a kind of rooster crest and her elbows were sharp through her thermal shirt. She took the stack of tests and started down my aisle, sorting through the papers.

I leaned forward in my seat. "Jenna—Jenna, do you have a pen?"

Jenna fished one out of her bag and handed it to me, smiling like a toothpaste ad or how a cat would smile if it had braces and highlighted hair and something to smile about.

I didn't have my notebook, so I started going through my pockets, looking for ticket stubs, gum wrappers, receipts. Finally, I found a piece of a band flier and wrote on the back, *Can I walk you home?*

When Tate got to my seat, I held out the note, but she didn't look at it. She turned the test facedown on my desk and went to keep moving down the row.

I caught her wrist. This wasn't something I'd planned ahead of time, and it took me by surprise. Her skin was cool and her bones felt small in my hand.

For a second, we stayed like that, me holding her by the wrist and her letting me. Then she jerked back like I was contagious.

She handed back the rest of the tests and took her seat without looking at Mrs. Brummel or at anyone else. I watched her, but she didn't raise her head or glance around.

We spent the class period going through the answers to the test and discussing each one in mind-numbing detail. I flipped through my textbook, looking for interesting pictures or maybe some magic solution to all my problems.

I was skimming the Romantics section when I turned the page to a photo of a painted jar. The people on the jar were all in profile. They danced and capered and sprawled around playing little flutes. They reminded me of the after party in the House of Mayhem, all celebration and awkward, spooky grace.

On the opposite page, there was a poem. It described how beauty and truth mattered more than anything else. They were the same thing.

But it didn't matter how pretty you painted the world. The fact was, my friends didn't know me, Tate didn't want me, and the truth was a really ugly thing.

I closed the book and stared at the clock, willing it to move faster.

In front of me, Alice and Jenna were discussing the Halloween party out at the lake and whether there'd be a bonfire this year or if the rain would mean they'd have to settle for little campfires in the barbecue pits under the picnic shelters. I watched them because they were both pretty and it was kind of nice to have something normal to distract me from my life.

Alice was wearing another installment in her wide selection of low-cut shirts, and I was enjoying tormenting myself a little, which Roswell would say is a very masochistic attitude. Also, self-indulgent, but her hair was honey brown and shiny, and thinking about Tate made me feel like an idiot.

Alice turned and caught me watching them. She gave me a bored look. "Are you going to the party, Mackie?" Her eyebrows were raised, but her lids were half lowered, like looking at me was making her tired.

On another day—*any* other day—I would have taken the question for what it was. Her version of being better than me, of writing me off and making me feel inferior. But things had been massively screwed up lately. They'd been downright obnoxious, and I just smiled, raising my eyebrows, leaning forward like I'd seen Roswell do a million times. "Why? Did you want to go with me?"

Alice opened her mouth and blinked. She closed her mouth, and I was surprised and kind of gratified to see that she was blushing. Beyond her, Tate was making dutiful notes on her test. I thought I saw her shoulders tighten but wasn't sure.

Alice gaped at me and then recovered. "Are you asking me to go with you?"

Her voice was playful, challenging, and I kept smiling, liking how her mouth looked soft and shiny. "Well, that depends on whether or not you're saying yes."

"Yes," she said, biting her lip, giving me a conspiratorial smile.

Behind her, Tate sat stubbornly at her desk, staring down at her test like the answers mattered.

CHAPTER 19

THE LAKE

It wasn't a date. Or at least, it made things easier to keep telling myself that.

It wasn't a date because I was meeting Alice there. But it was *some*thing, because I'd made actual plans to meet her, like normal people go to parties and make plans with girls.

Roswell was still intent on hooking up with Zoe, but the prospect didn't seem to cause him much anxiety. When I asked how I should proceed with Alice, he just shrugged and said, "Well, you could start by having a conversation."

After dinner, I went over to his house. His mom let me in with her hair up in some kind of fancy braid. She was in the middle of fastening the clasp on her necklace and gave me a smile. "He's in his room, getting all dolled up for his fans. Do you think you can prevail on him to drive responsibly?"

"I can try. I don't know how much influence I have."

That made her laugh, and when she did, she looked like him. Her eyes were the same shape and the same deep, frosty blue. She adjusted her grip on the necklace and gave me a one-armed hug. "Don't sell yourself short, buster. He listens to you."

Roswell was upstairs, trying to attach his enamel fangs. He'd put in a little more effort now that it was actually Halloween, and his hair was slicked back in a weird-looking pompadour.

I sat at his desk, which was covered with the pieces of his latest clock project, and watched him fumble with the tooth adhesive, squirting it on his fingers and then wiping it off on his jeans.

After he'd positioned the fangs to his satisfaction, he gave me a disapproving look. "What did you say to my mom to make her giggle like a schoolgirl?"

"Nothing untoward. Why does she always seem to think you drive like we're holding up a bank?"

Roswell grinned and rolled his eyes. "Because that's what teenagers do, right? They also carve swastikas into their arms, steal prescription drugs from old people, and freebase cocaine. I need to institute a policy where she stops watching *60 Minutes* and pretty much all public service announcements."

I studied the half-built clock. The housing was an old rotary phone, the dial replaced with mismatched foreign coins for the numbers. His desktop was covered with pins and little cogs.

I picked up a brass coin with a hole through the center and studied it. "She never says any of those things to me."

"That's because she thinks you're the good one."

"I *am* the good one. Where'd you get all these clock parts?"

"Where do you think? The twins gave them to me. Swear to God, every time Danny fixes something, he winds up with a whole shit ton of 'extra' pieces." Roswell folded his arms and looked me up and down. "No costume?"

I shook my head. "Since when do I need a costume?"

He grinned and thumped me on the shoulder. "Since you stopped looking all weird and cracked out on your own and started looking halfway normal."

I raised my eyebrows and stood up. "Hey, maybe this *is* my costume."

The lake was dry and had been since before I was born.

It sat on the outskirts of town, smelly and empty, a big muddy gouge. The shore was jagged with rocks, but out in the center, it had turned swampy as it filled with rainwater. The area around the lake bed had been a park, with picnic shelters and wooden docks for boating and fishing, but the recreational activities had all been abandoned when the lake dried up. People still went jogging on the paths and walked their dogs through the brush, but mostly, it was prime for minor drug deals and high school parties.

At the south end of the lake, we pulled up to a dilapidated cluster of picnic shelters. The fire pits were all lit, burning like lighthouse beacons. They flickered in a damp breeze as we turned into the gravel parking lot. The path to the shelters was choked with weeds and littered with fast-food wrappers and beer cans. The rain was the same thin drizzle that it had been for weeks.

Alice, Jenna, and Stephanie were huddled together in the middle shelter, wearing winter coats over their costumes. Alice was holding a beer can with both hands, standing close to the fire and hunching her shoulders against the cold.

Roswell and I came up to them and when Alice saw me, she smiled and waved me over to stand with her. Roswell tossed me a beer and I popped it open. It was disorienting to be standing at the center of things instead of watching from the periphery.

Jeremy Sayers came up next to me. He was dressed as a pirate, with a three-cornered hat and an eye patch. "Doyle," he said, clapping me hard on the shoulder. "You weird pansy fuck!"

It was hard to tell if the designation was supposed to be a compliment. He was smiling, so I took a shot at normalcy and smiled back.

Tyson Knoll squeezed in on the other side of our circle. Also a pirate. "Dude, did you tell him about the blood?"

I tried hard not to sound apprehensive. "What blood?"

"On your locker! Did you freaking love that or what?"

I took a drink of my beer and nodded, not sure what he expected me to say. I would have used a different word. Not love. Definitely not love.

Jeremy swung an arm over my shoulders. He smelled like Axe deodorant and hard alcohol. "Remember how Mason cut his lip in PE last year and you hit the court like a total pussy? Do you remember that? It was *so* freaking funny!"

I stood next to Alice, trying to look like the story was *not* completely embarrassing, but she just smiled up at me. I was surprised at how paranoid the years of keeping a low profile had made me. How every unusual occurrence was a threat and every encounter was suspicious. I'd spent so long protecting myself from everything that I didn't even know how to tell the difference between what was dangerous and what wasn't.

They were loud and unpredictable, and before, I'd always watched them with the same fascination I had when I watched Roswell. The way some of the less-popular girls were watching Jenna and Alice now, not resentful or jealous exactly, but like they just wanted to be them. Cammie Winslow stood by the railing, one shelter over. She was dressed in an oversized clown costume, looking lost and hopeful, like she would have given anything to be standing with the rest of us, laughing and drinking cheap beer with people like Jeremy and Tyson. And yeah, they were basically idiots, but I'd never known what it felt like to be included before and now, they were acting like I belonged there.

The air was damp and chilly, and the heat from the fire hit my face in a dry rush even though I stayed farther back than the others. The barbecue enclosure and the grate were steel, burned black and caked with soot, but a fog of iron still drifted out through the smoke. I was steady, though, and happy. Everything felt good, like this was how it should be.

Out in the gravel parking lot, some of the guys from the wrestling team were trying to get a fire started so they could burn a straw-and-burlap scarecrow of the Dirt Witch, but the rain was too heavy and mostly they just got a lot of smoke. It drifted toward us in dark billows and smelled unpleasantly like lighter fluid.

Alice moved closer, reaching for my hand. Hers was smaller and broader than Tate's, with smooth, soft palms and electric-blue nail polish. Her grip was firm and I thought of the Morrigan suddenly, how she always wanted to stand close or be touching me. Like a little kid, always reaching to make sure I was close by.

Alice was beautiful, though, nothing like the monsters in the House of Mayhem. Her beauty wasn't conditional the way Janice and Carlina's was, but stable and constant, catching people's attention, making them want her to notice them, even for a second.

We stood with the guys from wrestling and football while they told stories about dickish things they'd done to other people—in the name of fun, of course—and passed a bottle of Maker's Mark around the circle. Roswell and Zoe had gone off to talk, which probably meant to make out. I was on my own, navigating the world of normal people, but it was easier than I'd ever thought it could be. I wasn't failing at it.

I took the bottle from Alice, and when I drank, the heat felt good, burning all the way down. I thought I tasted a metallic whisper of her tongue stud but couldn't be sure.

Alice was looking up at me. Her eyes were deep, radiant blue and she was smiling that sweet smile, like everything was and would always be good. I put my hands on her shoulders and I kissed her.

The pressure of her mouth was warm. She tasted like Maker's and something indefinable, followed by a breath of surgical steel, making my head spin.

I kissed her again, moving closer. The fire was hot and the rain made soft pattering sounds out on the gravel parking lot. Her hands moved over my back and I was very aware of her body against mine and then her tongue, venomous with the barbell, moving over my bottom lip, sliding into my mouth.

Then pain.

For a second, I didn't know where I was or where the hurt was coming from. It was like a bright, scorching light. It glared down on me and there was nothing else in the whole world.

Alice pressed against me. She had her hand on the back of my neck, pulling me close to her mouth and her cold, excruciating kiss, holding me there. Then I jerked free and staggered back.

I stumbled away from the circle of firelight, bracing my hands on the wooden rail that ran around the outside of the picnic shelter, and tried to think. The pain was immense, like nothing I'd ever felt. I'd never known there could be so many different ways to hurt.

My arms were numb and heavy. I fumbled in my coat for the glass bottle, prying the cork out, slopping it all over my hands in the process.

I drank a huge swallow of the analeptic and pressed my forehead against the rail, curling in on myself as nothing happened, nothing happened, nothing fucking happened. Then something did, but it wasn't anything good. It came in a hard rush that wasn't fixed or better, and I hung over the wooden railing, retching. It was grim and miserable and went on forever.

Alice was saying my name, but I couldn't answer. The party seemed to be happening a million miles away from me, in another country. Another universe. There was just the ground and the railing and nothing else.

"He's tanked," Roswell said from somewhere above me, and then I felt his hand between my shoulders. "Shit, he's completely gone."

"Should we get him some water?" said Alice, and I kept my eyes closed, leaning on the railing as the cold got worse and then the shaking started.

Roswell stood next to me with his hand on the back of my neck. "It's cool, don't worry about it. I'll make sure he gets home okay."

"Yeah, that might be a good idea," Alice said, and the tone of her voice was flat and far away. "Jesus, that's nasty."

I was aware of certain things, that Roswell was holding me up, making me walk to his car. Stopping and letting me lean down so I could heave into the gravel. He dropped me into the passenger seat, cranked the window down, and closed the door.

Then he got in and started the car, glancing over at me.

"What's wrong?" His voice was loud, so sharp that he sounded angry.

I knew I should be careful, keep the secret, but I was too far gone to talk around it. My chest was working in huge spasms and I could barely breathe. "I kissed her."

"And then you went into anaphylactic shock?"

I closed my eyes and let the rain patter against my face

223

through the open window. "She has her tongue pierced."

Roswell didn't say anything else. He jerked the car into reverse and swung out of the parking lot, then turned down the bumpy stretch of dirt that led out to the main road. I slumped in the passenger seat, resting my head against the door and trying not to puke in his car.

Somewhere in the sickness and the pain, I remembered Luther's voice. It echoed in my head, that whispered declaration, *You're dying*. Before the ruinous kiss, the night had been almost normal, but it couldn't last. There *was* no normal. Not for people like me.

Out on the paved road, Roswell started asking questions again, sounding more agitated than ever. He was talking too fast, making it hard to follow the line of conversation. "Okay, what should I be doing? If you need to pull over, just tell me. Should I find you some water? Should I call Emma, tell her I'm bringing you home right now and you look like hell?"

"Take me to the dead end at Orchard."

Roswell took a deep breath, sounding rigidly calm. "Okay, you're slurring. Say that again, because it sounded like you just asked for something completely insane."

"You have to take me to the end of Orchard. I have to go to the slag heap."

CHAPTER 20

HORRIBLE LITTLE WORLD

Roswell parked at the top of the ravine and opened his door. In the glare of the dome light, I saw his face, hollowed by shadows and so rigid and watchful I barely recognized him.

I expected an argument, but he just pulled me out of the car and steered me down the path to the bridge. I reflected dully that he was a good friend, if you could call leaving someone half conscious alone on a bridge being a good friend.

As soon as I reached the bottom of the ravine, I felt desperately relieved. And much, much worse. I knelt in the mud, pressing my forehead against the wet slag, whispering for Carlina, Janice, anyone. When the door materialized out of the gravel, I slumped against it and fell inside.

The way down was choppy and disconnected, a series of slides that froze for a second and then switched over. Then I was back in the cavernous lobby, in the House of Mayhem, and I had the deep hopeless feeling that I was never going to get away from their horrible little world. My world. I had no place else to go.

The Morrigan was on the floor by the reception desk, running a little tin train back and forth across the stone. She glanced up when I stumbled into the lobby, and I knew then, from the look on her face, that it was bad. She jumped up, kicking the train out of her way, and came tearing across the room to me.

She grabbed my hand and tugged so hard I almost fell. "Goodness, what happened? Who did this?"

I shook my head, too far gone to explain that I was way more at fault than anyone else.

The Morrigan let me go and ran back to the desk. She opened the top drawer and pulled out a heavy brass bell. She held it over her head, ringing it and shouting, "Janice!" She went to one of the doorways, still clanging the bell, and I had a half-formed thought that I might black out from the noise. "Janice! Bring the exigency serum and the needle."

Then Janice was there, reaching for my arm, pushing back the sleeve of my jacket. "Here, keep still."

I steadied myself and tried to focus. She was holding a syringe, but instead of a steel needle, it was fitted with a brass tip that looked too heavy to pierce the skin. I realized with a numb fascination that she was going to stick me anyway, but my head was throbbing and I couldn't work up the kind of mental investment it took to care.

I had to lean against the reception desk just to stay upright. Janice positioned the syringe, placing the tip against the inside of my elbow and driving it in. A hot pain radiated up my arm as she pushed the plunger down. The serum was a deep brown, rushing out of the syringe and into my blood, burning as it went. I closed my eyes, tipping my head back as the pain peaked and then rolled off. Janice pulled the needle out and I started to shake. The feelings that came next were weak knees and dizziness, unpleasant but familiar. I sank down onto the floor.

Janice put away the syringe, and after a second, I could focus. She was standing over me in her romper and a long, embroidered bathrobe. Her hair was half up and half down, like she'd been asleep.

"I didn't mean to wake you up," I muttered, leaning back against the desk. "Thanks for the shot. I feel better now."

She crouched down, taking my face between her hands and staring into my eyes like she was checking my pupils. Then she yanked my mouth open and shook her head. "Are you *trying* to kill yourself? What the bloody blue devil have you been putting in your mouth?" She turned to the Morrigan, who was still standing rigidly by the desk, holding her bell. "He needs to lie down. Put him someplace quiet."

I'd never heard anyone in the House of Mayhem talk to the Morrigan that way, like they'd talk to a servant or a little kid, but she just nodded and took my hand. Hers was so warm that I almost couldn't stand it. She pulled me toward one of the narrow doorways and led me down a dark hall.

The room was a high-ceilinged bedroom, and I knew that it had to be hers. The floor was covered with a flowery green rug and there was a big four-story dollhouse in one corner, but most of the room was taken up with a giant canopied bed.

"Here," she said, pulling back the covers. "Rest here."

I sank onto the bed in my wet jacket and my muddy shoes, shivering and turning on my side.

The Morrigan stood over me. "Are you ever going to learn that you have certain limitations? You can get along in the world, you can survive, but you can't be like them. I don't have a serum or a tonic for that. It doesn't matter how you abuse yourself. You'll never be able to live the same life they do."

I didn't point out the absurdity of Them. Everyone in Gentry was a member of Them, but so was everyone in the House of Mayhem. I was the only one who was not a part of Them. I was just a wayward stranger, outside all of it.

"I don't want the same life as everyone else," I whispered, and my voice sounded breathless and ragged. "I just want to live *my* life."

"Well, you need the analeptic for that, and you need to start paying more mind to your health. You've been very careless with yourself, but you're here now, you're safe, and we intend to take good care of you."

The Morrigan took out a handkerchief and dipped it in a bowl of water by the bed. She wiped my face, scrubbing at the waxy streaks from Alice's whiskers.

Then she leaned close and whispered in my ear. "I thought my sister had done this to you. I saw you there at the door and I thought that she'd summoned the Cutter and ruined you."

I shook my head, trying to tell her that nothing was anyone's fault. That no one had ruined me.

"I loved my sister," she said, wiping my eyelids with the handkerchief. The water was cold and smelled like pond scum and dead leaves, but it felt nice against my face. I was starting to think that maybe I *was* home, even if it was a weird, creepy home where I didn't want to live. Her hands were small and careful. "I loved her so much, but in the end, I couldn't support her. Is it hypocritical to love a person and still find fault with their actions?"

I blinked away the water and didn't answer. The question didn't make sense. There weren't rules or instructions when it came to loving someone.

"I did a bad thing," the Morrigan whispered, climbing onto the bed and settling herself on my shins.

The room was soft at the edges, swimming in and out of focus, and above me, the canopy seemed to go on and on. I felt numb, like whatever Janice had injected me with might have taken care of the pain, but it made me dim and stupid, too drugged-up to function.

The Morrigan wriggled up to lie beside me on the pillow. "My sister takes children sometimes. Not for any real purpose, but just to keep them. She might take one because it's pretty or because it amuses her. And she took a girl, this lovely, clever little girl, and raised her as a toy."

I couldn't follow everything, but I got the part where somehow, the Morrigan thought keeping kids as pets was worse than taking kids to kill them. I closed my eyes, picturing a little girl with a blue church dress and blond hair. The image was faded and familiar, marked with creases like it had been folded, but my head was full of white lights and echoes, and I couldn't quite place it.

The Morrigan twirled the handkerchief, trailing the corner of it over my face. "I took her back. I went to my sister's rooms, deep into the House of Misery, and I took her. I brought her back to her family. It was the right thing to do, but my sister loathes me for it. The lake went dry shortly after and then came right back to devil us in the tunnels. She leeches all the joy from the town and sends rain." The Morrigan leaned close to my ear and there was a low, earnest sadness in her voice. "I betrayed her, and now we are estranged. She will punish me for the rest of my life, for one little girl."

I nodded, keeping my eyes closed. The damp cloth was cold on my face and I knew where the faded picture came from. I'd seen it a thousand times in the front hall, every time I passed the glass-fronted cabinet with the Dutch figurines and the teacups.

"My mother," I said, and my voice sounded harsh and unfamiliar, like someone else was whispering in my ear.

CHAPTER 21

BLESSED

I woke up in the dark, sprawled on the Morrigan's four-poster bed with the blankets tangled around my legs. The smell of the sheets was musty and unfamiliar, like the air in a strange attic.

When my eyes adjusted, I began to sort out objects. There was the giant dollhouse and, over in another corner, a heavy dresser with a hinged mirror. The Morrigan was asleep next to me, curled up with her thumb in her mouth and a filthy-looking doll clutched against her chest. Her hair had fallen back from her face and she looked uncommonly peaceful, like a little kid.

I untangled myself from the blankets and swung my feet down onto the floor. The inside of my arm still stung where Janice had stuck me with the syringe, but I felt better than I usually did after a reaction and much better than I had any right to, considering I'd recently had Alice's tongue stud in my mouth.

I left the Morrigan asleep in her massive bed and made my way back out through the lobby, up the corridor and into the rain.

When I got to Roswell's house, the porch light was off and his car was in the driveway. It was way past midnight and the ground floor was dark, but there was a light in his window. I stood in his mom's flower border, in the shadow of the garage, and texted him to come down.

He met me at the side door, looking like he was about to say something, but I shook my head. He shrugged and pointed toward Smelter Park. We walked the two blocks without talking.

At the park, Roswell headed for a wooden picnic table at the edge of the playground and sat down on the bench, leaning forward with his hood up and his coat sleeves pulled down over his hands. I had an idea that everyone was starting to get used to the weather, and if it went on much longer, we'd all just learn to live like this, no umbrellas and no raincoats. We'd all just be perpetually damp all the time.

I sat next to him, trying to formulate what I wanted to say, but my throat hurt and none of the words were even close to right. "So, what are you still doing up?"

He shrugged. "Working on the phone clock, waiting for a sign that you weren't dead. I tried to call you, but it wouldn't even send me to voice mail."

His voice sounded easy, like classic Roswell, but the way he was watching made me nervous.

He turned and put his hand on my arm, somewhere between hitting and grabbing on. "You scared the *hell* out of me. What happened?"

I looked out at the empty playground, the rusting slide and abandoned swings, trying to act normal. My heart was racing like it did when I got nervous before a class presentation. On the other side of a low fence, the dump hill was just a hulking outline against the dark backdrop of trees and sky.

I could feel Roswell looking at me, watching the side of my face.

"Okay," he said finally. "This isn't like a personal attack or anything, but lately you've been way weirder than usual. Would you please just tell me what's going on?"

My heart was beating so fast that it hurt. I closed my eyes before I answered. "I'm not a real person."

That made him laugh, short and hard, almost a bark. "Yes. You *are* a real person. Whether or not you're a *crazy* person remains to be seen, but I'm not sitting here talking to myself."

Hearing him say it was like being absolved. I was supposed to be happy, but instead I just felt awful. I hunched forward and covered my head with my hands.

"What's it like?" he said. His voice was very low. "Just tell me why you're like this."

Like I was missing some key ingredient that would make me as whole and as normal as everyone else. I looked down at the grass so I wouldn't have to look at Roswell. Then I told him the story in pieces. The open window, the screen, the crib and how Emma wasn't afraid of me, how she reached her hand in through the bars. How, on some fundamental level, I was nothing but a parasite, the same way cowbirds and cuckoos were.

I waited for him to call me a liar or tell me I was crazy. Gentry was good at keeping its secrets, and people were just so used to denying any part of the picture that didn't suit them.

The playground was at one end of the park, past the baseball diamonds and a big rectangle of mowed grass. When I was little, I'd wanted more than anything to play on the playground but had settled for games on the grass, first tag, then later, Frisbee and touch football, and Roswell had never minded that I had to stay far away from the monkey bars and the merry-go-round.

Roswell took a deep breath, glancing over his shoulder at the street. "It's never happened in my family," he said finally. "The stealing, the switching, whatever. It doesn't happen to us."

For a minute, I didn't even know what to say to that. It seemed like a bold statement, given the history of the town. "Are you sure?"

"Unshakably."

"It seems like it's happened to pretty much everyone in Gentry *some*where down the line. I mean, everyone's cousin or father or grandmother or great-uncle has a story about a relative who got really freaking weird and then died."

He grinned, shaking his head. "Sordid, right? But in the Reed household, it doesn't happen."

I stared at him. "Why not?"

He shrugged. "We're charmed." He said it like he was making a joke, but it was the truth.

Roswell was exuberant, indestructible. He was the kind of son a normal family should have. If I could have been like him at all, even a little, my entire life would have been different. I thought about what the Morrigan had said. Intent matters. If you believe you're charmed, capable, likable, popular, then you are.

Suddenly, Roswell's normal smile was gone. He was staring at his feet. "It's not like I feel *guilty*, exactly . . ."

"But you do."

He nodded down at his shoes, grinning in a bitter way.

"Is that why you hang out with me, do you think? Like, you don't mind how weird I am because when it comes down to it, you're kind of weird too?"

He quit studying his shoes and looked over at me. "It's not like that. I hate to break it to you, but there are other reasons to be friends with someone than mutual weirdness. You *are* actually kind of interesting, you know. And with you, I'm not always having to be happy or funny. I can say what I'm thinking. You pretty much suck at being honest, Mackie, but you're easy to talk to."

It was nice to think that Roswell could have a legitimate reason for being friends with me, besides the fact that our dads both worked at the church, but it didn't change the fact that I was something deceitful and strange. "Mackie Doyle's dead. I'm not anyone."

Roswell leaned forward with his elbows on his knees. "Look, Mackie is you. I started calling you Mackie in the first grade—*you*—not someone else. I've never known a Malcolm Doyle. If he's dead, then I'm sorry, but it doesn't *mean* anything. He's not you."

I couldn't look at him. "Are you . . . look, if you're dicking me around, I need you to tell me."

"Mackie, don't take this the wrong way, but all my life you've been the weirdest person I've ever met. That doesn't make you not a real person. In fact, it makes you pretty goddamn specific."

I dug my fingers into the edge of the picnic table. "This is the defining event of my life and you're treating it like it's normal. Like it's nothing."

He leaned back, looking up at the sky. "Well, maybe it should stop being the defining event. There's a whole lot more to an average life than something that happened before you were a year old."

I knew that he was right, but it was scary. I looked away because I didn't want him to see how lonely I'd been. It was disorienting to think everything that had defined me for so long was only circumstantial.

"I did something so stupid tonight," I said, hearing the catch in my voice.

"I figured. When you went all convulsive, I figured it was something big. Tongue ring, huh? Was it because you just like her that much—I mean, so much you'd kiss her anyway?"

I shook my head. "She . . . acts like I'm *normal*. Nothing different, nothing strange. Like I could be anybody."

Roswell laughed so loud I worried that someone might come outside to see what was going on. "And *that's* your criteria? A girl who makes you feel like you could be anybody?"

"No." I leaned back on my elbows and looked up into the rain. "I just mean, sometimes it's nice to hang out with someone who makes you feel like you're not completely freakish."

We sat on the picnic bench, staring out at the playground.

It was Roswell who spoke next, sounding like something had just struck him as funny and he was trying not to laugh. "Who would you get with, then, if normal wasn't an issue? I mean, if having them think you were ordinary and boring wasn't part of the equation."

"Out of anyone?" I ducked my head and pulled my sleeves down over my hands. "Tate, probably."

I waited for him to laugh, maybe ask if I meant Tate Stewart or if I was talking about some other girl who had the same name but a less dire attitude.

He just nodded and knocked his shoulder against mine. "So do that, then. Don't get me wrong, she's kind of terrifying, but she can be cool. I mean, at least she's not a sorori-whore in training."

I laughed, but it sounded fake, so I made myself stop. "There's no way. I pissed her off like you wouldn't believe. Way beyond repair."

Roswell shook his head. "Nothing's ever beyond repair. Jesus, the fact that the twins made a working snowblower out of two nonworking ones and some dryer parts should prove that. And people are pretty predictable once you know them. They don't change all that much. Do you remember in seventh grade, when we had to do current-issues debates and she and Danny got in that huge thing about capital punishment? She didn't speak to him for like a month, but she forgave him."

"Great. That was over a civics assignment. And she was twelve." I sighed and scrubbed my hands over my face. "Roz, you have no idea how hugely I've already screwed this up. If she's got any judgment at all, she hates me."

Roswell shrugged. "Fine, then she hates you. And if you

want to date her anyway, then you suck it up and you tell her you're sorry. If she's a reasonable person, she forgives you. If she's not, you might have to just let this one go and settle for girls who think you're normal. No tongue rings, though."

We sat on the picnic bench, not talking, not looking at each other, but being quiet and okay. The rain was almost gone, nothing but a thin, chilly fog. For now, I just wanted to sit on the picnic bench with him and not be anything but fine and uncomplicated.

CHAPTER 22

THE FIGHT

The next day was significant, mostly because it was the first day in weeks that it wasn't actually raining. The sky was still overcast, but the air was cold and dry. It was the first indication that the rain couldn't last forever and winter might be coming after all.

Drew and Danny were in a weird mood at lunch, looking pleased with themselves and grinning at each other. When Roswell asked what was so funny, they just looked at each other and started laughing.

I leaned on my elbows, trying not to yawn. "*You* look happy."

Danny tossed a french fry at me. "*You* look like shit."

"We fixed the Red Scare," Drew said. He was smiling, trying to keep it under control and failing. "Last night. It's kind of a MacGyvered mess, but it works."

I wanted to ask how they could stand to know the truth about anything when nothing good could come of it. How anyone could stand to be put on the spot. What it felt like to let someone else know their secrets.

After school, I started home the long way, skirting the edge of the parking lot and studying the soggy ground. I'd only gotten as far as the white oak tree when Tate and Alice came out of the school together. Which was unexpected.

They were side by side, talking as they cut across the blacktop. At least, Alice was talking. Tate was looking off at the blank suburban skyline like she was bored out of her mind.

When they stopped, it had the grim face-to-face look of a gunslinger showdown. Alice was smiling at Tate in a way that looked more like determination than goodwill. "All I'm saying is, you could make an effort. You don't have to go out and join cheerleading. Just be *normal*."

Tate didn't say anything.

Alice leaned closer. "You're just so weird. It makes people uncomfortable, and yeah, maybe no one else is going to say it, but it needed to be said."

"Okay," Tate said. "Okay, so you said it. Now can you go behind the bleachers and make out with someone?"

Alice laughed, and not in a nice way. "God, you're such a *reject*. How you ever thought you were going to wind up with Mackie, I have no idea, but you totally deserve each other."

Tate gave her a long, amazing look. The kind that burns people down. "You are *massively* unqualified to tell me what I deserve. I mean, Jesus, just because you choose to share details of your dating life with pretty much everyone does not make us dear, dear friends. In fact, it mostly just makes you sound like a huge bitch."

Alice slapped her. The sound was very loud and she looked surprised at herself.

Tate just tipped her head to the side. Then she reached out and slapped Alice right back, soft and quick and mocking.

Alice swung at her, and Tate skipped back, knocking her hands away. She moved quickly, like she was playing dodgeball or floor hockey and none of this was serious. Like it was all just a big, stupid joke.

Then Alice hit Tate for real. I don't even know if she meant to do it. It could have been some freak accident of hand-eye coordination or physics, but it worked. Blood spurted from Tate's nose, gushing down over the front of her shirt. She did nothing for a second. Then she smiled, which, when someone is covered in blood, is basically the most terrifying thing they can do. Blood was running off her chin, soaking into the collar of her T-shirt. I took my hands out of my pockets and started to walk across the lot. Then, when Tate knocked Alice down, I started to run.

People were crowding around, making a circle. Alice was

on the pavement, and Tate was kicking the hell out of her. The blood was bright on the front of her shirt, dripping off her chin, running down her neck. Her posture was straight and arrogant, like pictures I've seen of various British queens.

"Hey," I yelled. "Hey, hey, stop!"

I squeezed between people, trying to get a hand on Tate. I grabbed her by the shirt and she jerked away again. Alice was scrambling backward, trying to get back on her feet.

Around me, everyone was shouting, pressing close, but they weren't trying to break it up.

I elbowed my way into the middle of the circle and grabbed Tate around the waist. "Tate. *Tate!*"

Her body arched against my chest, rippling away like a fish. I held on tighter.

"Tate," I said against her ear. "Stop."

The blood on her shirt was burning my hands. Alice was still on the ground, scooting away on her butt. Her eye makeup made gray trails down her face and she was crying in short little gasps.

"Tate, *stop*." I wanted it to sound hard and authoritative, like someone in charge, but my voice was far away. My ears were starting to ring. "Please stop."

Her whole body was shaking against my chest. On the other side of the circle, Alice got to her feet. The look she gave us—gave me—was angry and complicated. Then she bolted into the crowd.

In my arms, Tate was unwinding, going limp. Suddenly, I had that prickly, floating feeling, like my body was very light. This is deceptive, because what it really means is, you're about to fall.

I let her go and staggered back, holding my hands away from myself. For a second, I was almost sure I was going to have to sit down, but it passed.

I started swiping at the blood, trying to scrape it off on the wet grass, on my jeans, anything just to get it off my skin. It had splattered on the backs of my wrists, but I wasn't graying out like I had during the blood drive. I walked into the building on my own, with Tate behind me.

In the entryway, I tripped on the last step and almost fell.

She put her hand on my shoulder. "What's wrong?"

"I need water." My voice sounded hoarse and she was standing so close that I could hardly breathe from the smell. "My hands."

She grabbed my hands and shoved them under the drinking fountain. The water was freezing, stinging the welts and the raw places. She stayed right behind me, holding me by the wrists, leaning on the press bar with her hip.

After the blood had run off down the drain, she let me go. I leaned back against the wall. My hands were nothing but nerve endings and a tiny static sea still roared in my ears.

Tate stood with her arms folded over her chest, squinting

at me. Blood was dripping from her nose and getting all over the floor. I watched her face, her mouth half covered in a red smear. Under all the blood, she was beautiful in the most unsettling way, and I smiled without meaning to.

She sighed and her shoulders relaxed a little. "Are you okay?" she said finally.

I nodded, patting my hands on the front of my shirt.

"I should get cleaned up, then." She turned and walked into the bathroom without saying anything else.

I sat on the floor and closed my eyes. My hands throbbed and I did my best to dry them on my shirt.

When Tate came out of the bathroom, she had a handful of paper towels against her nose, already soaked red. She crouched next to me and I turned away, holding my sleeve against my mouth.

She didn't seem to notice the way I was trying to avoid breathing her air, or maybe she just figured that was the least concerning aspect of the situation. She was looking at my hands. "Jesus, what happened to *you*?"

"It's okay, it's no big deal," I said, keeping my arm against my nose and mouth. " Let's just go."

Tate was still snuffling into the wad of paper towels. The smell of the blood was red and wet. "*Go?* I'm not going anywhere with you. Look, I'm sorry I had to punch your girlfriend in the face, but sometimes white trash moments are necessary, okay?"

"It's not *like* that. I just need to talk to you."

Tate stood up. She looked much scarier standing over me. "About what? How you insist on panting around after Alice despite the fact that she is mean as shit and hasn't figured where she left her brain? No thanks. I know that story already."

"Tate, please, just give me a chance. Just listen."

"Why?" she said, giving me the hardest, nastiest look. "As a certain selfless champion once said, what's in it for me?"

It wasn't the place I would have picked for a revelatory moment, sitting on the floor in the west entrance with Tate standing over me and narrowly avoiding dripping blood on my head. When I spoke, the words came out muffled against my sleeve. I couldn't meet her eyes.

Tate fidgeted and sighed. "I'm sorry, is my disdain making you nervous? Do you need some friendly reassurance? Do you need someone to tell you how you're doing great? That's it, Mackie—keep mumbling into your coat! *I* don't mind that you have this condition where you find it necessary to act like a huge douche!"

I clenched my jaw and said it louder. "Your sister isn't dead."

The change was instantaneous. Her hand dropped from her bleeding nose and she stared at me. Her eyes were wide and blood was running down over her lip, but she didn't seem to notice.

"Cover your face," I said into my sleeve, holding my breath, turning away.

She pressed the paper towels against her nose again, looking down at me over her hand. "Say that again."

"She isn't dead. At least, I don't think so. Not yet."

Tate took a long, shuddering breath and her eyes were so lit up she looked like she was carrying an electric charge. "I think you better tell me what that means."

"Look, let's not talk about this here."

"Oh," she said. "We are *going* to talk about it."

I pressed my fingers against my eyelids. "You were right, okay? You're right about this town. There are these . . . people. These weird, secret people." *People like me.* "They took Natalie, and they're keeping her alive until Friday."

"Okay. So, how do I get her back?"

I took my hands away from my face but didn't look at her. "I don't know."

Tate made a harsh, breathless noise, not a laugh. "That's great. That's beautiful."

"I don't *know*, but I'll come up with something."

She stood over me, eyes hard and paper towels bloody. "And why would you do that now? What would I have to do to earn the noble assistance of Mackie Doyle?"

I looked up at her. Her desperation showed on her face but just barely, like she was trying to hide it. "Please, can I walk you home?"

For a minute, I thought she was going to tell me I was disgusting, appalling, that I could go straight to hell, but then she nodded and started for the door.

Tate's house was older than mine, with a small, scrubby yard full of trash and dead leaves.

Inside, a skinny girl was sitting on the couch, watching TV—some rainbow-looking cartoon with a spaceship in it.

She glanced away from the screen when we came in, staring at Tate's handful of bloody paper towels. "*Oh* my *God*, are you suspended?"

"Connie, shut up."

The girl slid off the couch and went prancing down the hall to a closed door. "Mo-om, Tate's been fighting."

Tate took a deep breath, pointing to the stairs. "Go to your room. Now."

Connie stomped back into the living room and up the stairs. The door in the hall stayed closed.

Tate sighed and I followed her into the bathroom. She went straight for the medicine cabinet, scraping through tubes and prescription bottles with one hand and holding the wad of paper towels against her nose with the other. She found a bottle of peroxide and some cotton wool and slammed the cabinet shut. Then she dropped the paper towels into the sink and the smell rushed out into the room.

I grabbed for the shower curtain to keep from falling and

the sound made Tate swing around. "How you doing, Mackie?"

"Not great."

"You don't have to stay here. Sit down or go outside or something while I get cleaned up."

I went out into the kitchen and opened the freezer. There wasn't much in it—a few plastic containers with no labels and some toaster waffles—but there was an ice cube tray, about half full. I popped the ice and dumped it into a plastic grocery sack that was sticking out of the trash.

I filled the tray and put it back in the freezer. Then I sat outside on the front porch with my head in my hands and the bag of ice sitting next to me.

After a few minutes, Tate came out onto the porch and stood over me. Her nose had stopped bleeding, but she had a mess of scratches all over one cheek. Her hair was wet, sticking up like a hedgehog, and she'd changed her shirt. I had an amazing, torturous picture of her washing the blood off her neck, her bare chest. In my scenario, her bra was black and made of something lacy, but I couldn't really imagine Tate going into a store and picking out something like that.

She sat down next to me and held out a hand, still not looking over. I offered her the ice and she took it. Her hands were shaking a little, but her face was hard.

"Are you okay?" I said, but not very loud.

She ran her fingers through her hair. There was a small red mark just under her left eye. "No, but I'll live."

I wanted to smile because her voice was so tired and because her wrists looked unbelievably small compared to mine. We sat next to each other, not touching, not talking.

"I wish I could be like you," I said, and it was weird, saying the thing that I meant more than anything. I didn't just mean normal. She was sad and angry, but she knew exactly who she was.

She laughed. "Why would anyone—especially *you*—want to be like me?"

"You're always so good at acting like you know exactly what you're doing all the time."

Tate smiled a small, tricky smile. "What makes you think I don't?"

We both laughed, then stopped again just as fast. She'd slicked her hair back like a boy, but even wet haired and scrubbed pink, even on the sagging porch, she was beautiful.

"Tate."

She glanced over and the plastic bag rustled and crunched. "What?"

"I'm sorry."

She stared out over the yard and sighed. "I know."

"No, you don't. At least not all of it. It's . . . it's not like you think it is."

251

That made her set down the ice pack and turn to face me. "How do you know what I'm thinking?"

"Mostly? A whole lot of personal experience."

She turned and reached for me, pulling my head down. Then she kissed me, shallow and slow. It caught me completely off guard. I hadn't really bothered to hope that she'd let me anywhere near her again, but her arms were around me, her mouth was pressed against mine. And I'd given her nothing but the substantiation of something she already suspected.

I raised my hand, touching her cheek, the side of her neck. When she pulled away, her eyes were deep and alert. Her hair was damp under my fingers.

"What is it?" I said, letting my hand rest at the base of her neck.

She reached up and held on to my wrist. "Do you want to go up to my room? Come up to my room. Just for a little while."

"Are you sure that's a good idea?"

"Look, do you want to or not?"

I nodded, feeling electric and out of breath, trying to decide if we were back to the system of rewards or if she meant something more sincere. If a kiss could mean anything besides the acknowledgment that I'd given her what she wanted, I followed her inside because her hand in mine was warm and I could still taste her ChapStick.

Her room was a mix of personalities. She had posters all over the place, Quentin Tarantino and Rob Zombie and Sammy Sosa. Everything was neat, but not really how you'd think of a girl's room. The dominant color scheme seemed to be communist gray, except for a ludicrous flowered bed-spread.

When Tate sat down on the bed, I stopped in the door-way, crossing my arms over my chest. She leaned over to unlace her shoes.

"Tate?"

She raised her head and looked at me. "Yeah?"

"Why are you doing this? I mean, is this just what happens when I tell you what you want to hear?"

She was shaking her head as she peeled off her shirt. "No one tells me what I want to hear." She had on a very generic bra, off white, plain. Her body was thinner and harder than I'd imagined, but the tops of her breasts curved up soft and round like fruit. God, God, God.

She dropped her shirt on the floor and held out a hand. "Come here."

I sat next to her, feeling awkward and too warm, and she put her arms around my neck. Then she kissed me and I was kissing her back and nothing was awkward at all any-more. Outside, there was a flash of lightning. The storm was moving in, whipping up in gusts as the sky got darker.

Tate was yanking at my hoodie, sliding my T-shirt up. I

elbowed it over my head and got stuck in it and then unstuck. We were both laughing and I knew my hair must be all over the place because she smoothed it down.

I reached behind her to unhook her bra. The clasp was wire and it stung my fingers, but after a few tries, I got it. She slipped out of the straps, leaning into me, letting me slide my hands along her ribs and back.

When I touched her, she sucked in her breath. Her skin was prickling all over with little goose bumps. My heart was beating like crazy and I couldn't tell if I was more excited or more nervous, but it didn't matter. Both feelings were equally satisfying.

The wind picked up and branches rattled against the window. There was another flash of lightning, followed immediately by thunder.

Tate's eyes were squeezed shut, like against bright sunlight. I leaned down and kissed her along her jaw, just below her ear. She turned her face against my shoulder, my bare skin, and I had the feeling of rightness again, like I could just be this, now, and everything was where it should be.

There was a flurry of banging on the door. "Tate?" The knob rattled. "Tate, open the door."

Tate sighed and pushed me away, sitting up, reaching for her bra. Then she turned toward the door. "Is it an emergency?"

"Tate, I mean it—just let me in."

"Connie, is this an *emergency*?"

"Yes!" Her voice sounded high and panicked. The next words were almost lost in the rising wind and the thunder. "Smoke—at the church! Something's on fire!"

Tate was already hooking her bra, wriggling back into her shirt and throwing mine at me. I put it on in a fumbling rush and we pounded downstairs and out onto the porch.

CHAPTER 23

OUR TRESPASSES

The smoke was oily black. It rose in a column, a hundred feet, two hundred feet over the town, like the Israelites' pillar of fire.

"Shit," I said, and my voice sounded completely flat. "*Shit*. The church is burning."

Tate was on the porch next to me. She put her hand on my arm, but I barely felt it. Thunder rumbled above us and the wind gusted, but under it, I heard the low roar of flames. I bolted down the steps and took off toward the blaze.

On Welsh Street, the whole block was in chaos. Even as I turned the corner, I could feel the heat pulsing out in waves, smell the sharp, dry smell of smoke and ashes. The street was full of lights and sirens, trucks parked at angles blocking off traffic. The church was a surging ruin of flames. They licked up the sides of the building in orange tongues, blackening the brick. There was a jagged hole at the base of the steeple, and smoke was pouring out in billows.

The gutters still ran, but the water came from the hoses and not the sky. It spilled along the sidewalks and into the street, black with soot, glittering with sparks and loose embers.

Firefighters were jogging back and forth on the grass, leading people out in twos and threes away from the building.

I found Emma on the lawn of the courthouse. She was standing by herself, hugging her elbows and watching as the Sunday school burned. I came up next to her, reaching for her, pulling her toward me. When she looked up at me, her face seemed to crumple.

"How did it start?" I asked, keeping my arm around her and letting her hang on to me.

"I don't know—lightning, maybe—there was lightning. The chapel caught before the trucks could get here. I don't think they can save it. The roof's gone."

"Where's Dad?"

Emma shook her head. Her mouth was open, but not like she had anything particular to say.

"No, Emma, where's Dad?"

"I don't know, I don't know. There were so many people—women's choir and Bible study and the cleaning crew." She was shaking her head, not stopping. "There had to have been at least thirty people in there."

I splashed through the street to the church and crossed the police line, ducking under tape and around stretchers through the crowd to the service driveway, where paramedics loaded choir members into the ambulances, oxygen masks strapped over their mouths. I looked for him in the coughing crowd of people wrapped in fire ponchos and blankets, and when he wasn't one of the stragglers filing out, I looked for him on the stretchers.

One of the gurneys was covered, and my chest tightened with a deep, wordless dread, but even before I got close, I knew it couldn't be him. The body was small and delicate under the sheet. The body of a woman. Or a girl.

I came up to the driver and grabbed his arm. He wasn't part of my dad's congregation, but his face was familiar from years of hospital picnics, Brad or Brian—some safe, pleasant name—and I held on, turning him toward the sheet. "Who is it?"

He shook his head. "We can't disclose that. She has to be pronounced." His voice was helpless and he stared at me with a stark, jacklighted expression. "I can't pronounce her. She has to be identified by the doctor or the coroner."

I let him go, staggered by the utter formality of pronouncing someone dead. I knew it already, and so did he, without confirmation from the coroner. Her body was there under the sheet in front of us, and what difference did it make who said it? Nothing would be different if it was a wide-eyed paramedic who called her dead and not someone else.

I looked down at the covered body. The rain was just a fine mist, soaking slowly through the fabric. The shape of her profile was unclear. But I knew her shoes. The toes stuck out from under the sheet, just barely, just her toes.

The shoes were flat bottomed, made of black rubber and red leather, with little flowers cut out on the toes. I could see her socks through the openings of the petals. I'd noticed them at Zoe's Halloween party. They'd looked so wrong with the rest of Jenna Porter's costume.

I raked my hands through my hair, trying to find the right set of feelings. She'd been nice. Thoughtless or shallow, maybe. But nice. She hadn't deserved to die like this, sucking down smoke until her lungs stopped. She'd said hi to me in class and lent me pens and stayed quiet when Alice said nasty, malicious things to other girls—and she did, I'd always known that, even when I was busy being awed by her eyelashes or mesmerized by her hair. But not Jenna. She'd never done anything to anyone.

I backed away from Brad, who was looking slack and shell-shocked, then turned in a circle, scanning the crowd for my dad, until finally I found him. He stood in the middle of the street, in the dark blue suit that he always wore for office hours. His hair was wet and his white button-down shirt wasn't all that white anymore but streaked gray with soot.

He stood with his arms at his sides and his face turned toward the church as it blackened and crumbled. His expression was bare and helpless, and he didn't see me. The only thing in his field of vision was the ruined church. It was a landmark, one of the oldest buildings in Gentry, and now it was nearly gone. I stood next to him and watched it go, thinking how strange it was that something could stand for so many things. It was Gentry, like Natalie was Gentry— just a symbol of a town, the particular warm body that represented everyone else.

I watched the smoking church, the demolished Sunday school, feeling a kind of surreal tenderness for it. It had been built to withstand disasters and acts of God. There were lightning rods on two corners of the roof and one on the point of the steeple, and that was where the lightning had hit. The strike had made contact six inches from the tallest lightning rod. It had arced *away* from the metal, and that was not consistent with lightning, but pretty goddamn consistent with other types of disasters.

I turned away from the smoke and chaos of the blackened church, away from Jenna's covered body and my devastated father, and headed straight for the slag heap.

*

On Concord Street, the gutters ran high and fast, and the storm drains were clogged with leaves.

"Mackie! Mackie, wait." Carlina was hurrying up the sidewalk after me. She was wearing her coat and had wrapped a scarf over her head.

The rain was so thin it was almost fog, coming fine and sideways under the streetlights. It dripped off the bottom of her coat in a little fringe, splashing around her feet.

"Where are you going?" she said, stopping under the streetlight.

"Where do you think? I'm going down to ask the Morrigan where the fuck she gets off torching community property! The church is *gone*, Carlina. The whole thing, it's just gone."

She pressed her hands against her face, letting her shoulders slump. "It's not like that." Then she said it again. "It isn't like that."

"Tell me what it *is* like, then. Tell me what happened to the church. Did you burn my dad's church?"

"We're not monsters, Mackie. We didn't do this."

Her face was strangely plain, and I was struck again by how different she looked from the woman onstage. Carlina Carlyle meant smoke and colored footlights. This new woman was mysterious and still. In the street, the air was hot and used up.

261

"Who are we?" I said, and I sounded tired, like I didn't even care anymore.

"We don't really like names. When you name something, you take away some of its power. It becomes known. They've called us a lot of things—the good neighbors, the fair folk. The gray ones, the old ones, the other ones. Spirits and haunts and demons. Here, they never really named us. We're nothing."

It was a minute before she said anything else, and when she did, her voice sounded strange. "The Lady is the kind of person who likes to make the town hurt. She's the kind of person who sets fires."

"Where is she?"

"There's a door in the dump hill by the park. But you don't want to go there. She's incredibly dangerous, and the Morrigan will be furious."

"Then she can be furious."

Carlina turned and looked out over the road. "You need to think about what you're doing. You can be angry at the Lady for doing this, but it's not your job to stand up for them."

"Stop talking about *them*. I *am* them."

Carlina nodded, eyes huge and sad. "Then take a knife with you." Her voice was low. "Just a regular kitchen knife. Wrap it in a dish towel or a handkerchief if you have to, but take it and stick it in the ground at the base of the hill. The door won't open otherwise."

262

"And that's it, just stick a knife in the dirt and the door opens. What then? I just smile and walk right in?"

Carlina shoved her hands in her pockets. "Castoffs are always allowed to come home if they want to. She might be a nasty piece of work, but she owes you that much."

The rain was thin and constant. *Castoff* was like a slap when Carlina said it.

Maybe she saw something on my face because she folded her arms and looked down. "What I mean is, good luck."

PART FOUR

THEM

CHAPTER 24

THE HOUSE OF MISERY

At home, I wrapped a dish towel around my hand and dug through the cupboard over the refrigerator, feeling around in the mess of forbidden cutlery for a paring knife. I was shaking, and my fingers skittered over forks and ladles before I found the knife my dad had been using on his apple the other night. The blade was only about three inches long, not particularly sharp. It had a wooden handle, and the finish had started to wear off. I wrapped it in the towel and put it in the pocket of my coat. Then I put up my hood and started for the park.

At the intersection of Carver and Oak, I cut across the grass, past the picnic shelters and the playground. The swings were squeaking to themselves. The park was empty and smoke hung over everything.

On the other side of the baseball diamonds, the dump hill rose dark and hazy through the rain. The ground was swampy with standing water.

I jumped the fence, wading through a tangle of weeds. At the base of the hill, I stuck the knife deep into the loose gravel and the fill. The door was there almost at once, so dull and worn out that it was almost invisible. There was no handle, so I knocked and stepped back. For a second, nothing happened, but then the outline flared from inside, lit with a warm glow. From far away, I heard the sound of bells and was blindsided by a strange feeling of inevitability. The hill had always been there, looming over the park, right there on the other side of the fence. Waiting for me.

When the door swung open, no one was waiting in the entryway. Glass lanterns lit the corridor in two rows. The panes were set in a network of lead, arranged in fancy diamond patterns. When I pushed my way inside, the door swung closed behind me. The knife lay on the floor and I bent and picked it up.

The Lady's hill was nothing like Mayhem. The walls were paneled in dark, polished wood, with an intricately tiled floor and carved baseboards. Everything was clean and symmetrical and shiny. Stained glass windows hung in rectangular alcoves along the hall, the pictures lit from behind with oil lamps. The air smelled nice, like cut grass and spices.

At the end of the hall, there was a little table with a shallow silver dish on it.

A boy stood beside the table, wearing dark blue knickerbockers and a matching jacket. He looked maybe twelve and was looking up at me, holding out his hand. "Your card, please."

I stared down at him. "*Card?* What the fuck are you talking about?"

"Your calling card. Present your card and I'll announce you."

"I don't have a card. Take me to see the Lady!"

He looked at me a long time. Then he nodded and gestured for me to follow him. "This way." He led me through corridors and doorways into a warm, lamplit room.

There were rugs on the floor and a fire burning in a marble fireplace. All of the furniture was the fussy old-fashioned stuff my mom liked.

A woman sat in a high-backed chair, embroidering a cluster of poisonous-looking flowers onto a piece of cloth. She looked up when I came in. The skin around her eyes was pink, like maybe she'd been crying. When she raised her face to the light, though, I saw that her eyelashes were crusted with something yellow and diseased. She looked young and like she should have been delicately, strikingly beautiful, but it was spoiled by her unhealthy appearance.

"Are you the Lady?" I said, standing in the doorway.

She sat perfectly still, holding the needle out from the cloth and watching me. The front of her dress was a complicated arrangement of creases and folds. Above that was a high fitted collar made of lace. She smiled and it made her look frail. "Is that any way to greet someone?"

Her voice was sweet, but it had an icy undertone that cut through the harmony. Her expression was so peaceful it looked arrogant, and I could feel myself getting angrier. "You burned down my dad's church! Is there a formal greeting for that?"

The Lady set down her embroidery. "It was a necessary evil, I'm afraid. My dear sister has been scampering around like a trained dog, playing jester and fool to people who are already dangerously close to forgetting us. It was time to remind the town what really defines us."

"*That's* your reason—to put the fear of God into a bunch of people who don't believe you exist? You just destroyed a two-hundred-year-old building! A girl is *dead*!"

"The fear of God is nothing compared to the fear of tragedy and loss." She tilted her head and smiled. Her teeth were small and even, perfectly white. "But in the main, it benefits us in other ways. After all, the tragedy has turned sweet and brought us a visitor."

At first I thought she was talking about herself in the plural, the way that queens did, but then I looked around. On a big pillow near the writing table, there was a little kid wearing button boots and a white sailor dress. She was playing with a wire birdcage, putting a windup bird inside and taking it back out. She had a wide ribbon tied around

270

her waist. The other end was fastened to the leg of the table.

"Do you like her?" said the Lady. "She is such a sweet thing."

The girl was maybe two or three, with hazel eyes and small, even teeth. She smiled up at me, and one cheek dimpled so deep I could have gotten my finger stuck in it.

I sucked in my breath. She wasn't how I remembered, but I knew her. Through all the bows and the ruffles, I knew her. She was human. I'd seen her every week in the church parking lot or playing tag with Tate on the lawn in front of the Sunday school. Natalie Stewart sat on the floor, looking at me over the top of the cage.

She waved the clockwork bird, and the Lady reached down, touching Natalie's hair, patting her cheek.

I remembered what my mom had said about sitting on a cushion at the Lady's feet. Natalie was so clean that she looked artificial. "So, she's like your *doll*?"

That made the Lady laugh, hiding her mouth with her hand. "I do love a pretty child, don't you? And she complements the room." She gestured around us. "As you can see, I am a great lover of beauty."

The walls were covered with glass display cases holding seashells and pressed flowers. The biggest case hung over the back of a velvet sofa. It was full of dead butterflies on tiny brass tacks. Two of the walls were lined with built-in shelves, like a library, but there were no books. Instead, there were birds—robins and jays, mostly—and a huge stuffed crow with orange glass eyes.

While I looked around at all the butterflies and birds, the Lady sat at her table, watching my face. Then she stood up and turned her back on me.

"Please, sit," she said, gesturing to a chair by the fireplace. "Sit and warm yourself."

I sat down on the edge of the high-backed chair, leaning forward a little. My jacket was wet and I was dripping on the upholstery.

Natalie put down the cage and came as close as the knotted ribbon would let her.

The Lady smiled. "And what does one say to our guest?"

Natalie tucked her chin and didn't look at me. "How do you do?" she said, rocking back on her heels.

When she rocked forward again, she held out a hand, offering me a crumpled ribbon with a little charm strung on it. When I reached for it, she dropped the ribbon into my hand. Then she smiled and backed away, tugging a handful of hair across her mouth and sucking on it.

The Lady stood very still, staring off at nothing with her hand at her throat. She kept touching a carved oval on a velvet band, brushing the profile with one finger.

Then she turned to look at me. When she smiled, it looked savage. "My sister used to be a war goddess. Or didn't she tell you? She used to sit at the ford with an ash branch in her hand and a crow's wing tied in her hair. She watched as armies crossed the river and chose who and in what order they would die. And then she let herself be ruined, like everyone lets themselves be ruined, shrunken down to fit the visions of the ignorant. All except me."

"I don't understand. Why do you care so much what people think about the Morrigan?"

"No one is immune to disbelief. Their weakening faith can destroy us all." She turned and looked me full in the face, biting down on the word *all*. Her eyes were dark and bloodshot, caked yellow with infection. "We have always gloried in our strength and our power, even when it made us monsters. But now, they diminish us in their stories, making us spirits and sprites. Trivial people, bent on mischief, petty in their dealings. Petty and spiteful and powerless." She raised her head and looked me straight in the face. "I assure you, Mr. Doyle, I am not powerless."

I didn't say anything. She might look sick and frail, but in that moment, she also looked unbelievably cruel.

"We are changing," she said. "They've ruined my sister and robbed her of her power. We're a fabular people, defined by the whims of their lore and their tales. They have always told us what we are."

"Why stay here, then, if it's so bad? Why stick around and wait for them to ruin you?"

"The town is bound to us. From the earliest days, we've helped them where we could, and they've helped us."

"By help, do you mean blood?"

The Lady drew herself up. "We are entitled to payment for the assistance we provide. We gave them prosperity. We made them what they are—the finest, the most fortunate hamlet in the region, and in turn, they remembered us as tall and proud and fearsome. Their belief has been enough to keep us whole."

But it wasn't enough. The roofs leaked, the topsoil was washing away in the rain, the rust had settled in, and now Gentry was coming down in pieces. She was pale, red around the eyes, and they needed blood and worship to survive.

I shook my head. "You take kids away from their families, and you kill them. Are you saying that everyone should just sit back and let it happen?"

"We are as much a part of this town as they are—vital to their way of life. And they love us for it."

I stared into the fire, shaking my head. "That's not true. They don't love or need us. They *hate* us."

The Lady made a breathless little noise, almost a laugh. "People are very disingenuous, dear. They talk and arrange meetings and generally make a great to-do. Do you know how one can tell which of the chorus are sincere?"

Her smile was cold. She could have been made of wax or

porcelain like a doll, but her eyes were wicked and bright. "The ones who are sincere *leave*. The others sink their roots in this quiet town and wring their hands and bemoan the loss of their children, and all the while, they take their payment, and they keep the town and they feed it, just like they've always done."

Her eyes were dark and awful. I had an idea that she never stopped smiling.

"So, killing kids isn't something you do because you're morally bankrupt psychopaths, but more like a public service." My voice was hard and that made me feel braver. "You're doing it for *every*one, right? Not just to feed yourselves, but for the town because the *town* needs devastated parents and dead kids. And hell, might as well burn their churches down as long as you're at it."

"Yes," the Lady said, very calmly. "Their blood is their blood and when they honor me with it, I receive it and then give that power back to them. I make them prosper." She reached up and tried to touch my face. "Just accept it, dear. Everyone else has."

I pulled away, twisting out of her reach. "If you're just going to go around bleeding the town, why bother with the church at all? Why make them suffer if you're going to take their blood anyway?"

"Because my wretched goblin of a sister has fallen well outside the bounds of my authority, allowing her fiends to

275

show themselves in the streets at every opportunity. Her cavalier regard for prudence might seem precious now, but it undermines us all. They won't be joyful enough to give her what she wants if they're looking to their own tragedy."

"So you're punishing her."

The Lady smiled and her mouth was beautiful and cruel. "I only want us to be amicable, to reach a compromise. But if she refuses to see reason, then there's nothing I can do and she must be punished. Will you tell her so when next you see her? Tell her all this could have been avoided."

"I'm not your messenger. I work for the Morrigan, and it's not my job to tell her what she's doing wrong."

The Lady smiled, eyes downcast. "Oh, my naive darling, the Morrigan doesn't command you. You're a creature of free agency who came to me tonight of your own accord. She would have held you back had she been able. On occasion, you might dally in her pitiful circus, but your will is your own."

"At least your sister cares about something besides *herself*. She saved my life, so stop talking about her like she's so beneath you."

"She *is* beneath me. She has no pride and no dignity. She sends her creatures out to dance like monkeys and degrade themselves before the town."

"And so you decided to hate her?"

The Lady shook her head, looking off toward Natalie.

276

"She lied and deceived me. She stole a child from my house and brought it home. She defied me and threatened us with discovery. She nearly destroyed the town."

"She thought it was disgusting to keep kids as toys and pets, and she's *right*. What are you going to do with your new toy? Pin her on a corkboard and then show everyone your collection and talk about how pretty she is?"

"This little imp? Nothing so significant. She'll go to the earth like all the rest, completely unremarkable."

"She doesn't have to be remarkable to *matter*. She's a kid with a family. She's someone's *sister*."

"Just so. And now she's nothing. She'll go to the unholy ground in the hour before dawn as All Souls' passes into a forgotten saint's day, and she'll die for the renewal of the town."

"And that's all it takes to make you happy? You kill little kids, then go home and wait until it's time to do it all again? What the hell kind of existence is that?"

The Lady raised her head, looking off at something in the distance. "They used to honor us with *warriors*." She glanced over at Natalie, like the idea of using something so powerless disgusted her. "And now we've been reduced to sprites and goblins, and only the slaughter of the weak keeps us alive."

I backed away from her. The room was full of glass-eyed birds and dead butterflies and big, old-fashioned furniture.

All these things were very clear, like they were the only things that had ever happened in my life.

The Lady went across to the table and picked up a little brass bell. When she rang it, the sound was high and clear.

Then she sat down, looking at me steadily. "This meeting has gone on long enough, sir. I thank you for your company and bear you no ill will, but I can't take back the destruction of the church or give you what you want. The Cutter will escort you out."

I remembered what the Morrigan had said about the Cutter. For one second, I could almost picture him—a massive silhouette, huge and hulking. Then it was gone. Instead, there was just the image of a woman. She lay on her back in a pool of murky water, face mangled, arms strapped to her sides.

"No," I said, already knowing that the word didn't matter but needing to say it. "I'm not leaving her here. She's little, she's just a kid."

"It's no use arguing," the Lady said. "I won't cede her to you willingly, and you can't stand against the Cutter. None of us can."

I tried to think what a brave person would do. What Tate would do. But Natalie was her family, and I was underground with a woman who emptied entire lakes and then dumped them in her sister's living room when she was feeling particularly vindictive. Who called up endless rain and burned down buildings just to make sure that no one forgot her. Compared to her, I was useless.

When the door swung in, Natalie cringed, shrinking against the Lady's skirt and holding on to her birdcage. The Cutter stood in the doorway. He was thin, taller than the Lady. He could have been her brother. He had the same dark hair, the same watery, diseased look around his eyes.

Everything about him was familiar in flashes—the black coat, the thin, colorless mouth, the bones in his face—all vague and uneasy, like something from a dream.

He touched his forehead, even though he wasn't wearing a hat.

When I looked at him, I remembered being small, just the right size to fit in the crook of his elbow. He was creeping into the bedroom, taking the rightful baby out of its crib, closing the window. Leaving me behind. He was the only thing I remembered from a life before Gentry.

The Lady rose from her chair, giving him a wide path, and he watched her back away. His eyes were sharp and narrow.

When the Lady spoke, she was looking away from him. "Show our guest out if you please, sir."

The Cutter smiled—a strange, empty smile—and bowed to me, and then I smelled the smell that was seeping out of his skin. He smelled toxic, reeking with iron. I could feel my heartbeat—not just in my chest, but in my arms and hands and throat.

The Lady had covered her face with a handkerchief, and my question wasn't so much curiosity as numb confusion. "What *is* he?"

She looked at me over the lacy edge of her handkerchief and her answer was muffled. "A sadist and a masochist. He endures tremendous suffering because it pleases him to see the suffering of others."

The Cutter didn't look particularly miserable or suffering. His eyes were red rimmed and bloodshot, but he moved quickly. "Come along," he said in a hoarse whisper, and grabbed me by the arm.

As he pulled me out into the hall, I looked back. The last thing I saw was Tate's sister, settling back down onto her pillow, hugging her birdcage.

Then the fumes washed over me and I staggered. The Cutter held me steady, digging his fingers into my arm. His expression was polite, like a gentleman in a movie about people who rode around in carriages, but his voice was deep and rough and should have belonged to someone else.

"Easy does it," he said. "You're all right."

With his hand on my arm, he led me along the hall.

"Tell me, cousin, how's the weather up in the park tonight? I thought it smelled like rain."

When I didn't answer, he gave me a little shake and

tightened his grip, dragging me along by the elbow with his coat flapping behind him. "Don't go faint on me now or I'll have to slap the sense back into you. Maybe you think I haven't a care for what happens up ground, but God help me, I love that town. The Lady, she pines after the old days, but tribes and villages can't match the hospitality we've seen here."

I concentrated on putting one foot after the other, keeping myself upright and my eyes on the floor in front of me.

"Let me tell you a story," he said. "A story about us and about the people who live just above us. It was a miserable, desperate time, and they looked to us for salvation. Cousin, we had more blood than any hill's ever had in a single year. We bled their lambkins on all the old feast days—Imbolc and Beltane and Lammas—and on every holy day." He smiled over his shoulder, showing small, even teeth, but his gums were raw and infected looking. "There are a lot of holy days, cousin."

"In the Depression," I said. My voice sounded thick and disjointed.

"The what?"

"In the Great Depression, you took that blood from the town. You took their children and they blamed it on Kellan Caury. They hanged him out on Heath Road for stealing kids."

The Cutter stopped walking and turned to face me. Then

he grinned—a wide, leering grin that took over his whole face. "Oh, Caury did it, all right. Make no mistake. He took them."

The smell that came off him when he talked was thick and scummy, like flaking rust and old blood. I yanked my arm out of his hand and leaned against the painted wallpaper. "What are you talking about? He wasn't a kidnapper. He just wanted to live a normal life."

The Cutter laughed. "Sure. Sure, he wanted to live peaceful and idyllic, tending his shop and stargazing with his girl. And we wanted something else. We get what we want."

For the first time, I looked at the Cutter—really *looked* at him. His face was symmetrical, with a straight nose, a sharp chin and jaw, but the tightness around his eyes made him look hollow and vacant.

Except for the pack of rotten girls, people in the slag heap seemed healthy. They were strange and sometimes ugly, but their faces were painless and their eyes were clear. The Cutter looked contagious. I took short, shallow breaths. My vision was starting to tunnel, and I couldn't do anything to stop it.

He grabbed my arm again and gave me a hard shake. "Stay with me, cousin. We're almost to the door."

"How did you get it—what you wanted from him?"

"Caury? That was simple. He had a sweet, pious girl that

played piano in the church on Sundays and didn't mind much that he was a right oddity. Maybe he didn't start out begging to do our work, but he was willing enough in the end." The Cutter's voice sounded eager suddenly. "By the time I got through, that little tart was half what she'd been before, and he'd have done anything just to see that she didn't lose any more fingers."

I felt light-headed, sick in waves. "The way I heard it, you didn't kill him. It was the sheriff, the deputies—they got together a lynch mob."

The Cutter shook his head. "Oh, we killed him. Make no mistake. The town came for him, but we were the ones who killed him. They delivered him down to the killing ground, and maybe they didn't even really know why, but they got him there all right. They bludgeoned him first, beat him in the street like a dog, but there was still enough life in him to scream."

"You murdered one of your own people."

He was pulling me along, winding through hallways with fancy carved baseboards and painted wallpaper. We turned a corner and I was back in the entryway, with its smooth floor and its elegant wood-paneled walls. Everything seemed to blur and swim.

The Cutter unlatched the door and pushed it open. "Get along to your little friends, then."

On the other side, I could smell dead leaves and fresh air.

I needed to be out in the park, out where I could breathe, but Tate's sister was tied to a fancy plush armchair and I turned to face the Cutter with the room tilting all around me. "What if I don't?"

He stood beside the door, straight and perfect like people in the court were supposed to be perfect, but his mouth was thin and the purple shadows under his cheekbones made his face look like a skull. "You will because I tell you to, and if you don't, then you can get along to hell. You might be fine and good and fair, cousin, but you're no cousin of mine."

His hand hit me between my shoulders then and he shoved me in the direction of Gentry and the outside world.

I stumbled into the drizzle and landed on my hands and knees, leaves cold and slick between my spread fingers. Behind me, the door swung shut and melted back into the shadows.

I got to my feet, gasping and coughing, and started across the park. At the corner of Carver Street, though, I stopped. I stood in the wavering halo of a streetlight, looking at the charm that Natalie had given me. The ribbon was sticky and frayed and the charm was nothing but a zipper pull, made of pink plastic and shaped like a teddy bear.

I crossed the grass to the solitary picnic table where Roswell and I had sat the night before and collapsed on the bench to think.

I was exhausted. My lungs ached and my clothes smelled

like smoke, my dad's church was gone, and Natalie Stewart wasn't dead, but she was about to be.

I wanted to turn invisible, to disappear. I wanted to lie down and sink into the ground. That way, I wouldn't have to feel or think. I could be earth, roots, grass. Nothing.

My phone buzzed in my pocket and I took it out to see who was calling. Emma. I knew I should answer, at least tell her where I was and that I was okay, but the conversation seemed impossible. I stared at the phone, at her name glowing on the screen. Then I turned it off.

CHAPTER 25

SACRED

I woke myself up shivering, curled awkwardly on the picnic bench. The ache in my neck was unreal and my toes had fallen asleep. It was six o'clock in the morning. I had nine missed calls from Emma and two from Roswell.

School wasn't exactly a priority for the day. My hands and feet were freezing, and I needed to go home, to take a shower and sleep in a bed. But in the daylight, I knew that I had to talk to Tate first, so I took the long way home, down Welsh Street so I'd pass her house.

She was out in the garage with the door up and I guessed that she was either planning some truancy of her own or, more likely, someone had notified the administration that she'd kicked the holy hell out of Alice. The punishment for fighting on school property was suspension.

The hood of the Buick was propped open and she was knocking around under it. As I came up the driveway, she hit her head on the underside of the hood and dropped a wrench. It clanged against the cement, then bounced under the car.

She kicked the bumper and hopped back a little, wincing.

"Tate," I said. And then I didn't say anything else. My voice sounded hoarse and used up.

She turned, already starting to smile, and then the smile faded. "What's wrong? What are you doing here?"

I shook my head, catching her by the sleeve, pulling her away from the car and toward the weak daylight. "Have you seen this before?"

"Hey—" She reached for the zipper pull. "Hey, where'd you get that?"

I tried to make her see the answer in my face, no completely inadequate explanations, no words, but she just stared up at me with a panicked look.

"No, where did you get it? Did you find it somewhere? Where the *hell* did you get that?" Then she snatched it out of my hand and held it up. "You see this? Do you see this piece of plastic in my hand? You need to tell me where you got this."

I looked down at her. The truth was awful and I had no name for myself and none for what was happening under our town. "Wherever you think it came from, that's where."

She looked down at the little charm, and I could see the change happen on her face, like something inside her cracking and then, just as fast, fusing back together. "You saw her."

I was struck, suddenly, by how dry my mouth was. "Underground."

Tate stared at me. "But you *saw* her. Right now, she's alive, and you saw her and you didn't do anything—you didn't bring her *back*?"

I shook my head, feeling helpless and ashamed. "I couldn't, Tate. They're so used to just being allowed to do this, and no one ever stops them, no one does anything. I don't know *how*."

"Well, you better figure it out!"

I thought of my mom, weird, distant, cold, and sad. "Are you sure that's what you want?"

"Yes, I'm fucking *sure*. She's my *sister*!" Tate screamed it, slamming her hands down on the hood of the car. "Why would I not do everything I can to get my *sister* back?"

I didn't know how to explain life at my house, how bad and weird and creepy it could get. How my mom was still being punished just for surviving, and they'd waited fifteen years to get revenge, because to people like them, fifteen years was two seconds and nothing was ever really forgiven. They could make you pay for the rest of your life.

"It's just going to mess up your family," I said.

Tate took a long breath and reached for my hand, not like a girlfriend, but hard and panicked like someone

288

drowning. "Mackie, my family is already so messed up that I can't think of a single thing anyone could do right now to make it worse." She squeezed my fingers, staring up at me, and everything smelled like metal. "Just tell me what to do."

I shook my head. Tate never asked anyone what to do, and I had no answer, no secret knowledge. This was just what always happened and what had been happening for decades. Maybe centuries.

Tate's eyes were hard and shiny, but not like tears. Her gaze was brutal, and she wasn't the kind of girl who begged for anything. "There has to be something I can do because I'm not going to just sit around and do *nothing*!"

I held her hand in both of mine, gripping her by the wrist, holding her still.

They'd had to work on Kellan Caury a long time before they finally made him their man, but the Cutter had figured it out eventually. You can get a lot from a person if you cut the fingers off his girlfriend.

"Stay inside," I said with my hands locked around hers.

The look she gave me was terrible. "No—no way. You're talking about my *sister*. There is no way I'm just going to sit home like a good little girl and wait for you to decide whether or not you're going to do something!"

She was so brave and so reckless, and I wasn't lying when I said, "Look, this is how it *is*, and you can't do anything to help her. You need to go in the house and lock the doors. I'll figure something out."

Then I kissed her fast and ducked out the open garage door before I could see the look on her face.

I'd been relatively sure that Tate would follow me, but she didn't. When I'd gone a block and a half without her screaming obscenities at me or chasing me down, I let myself hope that for once, she might actually be listening to me.

I headed home, making a mental inventory of my resources. They weren't very encouraging. The Morrigan might hate her sister, but she wasn't going to help me save Natalie because apparently human sacrifice didn't fall under her classification of inappropriate reasons to steal kids. Or maybe it was just that the Morrigan was scared of her sister—like everyone else. Scared of what happened when the Lady caught someone doing something she didn't like.

I didn't have a solution, I didn't have a plan. I had half a bottle of analeptic and an old paring knife, neither of which was that much help in the greater scheme of things.

At the corner of Concord and Wicker, I stopped. I stood on the sidewalk for a long time, looking at my house like it was one of those find-the-hidden-picture games. The yard wasn't right, and there were too many wrong things to count.

The stepladder was out, but it was tipped over, open so it made a capital *A* on the lawn. There were long smears of dirt on the front walk. The grass was mashed down flat in places. The gutter was stopped with twigs and dead leaves, and water ran in a steady fall down onto the front steps.

I tried the door, but the knob was locked and so was the dead bolt, and I had to go scraping around in the bushes for the hide-a-key. Some of the edging was torn up and tulip bulbs lay brown and papery on the cement.

A jack-o'-lantern lay smashed in a pulpy mess on the porch. Its eyeholes gaped up at me, candle scorched, half caved in.

When I stepped into the front hall, I was struck by how deserted the house was. My dad was probably at the police station or maybe helping Jenna's family make preliminary arrangements for the funeral. He'd be comforting the masses, managing the chaos, and my mom would be at the hospital, working the morning shift, but Emma didn't have class until noon. Her bag was hanging on a hook behind the door. I waited a second and then called her name.

There was no answer. Her coat lay on the bench by the mail table. All the lights were out and I moved slowly, staying close to the wall.

The kitchen was empty, but I had a soft, creepy feeling on my neck, like I wasn't the only one in the room. I listened a long time before I heard it. Not a cry, but a breathless gasp. Then nothing.

"Emma?" I flipped the light switch and knelt on the floor.

She was sitting under the table. All the stainless steel flat-ware and the good knives were lined up in a circle around her, and she had her arms pulled close against her chest. She was holding a butcher knife. There was a bruise coming out on one cheek.

"Emma, what happened?"

She opened her mouth but didn't say anything, looking out at me from under the table, shaking her head.

I reached for her and the metal circle sent a flash of pain up my arm. I sat back hard on the floor, closing my eyes as the kitchen spun. "You have to move that stuff."

She shook her head again, a quick, frantic little shake.

I yanked my sleeves down over my hands and raked away the knives, reaching for her, pulling her out from under the table and dragging her across the linoleum into the light.

Dead leaves and little twists of brown grass were stuck all over her clothes and in her hair. Her T-shirt was muddy. Her arms were bare, covered past the elbow in thin, spiral burns. They ran in crazy squiggles, oozing clear and yellow. When I touched one of them, she gasped. The skin around the burn felt sticky. I didn't do it again.

I put my hands on her shoulders. "Did they come in the house?"

"No," she whispered. "They were out in the yard. I was on the ladder, you know, to clear the gutter. It was running over. They—uh, they were laughing."

"What did they look like? Were they like me?"

The look she gave me was agonized. "No, they weren't like *you*. They were—" She took a short, hitching breath. "They were *ugly*."

I realized I was squeezing her and made myself stop. "Ugly like how?"

"Like bony and white and . . . rotten." Without warning, she mashed her face against my chest so she was talking into my shirt. "They were *dead*, Mackie."

Pain seared across my ribs and I gasped. "*Ow*. Put that down."

She looked at the knife in her hand like she was surprised to see it there. Then she tossed it away. It spun like a dial on the floor. When it stopped, it was pointing to the refrigerator.

She took a deep breath. "They came up on the lawn and stood around the ladder." Her voice was hard. "They asked me if I wanted to come and visit them. They said they ran a sanitarium and I was just the kind of girl they needed on their staff."

"Then what?" I was brushing at the grass on her T-shirt, picking leaves out of her hair. "What did they do to your arms?"

"They knocked me off the ladder. They had fingernails—long fingernails—and then . . ." She held out her arms and didn't finish.

The burns were wet and raw. They gave off a bright ozone smell that reminded me of lightning storms. "How did you get away?"

She smiled and it was the most ironic expression I'd ever seen. "I said the Twenty-third Psalm."

"You chased them away by quoting *Bible* verses?"

"I read, Mackie."

"So, what you're telling me is, you have a book that says if a pack of rotten girls shows up at your house and starts burning graffiti all over your arms, recite a couple of psalms and they'll go away?"

"Revenants," she said, with her head against my shoulder. "When a person comes back from the dead, they're called a revenant." She sounded fussy and serious, even with her scorched arms, her wet hair soaking through my shirt to the skin. She squeezed me hard and raised her head again. Her arms were a raw, oozing mess and she was holding them stiffly away from her body like she was trying not to show how bad it hurt. "It's . . . I just didn't know what else to do."

"Emma, I'm sorry. I'll get you peroxide or iodine or something. We'll get you cleaned up. Just tell me what to do."

"It's okay," she said. Water was dripping down the sides

of her face. "I'm okay. They didn't even come in the house. And it's not as bad as it looks. It hurt a lot, but it's better now. I can hardly feel it."

I looked at her arms again, then held her away from me, staring at her hands. "Are you cold?"

"A little. Not too bad, though." Then she looked down.

Her hands were pale blue and going bluer as we watched. The veins stood out in a dark network under the skin. Her fingernails had turned a deep bloodless gray.

"They took my work gloves," she said in a thin, shuddering voice. "They have my gloves."

I stood up. "Okay, turn on all the lights and lock the doors. I'll be back as soon as I can."

She reached out, grabbing at my sleeve. Her fingers slipped and fumbled on my jacket, like she couldn't quite make them work. "Wait, where are you going?"

"To get your gloves back."

CHAPTER 26

THE PRICE

Under the slag heap, the House of Mayhem was humid from the rain. At opposite ends of the lobby, the two huge fireplaces had been lit and the room was warmer than usual.

The flock of rotting blue girls huddled together around one of the fireplaces. They were sorting through trays of Janice's bottles, melting wax over the tops and pasting on labels. They worked in kind of an assembly line, passing the bottles along and talking in low voices. Behind the reception desk, the Morrigan was sitting on the floor, playing with a doll made of feathers and dirty, knotted string. I came around the desk and stood over her.

"Hello, castoff," she said without looking up. "Are you here to tell me how sorry you are for running off to beg favor from my sister?"

"No, I'm here to tell you that you just made one huge fucking mistake. And stop calling me that."

296

"What would you prefer? Foundling? Changeling? Child left in someone else's bed?" She dropped the doll and stared up at me. Her teeth reflected the firelight back at me in bright pinpricks. "I gave you cures and medicines, cared for you when you were ill. Without my mercies, you would have died, and still you disregard me, you *slight* me for my sister?"

"Yeah, I talked to your sister, okay? Fine, I'm a terrible person. Tell your rancid hookers to give Emma's gloves back."

The Morrigan nodded toward the far side of the room. "Tell them yourself."

The girls were clustered together on the floor, laughing in a soft, breathless way. One of them, starved looking, with matted hair and ragged gashes down her arms, was wearing a pair of pink suede gardening gloves.

I crossed the lobby and stood over them. Close to the fire, they smelled worse—all wet dirt and rank, decomposing flesh. In the flickering light, they looked greenish under the skin.

"May we help you?" said the one wearing Emma's gloves. She smiled a loose, mushy smile, showing black teeth and rotting gums.

"Yeah, give me those."

"Give you which?"

"Give me my sister's gloves. I'm through dicking around."

The girl next to her leaned in and elbowed her, grinning up at me. She was holding a smoldering stick of wood and a lump of half-melted wax. Her tongue was blue and her whole mouth was crawling with little white maggots. "How will she be compensated for her cooperation?"

"Kiss her," whispered the girl from the Halloween party.

The others laughed and covered their mouths. "Yes, kiss her, kiss her and we'll let your sister's hands go."

The one with the gloves got to her feet, stepping close and smiling up at me. "Just once," she said, and her voice was softer than the others'. Almost sad. "Kiss me once, and I'll give them back to you."

I looked down at her. Her eyes might have been green once, but now they were cloudy and pale.

"It doesn't have to be passionate," she said. "You don't have to convince me that you mean it. Just give me the chance to pretend you don't find me revolting."

The other girls watched, hungry and eager, but the girl with the gloves just looked cold. She wasn't laughing.

I bent and kissed her on the cheek, close to the corner of her mouth. The smell was bad. She reeked like ground-water and decay, but underneath was the thin fragrance of church incense and funeral flowers, the dismal aroma of grief, of never really dying.

I stayed with my face close to hers, my mouth against her cheek, even after I'd given her what she asked for. The only thing she'd wanted. I wanted to make it count because I was sorry for her. Because she was dead and I wasn't.

When I finally straightened and stepped back, the girls on the floor muttered restlessly, but the one with the gloves just gave me a wistful look.

"That was nice," she whispered, holding out her hands.

I took the gloves by their fingertips and slid them off. Underneath, her hands were a healthy pink, but even in the firelight, I could see it draining out of her. The warm tinge faded, and her fingernails went an ugly bruised color. She sighed and smiled at me. The smile made the skin on her lips crack.

I jammed the gloves in my coat pocket and crossed back to the desk, where the Morrigan sat playing with her doll, dancing it along the floor. I could still smell the chilly stench of the girl's skin, this ghostly miasma that drifted and clung to me. The Morrigan was humming and it made me want to kick her.

"Why did you let them do that to Emma? I thought the whole agreement was that you would leave her alone if I worked for you. I thought she and Janice were supposed to be *friends*."

The Morrigan glared up at me. "You chose to appeal to my sister. You ran to her at the first opportunity. She did her best to break the town, and you went to *bow* to her." She swung the doll against the leg of the desk. Its head made a hollow noise when it hit. "They don't have the will to give us favor when they're sad. They're too caught up in their own misery, their own tragedy, and then they don't love us."

"Look, you started this. You called out the Lady when you stole my mother back."

The Morrigan sat with her legs folded under her, hugging the doll against her chest. "And look at where it got us. The town is *sick*. It gets worse every year, and now the buildings are falling, the house of God is destroyed, and even the train tracks and the trestles rust."

I let my breath out between my teeth and then held out the zipper pull. "They're going to kill a three-year-old girl. Not a warrior or a king. She's a little kid—she's like you."

The Morrigan took the plastic bear, turning it over in her hand. Then she looked up at me, teeth sharp and glossy. "No, not like me. I'm quite sturdy. She, on the other hand, is going to bleed a river."

When I finally spoke, my voice sounded dry. "What is your problem?"

She dropped the doll into her lap and looked up at me, still holding the plastic zipper pull. "You choose them over us. Every single time."

"And I'll keep doing it! This isn't about picking sides. The Lady is completely out of her mind, and you know how to stop her. Tell me what I need to do to steal Natalie."

The Morrigan seemed to consider that. Then she gave

me a sly look. "Dead is dead," she said. "But my sister is plenty cold herself. Sometimes she can't tell the difference."

"Okay, but what does that *mean*?"

"Only that there are always spare children, dead in borrowed beds, buried in borrowed clothes, waiting to be made use of." Her smile was wide and it was hard to tell if it was cruel because she was cruel or if that was just her smile.

"No." I shook my head. "That's not what you're talking about—not children. You're talking about bodies. About grave robbing."

"Call it what you like. You asked how I managed it, and I've told you. The night was long, and in her sitting room full of dead beauties, I exchanged one more dead thing for a live one, and it was hours before she knew. Before she realized that her prize was gone and the silent child in her sitting room was one of ours."

I took a deep breath and felt a little sick. "Tell me how. How you made the Lady believe the body was real."

The Morrigan smiled, shaking her head. "Dearest, it *was* real."

"How you made it seem believable, then, how you replaced something alive with something that wasn't."

She fidgeted with the zipper pull, rolling it between her fingers, humming and rocking. "Our children rot, but not as readily as theirs do. They're restless things, the failed replacements."

Over by the fireplace, the blue girls whispered and snickered, braiding each other's brittle hair. The one I'd kissed was looking back over her shoulder at me, just once. Then she turned away, keeping her head bowed.

The Morrigan stood up, facing me with the mangy doll in one hand and the zipper pull in the other. She looked like a little girl, old-fashioned and strange, but her teeth were brutal, and her eyes were wide and black. "I'm not your keeper and I don't owe you anything, not anymore. If you intend to cross her, that's not my business, but you should know the cost. A person should always be familiar with the cost of his actions."

"What's the cost?"

She dropped the doll and it landed spread-eagle on the floor, its arms and legs sticking out at awkward angles. "If you don't know after this morning's escapades, I'm certainly not going to tell you."

She smiled up at me and held out the plastic bear. After a second, I took it.

CHAPTER 27

RAISING THE DEAD

When I came in out of the drizzle and the fog, I was relieved to see my dad's black overcoat hanging in the hall. He was sitting in the kitchen with his back to the door. The kettle was boiling on the stove and there were cups on the counter, but Emma wasn't with him and I wasn't brave enough to go in and ask how he was.

His shoulders were too defeated. His head was bowed like he might be praying. Praying or crying, and neither was something I could deal with. I took off my shoes and went upstairs.

Emma's room was a mess of books and flimsy plastic trays full of sprouts and cuttings. Her shelves ran all the way up to the ceiling and the walls were covered in tacked-up post-cards and pictures of greenhouses and gardens cut from magazines.

She was sitting on her bed with her arms crossed over her chest, holding on to her shoulders and looking small. Her hands were their normal color again and she'd put Band-Aids over the scratches on her arms. She glanced up with a wary expression. "Hi."

I didn't have the energy to say it back. I wanted to ask why she wasn't downstairs with our dad. Her hands were warm and alive. The blue girls' assault on her that morning couldn't be the reason they were sitting in different rooms.

The smell of smoke still lay over everything. It was on my clothes and in my hair. Emma's jeans from yesterday were crumpled on the floor and I smelled the black tar smell of shingles and burned copper wiring.

Emma sat rigidly against the headboard of her bed with her hands cupping her elbows. "Why did they do that to me?"

"Because I pissed someone off."

"Was it over something important?" Then she turned so I couldn't see her face, looking away, in the direction of the window. I didn't know what to say. I'd thought so at the time, but what had I really accomplished?

"I got your gloves back." I pulled them out of my pocket and tossed them on the bed next to her, and then they just sat there, pink and dirty.

Emma picked them up. After a second, she put them on.

I sat next to her and looked around at all her clutter. There were books spread open on the desk and the floor, pages marked with sticky notes and colored paper clips. Volumes of chemistry and folklore and a little dog-eared paperback of *The Ballad of Tam Lin*.

Emma slumped next to me. She rested her head on my shoulder and took a deep breath. "What's happening, Mackie?"

Her voice was barely a whisper, and she sounded sad, like she knew there was no way the answer would be good.

I leaned my cheek on the top of her head. "The same thing that always happens."

Emma nodded and I wondered if she knew what it was that always happened or if that was part of the creepy thing about Gentry. You always knew that something was happening, but you never knew what it was.

"I know what's wrong with Mom," I said.

"A little chunk of granite where her heart should be?"

"Sort of, yeah. You know how I came from somewhere else? For her, it's backward. They stole her away, then brought her back, and she couldn't ever figure out how to be normal after that."

Emma was still watching the pink gloves. "Are you sure?" she said.

I nodded.

She leaned against me suddenly, letting her head drop against my shoulder. We sat like that, leaning against each other. Outside, the sky was dark and heavy. Rain pattered on the window and ran down the glass, reflecting yellow and red in the light from the street.

"We have to do something terrible," I said. "We have to dig up—" I stopped. "There was this thing that replaced Tate's sister. We have to dig it up."

Emma pulled away from me. "What are you talking about?"

I didn't want to take the conversation any further. Digging up a grave was the worst kind of desecration, but I knew there was no other choice. Even if I stood back and let Natalie die, none of the bad things would stop. Kids would keep being replaced. Gentry would keep looking the other way, just like it always had. Except that then, I'd have to live with myself.

I took a deep breath. "Natalie Stewart's alive and I think we can save her. But we can't do it unless we have something to leave in her place. If we can get the body back, there are ways of waking them up. I'm not sure how, but I know there are ways."

Emma's gaze drifted to her bookshelves. "I've read about replacements coming back from the dead, but you need the blood, or sometimes the possessions, of the people they replaced. We'd need something of Natalie's. You could call Tate, right?"

"I really don't think that's a good idea. Anyway, I've already got something." I took the zipper pull out of my pocket. "It's not much, but it's Natalie's."

Emma gave it a doubtful look. "Okay," she said finally. "I'll start going through folk stories, scholarly essays, anything that might give us instructions. But this is going to be pretty bad. And it's going to mean a lot of digging."

"I know. I think we should call Roswell."

"Excuse me?"

"He'll help," I said. "He might not be thrilled about it, but he'll help."

Emma sat very still, eyes fixed on some unlikely point just past my shoulder. Finally, she pushed away the quilt and stood up. She yanked her hair back into a ponytail with one hand and went to her dresser for a rubber band. Her face was sober and her hair was already slipping down again, drifting in mousy wisps around her clenched fist.

"Okay," she said, snapping the band around her hair. "Okay, but we need a plan. This is serious, what you're talking about."

"Yes, but it's not a break-in." I tried to keep my voice steady. "It's not a covert operation. Everyone in charge of anything is down at the hospital or the police station, Dad's at home, the church is wrecked. We'll wait until dark and then sneak in. No one's going to be looking out for trespassing or vandalism. The whole town is too busted up to care what someone's doing in the graveyard."

*

I lay on my bed, trying to get some sleep and failing completely. Planning to dig up a body pretty much ruled out any peace of mind.

Tate called twice, but I didn't answer and didn't listen to her messages. It was hard enough to contemplate the night's work without her getting involved. If she knew what I was going to do, she'd be horrified. Or worse, she'd want to help.

After half an hour of dozing off and immediately jerking awake again, I got up and went downstairs. I found my dad in the kitchen. The kettle was still rattling on the burner and he hadn't moved since the last time I'd looked in.

I crossed to the stove and turned it off. "Dad?"

He glanced up and his face was hollow, raw around the eyes. "Yes?"

"The building doesn't matter."

He straightened in his chair, looking up at me like he was trying to figure out if he should be angry or hurt or something else just as bad.

"It doesn't matter," I said again. "The church is you and the town. *Where* doesn't matter. You'll build a new one and the congregation will be there with you, and that's what you love. Them, not the building. It will be as good as it always was."

For a second, I thought he'd tell me I was disrespectful, out of line, that I didn't understand how important that building had been. That someone like me could never understand. He sat with his hands resting slack on his knees and his jaw working. Then he stood up.

He crossed the kitchen and I tried not to tense my shoulders. I was completely unsure about what was going to happen, and for a second, the look on his face was so intense, I thought he was going to shake or hit me. Instead, he grabbed me in a rough hug, one hand on the back of my head, fingers digging into my scalp. He smelled sharp and exhausted and everything was still acrid with smoke. We both were. He was leaning against me, holding on like he was looking for rescue.

I stood out in the driveway, waiting for Roswell and holding my dad's work gloves. It was nine o'clock and pitch dark. The cloud cover was heavy and the drizzle made puddles and soggy places on the lawn. The teddy bear charm was in my pocket and my heart was beating hard with the idea of digging up something that ought to be buried. This was the kind of thing that only desperate people did. The last resort, the only thing left, and so I must be desperate.

When Roswell pulled up to the house, he was wearing his other jacket. The black one. I hadn't said anything about appropriate clothing.

We stood in the street, looking at each other over the hood of his car. The neighborhood was silent. No other cars, no wanderers. Gentry knew enough to be afraid of the dark. A few jack-o'-lanterns still glowed on porches, grinning crumpled grins.

"What's up?" he said, like the church was always burning down and I always called him on a school night, telling him to come over after dark and to bring a shovel.

I swallowed, trying to keep back the panic that was rising in my chest. "I need your help. We have to do a bad thing. We have to dig up a grave. Don't look at me like that—the girl who's supposed to be buried isn't dead. I saw her tonight. But we need what's in the box."

Roswell didn't look confused and he didn't ask me to repeat anything. "Grave robbing. That's what you're talking about."

I pressed the heels of my hands against my eyelids. "They kidnapped Tate's sister and we can't get her back unless we have the thing that was buried in her place."

When I took my hands away, Roswell was still watching me, but I couldn't look at him. I stared across the street at the Donnellys' jack-o'-lantern.

"They?" he said, sounding apprehensive.

"Me. They're like me."

"Don't be a jackass," Roswell said, but not meanly. "No one's like you."

Emma came around the corner of the house, dragging the stepladder behind her. She was carrying a roll of canvas under her other arm. She had a duffel bag hooked over one shoulder and a scarf tied over her hair.

Roswell glanced from me to her. "We're really doing this, then?"

And I'd known he'd come through, because he always did, but I was still so unbelievably relieved to hear him say *we*.

Emma handed me the ladder. Her expression was tense and her hands were shaking. She hitched the duffel bag higher on her shoulder, and when she looked at Roswell, he took the bundle of canvas and tools without having to be asked. The three of us stood in the yard, watching each other. Then, without saying anything, we stepped off the curb and started for the church.

At the cemetery gate, Emma dug around in the duffel bag, took out a flashlight, and handed it to me. The lens was covered with a sheet of heavy paper and when I switched it on, the light shone through in a narrow beam. It sliced palely through the gloom, sweeping over the ground. Everything else was dark. My dad's church was gone, but the graves were untouched. The only part of his whole life's calling that had survived was the dead part.

I held the doctored flashlight up to my face. "How are you suddenly an expert on breaking into cemeteries?"

"I don't like to go into things unprepared." She held up the keys. "And it's like you said, we're not breaking in."

When she turned the lock, the gate squealed open. It was the strangest feeling, standing there on the footpath. I'd never been in a cemetery in my life. We stuck to the unconsecrated side, following the northern path that ran by the unnamed graves and the crypt. I could smell the smoke, much stronger now that we were near the black wreckage of the church. It sank into the town, leaving the air stale and unbreathable. The whole place was still and eerie. Completely silent, like the silence before an electrical storm, like everything was hunkered down, waiting for the worst of it to pass. It occurred to me that it was completely irrational to think that way about dead people. This was how they always sounded.

Emma led the way toward the back of the cemetery, picking her way between the headstones, where the ground was unconsecrated, reserved for suicides and stillbirths. But that wasn't the truth, was it? It was reserved, but for abandoned monsters in borrowed clothes.

We made our way past the mausoleum, heading toward the back wall, where the white headstone sat small and pale in the dark.

At the edge of the grave, Emma dropped the tarp, then reached into the bag and started bringing out hand tools. She lined them up across the canvas like she was doing surgery. "Hold the light close to the ground."

I shone the beam over the grave, muddy and bare, still

waiting for the turf to be laid over it. After we'd scraped the worst of the mud away, Emma adjusted her tarp, lining it up along one side of the grave. "Shovel onto that and try to keep it neat. That way we can put things back when we're done."

Roswell and I took turns, trading out while Emma stood up on the edge of the grave, keeping track of the dirt and handing down tools.

The night seemed to stretch out forever. I was in the little grave, digging deeper, deeper. Like the hole was so deep that I wouldn't ever be able to get out. The dirt piled up on the tarp and trickled back down in streams, getting all over my hair and my clothes and the ladder.

The air was cold and smoky. My arms and back hurt, and even through the chill, I was starting to sweat when my shovel hit something hard and flat. I scraped the dirt away and Roswell jumped down to help me.

The box was small, maybe four feet long. It was heavier than it looked, but we got it loose between us, levering with the shovels, then getting under one end and shoving it up onto the grass. The wood was damp, slick with grave mold or moss. It had only been in the ground a few days, but it already smelled like it was starting to rot.

"It's a cremation casket," Emma said in a voice so low that I could barely hear her. She was kneeling down,

313

running her hand over the lid. "It's not a real burial casket."

"They're cheaper," Roswell whispered, and he sounded hoarse.

Emma picked up a screwdriver and started working at the latch. It had already begun to rust. When the screws stripped, she jammed the blade between the metal and the wood. Suddenly, she gasped and the whole latch peeled away with a squealing sound.

We just sat there for a minute, kneeling in the grass, looking at the closed casket.

Then Emma took a deep breath. "Okay, hand me the flashlight." Her hands were steady, but her voice was high pitched.

I gave her the light and she inched forward and lifted the lid.

The body was small and weirdly perfect. Then Emma shone the beam over its face and the eerie sense of flaw-lessness was gone.

The nose was losing its shape, starting to collapse. The smell came rushing out of the open box, rising in clouds. The odor on top was thin, a sweet layer of rot that seemed to float and twinkle in the air, and under that, a hard, chem-ical stink that might have been embalming fluid.

Emma was on her feet, stumbling back. The flashlight fell and rolled across the grass. Light splashed over the headstones and the weedy graves. She had both hands against her mouth like she was trying to cover her own screams.

Roswell stepped around the pile of dirt and reached to grab her, but I couldn't move. I stood looking down at the little body, half in shadow on the satin lining. "We have to take it out." The sound of my own voice seemed flat and far away.

"You okay?" Roswell asked, looking over at me, covering his mouth and nose.

I nodded. The rain made everything waver and blur, and three of us stood looking at the body.

After a second, I collected the dropped flashlight and stood over the casket, too numb to tell that I was shaking except for the way the light jumped and fluttered. I tried to hold it steady, but I couldn't feel my hands.

Roswell was the one who got down on his knees and reached into the casket for the body. For the baby. He leaned over the casket, wincing, but reaching in anyway, gentle, cautious. He was so brave I felt sick.

I held the barrel of the flashlight tighter and cleared my throat. "Will it be okay, or is it too rotten to pass?"

"No," he said, with his fingertips under its chin. "It's in really good shape. *Really* good. I don't think there's any way it could have been human."

His voice was like cotton wool, like it was coming from far away.

I handed Emma the light and put my hands over my face. I'd known. Of course I'd known. Hearing him say it just made it the truth. Someone would send a baby out to suffer and die in a poisonous world without regretting it, without feeling guilty at all. It might as well have been me.

Roswell straightened and then got to his feet. "Mackie."

I didn't answer. My throat was so tight it hurt to breathe.

He stepped around the casket and hugged me. I didn't want him to. I wanted him to let me stand back in the shadows and be nothing. I wanted to stop seeing. Roswell was always hugging somebody, but not seriously, not like it meant anything. This time, he pulled me hard against his shoulder, holding on to the back of my jacket even when I tried to pull away.

All my life, Roswell had been rescuing the moment, saying the right thing, but this time he didn't say anything. The rain was slow and cold and I didn't think I could stand it if he tried to make things better.

Then Emma was there, reaching for me. She had both arms around me and was pressing her face against my shoulder. I let her hold on to me and she was warm through her sweatshirt. She smelled like autumn and dirt and home, like the burned-out church and the grave. I leaned against her, thinking how strange it was that I hadn't ended up in a little wooden box years ago, that anyone in the world loved me that much.

When she let me go, I felt light and far away, numb from the cold. Numb enough to touch the body. It lay in the box, chilly and stiff like a doll. Roswell and Emma looked up at me expectantly from where they knelt on either side of it, not speaking.

Finally, Emma took a little hitching breath and whispered, "Should we take it out?"

We lifted the body from the coffin liner and wrapped it carefully in Roswell's jacket. Its hair was dark and thick but brittle. Its skin was gray. It was nothing like the true, living girl tied to the Lady's armchair.

Emma stroked the dull hair, cradling the body in her lap. After a minute, I tied the charm around its wrist, not knowing what else to do. The body lay stiffly in Emma's arms, looking pathetic and horrific in the ruffled funeral dress and the makeshift bracelet.

I stood over them. "What now?"

Emma looked into the emaciated face. "In the stories, people talk to them, but none of the accounts have a script or anything. I don't know what to say."

"It's okay. I think I do."

I leaned down and whispered in the replacement's ear all the things I'd wanted to tell the blue girl in the House of Mayhem. What someone else had done to her, and it was okay to be gruesome and frightening because it wasn't her fault.

317

When the bundle in Emma's arms began to move, I wanted to look someplace else. The squirming body was worse than the still, tragic one. It fidgeted in Emma's lap and she stared up at me with a mute, hopeless expression.

I crouched over it and pulled Roswell's jacket open.

The thing was small and delicate, almost like a real kid. It wasn't a perfect replica, but it resembled Natalie. It blinked slowly at me, reaching up with a tiny hand. Its eyes were blank and a little cloudy, but they were hazel like Natalie's. Like Tate's.

"We have to hurry," I whispered, thinking of Emma's hands when the blue girls had taken her gloves. How they'd started rotting.

Emma breathed out in a long, slow sigh. She held the wriggling, squirming thing in her lap, looking up at me from the muddy ground. Her eyes were full of tears, like she wanted to put it down.

"Jesus Christ," whispered Roswell. He was holding the shovel, standing stiffly by the open grave. "That's about the freakiest thing I've ever seen."

I shook my head, looking down at the thing in Emma's arms. "It's just a body someone didn't want. It's not any worse than me."

CHAPTER 28

THE REVENANT

Roswell closed the casket and we dropped it back into the grave. It thudded in the dirt and I flinched. After a minute, Roswell started to shovel the dirt back in.

The grave was nearly filled in when my phone started buzzing. Tate. When I didn't answer, she called twice more, then texted the words: *total bullshit, mackie. i'm coming over.*

I turned off the phone and shoved it in my pocket. There was no way to head her off. I could only hope that when my dad opened the door, he would see a distraught, grief-stricken girl and decide she was in need of some counsel. I didn't have much confidence in that scenario, though. I knew from experience that once Tate got going, she was nearly unstoppable, and my dad was more broken up than I'd ever seen him.

She'd just have to show up at the house and then do whatever reckless, ill-advised thing she was going to do when she found me gone. It was not a comforting thought.

"So, what's the plan?" Roswell said, tamping down the last of the dirt with his shovel.

Emma was sitting on the muddy ground holding the revenant, but now she stood up.

I leaned on the handle of my shovel, breathless and dizzy from the steel, soaked from the rain and still too hot. "Go down into the house under the dump hill and take Natalie back."

"And they're not going to have a huge problem with that?"

I gave him a helpless look. "We need a distraction. Like, an offering or a present. The woman in charge there loves it when people pay their respects to her."

"What does she want that we could give her?"

I thought about that, about how angry she'd gotten at the Morrigan—so angry that she'd flood them out slowly, over years, instead of just punishing them once and getting it over with. "She wants to be able to control everyone—the whole world. She wants to make sure that everyone is so scared of her that they'll never disobey her, never trick or lie to her."

Emma moved closer to me with the revenant against her shoulder, looking uneasy. "Like we're about to do, you mean?"

"Pretty much. I guess you could say that people tricking her is her biggest ongoing problem, but I don't really have a solution for that, and neither do you."

Roswell nodded, looking thoughtful. "But we know some people who do."

The twins were not happy about being dragged out into the rain in the middle of the night and less happy about being asked to part with the Red Scare, but they showed up at the cemetery in under fifteen minutes. Danny was carrying the polygraph. It had a handle, like an old suitcase, but he held it carefully in both arms.

The twins could generally be depended on to be completely unshocked by anything. They took the revenant with less self-control than usual.

"*Jesus*," said Danny, staring at the thing in Emma's arms. "What have you guys been doing? Are you out of your minds?"

Drew didn't say anything. After a second, he reached out and touched the revenant's arm. It twitched irritably and he stepped back.

I explained the plan, such as it was, and Drew nodded, still watching the revenant with a kind of wary fascination.

Danny was less accepting. He held up the polygraph. "Okay, I'm all for not letting Natalie Stewart get murdered—that's not really in question. But why are we giving away our most successful project again?"

I tried to think how to explain the Lady and her appetite

for power and control, but it was Roswell who answered. "We need a convincing present for the woman who has everything."

Danny nodded, looking resigned. "Everything except a portable McCarthy-era polygraph, apparently."

"Well, come *on*," said Drew. "That's pretty much every-one."

The walk to the park seemed longer than it ever had.

Emma was a trooper about the revenant. She carried it wrapped in Roswell's coat. It didn't seem to mind, just rested its head against her shoulder and kept quiet.

At the dump hill, I reached to take it from her. "We can't all go—it just doesn't make sense. And Mom and Dad are going to be going crazy wondering where we are. I think you should go home."

Emma backed away, clutching the revenant and shaking her head. "No. I'm going with you." There was dirt smeared all over her face and her neck. She looked like she'd escaped from somewhere.

I stood looking at her. She'd always been willing to do whatever it took. Always. She'd been going with me my whole life. "You can't. There's no reason to, and it might be dangerous."

Emma moved very close. "Listen to me." The thing in her arms began to fidget and whine, and I had a feeling she

322

was squeezing it. "I have spent *years* making sure you don't die."

"And I never *asked* you to—you didn't have to follow around after me, taking care of me. You could have had your own life."

"I know. Listen to me. When it's been a choice between you and anything else, I've always picked you. I'm not sure I always made the right choices, but it doesn't matter. *I* made them—me. You didn't do anything to me. I picked you and I am *not sorry*."

We stood in the dark at the base of the hill. Roswell and the twins were standing back, staying out of it. The argument was ours—mine and Emma's. We'd been talking to each other in the dark for pretty much my whole life. The thing is, you don't realize how much people lie with their faces when they talk. Emma's voice was always honest, the realest, truest part of anything she said. It was scary to hear how much she meant it.

I looked down at her and said, "Please, Tate is on her way to our house—she might already *be* there—and I don't know what she'll do when she finds out we're gone. I think she'll come looking for us, and you have to stop her. Keep her away from the park, away from the cemetery. If she gets involved, it's going to be a disaster."

Emma didn't say anything, but after a second she nodded and let Roswell take the revenant.

323

"Emma," I said. "Thank you."

She went on tiptoe and kissed me on the cheek. "Just come home, okay?"

Then she turned and started toward Welsh Street. I watched her walk away through the playground with her head down, not looking back. I knew she was crying, but there was nothing I could do except keep moving forward. We jumped the fence, and I led the way to the base of the dump hill and used the paring knife to open the door to the House of Misery.

In the entryway, the boy with the footman's uniform asked for my card and I told him I didn't have one. He gave me a disapproving look and I told him he could fuck right off.

Behind me, the twins were staring around the hallway incredulously. Roswell seemed beyond comment, which wasn't that surprising, considering the fact that he was holding a squirming, rotting baby that had been dead an hour ago.

"It's very ill mannered to bring guests without an invitation," the boy in uniform said.

"We have a present," I told him. "It's rare and valuable, and she doesn't know it yet, but she wants it bad."

The boy nodded and started away down the hall into the House of Misery, but he didn't lead us back to the reading room. Instead, he showed us down a wide gallery and through a pair of double doors.

"She will receive you in the formal parlor."

The room was fancier than the Lady's reading room, with an intricate rug and painted vases in niches along the walls. There were bronze sculptures of soaring birds and shepherdesses placed on tables around the room. The Lady was reclining on a long dark-colored sofa. When we stopped in the doorway, she looked up and smiled like she'd been expecting us.

Danny and I stepped into the room, while Roswell and Drew hung back in the doorway, with Drew slightly in front so he was shielding the revenant from view.

"Mr. Doyle," the Lady said. "It is so lovely to see you again. To what do we owe this pleasure?"

I kept my expression neutral and pleasant. "I was thinking about some of the things you said before. I was pretty unfair—I know that—and I wanted to bring you a present."

The Lady smiled at me expectantly. Then she looked past me and the smile disappeared. "Send them out," she said, looking thunderous. "Out, now!"

My first thought was that she'd seen the revenant, and it took me a second to realize that she was talking about Drew and Danny. I stared at her, shaking my head. "They can't both go. They're the reason we're here."

"You brought unnatural monsters into my house? How dare you? How dare you presume to defile my house!"

I glanced back at the twins. Their resemblance had never

seemed shocking or even very unusual. Or at least, they'd always seemed a lot more normal than I was. Apparently, freakishness was a little different for everyone.

I moved toward the Lady and held up my hands. "*Wait*, if Drew goes, can Danny stay and show you the present? One of them has to stay and show you how it works."

The Lady watched me, her expression wary. "Very well. You, with the gift. You can stay. Make the other wait in the hall."

Drew and Roswell beat a precipitous retreat and the Lady turned her attention back to me. "What gift do you have for me?"

"I wanted to bring you something that would help you. You were talking about how the Morrigan lied to you, and up in town, they have a solution for that. This would keep anyone from lying to you ever again."

The Lady smiled and her eyes were hungry. "That would be a precious gift indeed." She barely glanced at me. Her gaze was on Danny and the suitcase. "But it looks so ordinary."

He was kneeling on the floor, opening the suitcase. "That's part of how it works. No one knows you've got it until it's too late."

I began to back toward the door. "While you're seeing how it works, do you mind if I check on my friends?"

The Lady didn't even look up. Her eyes were fixed

lovingly, greedily on Danny's hands as he undid the clasps and opened the Red Scare.

Roswell and Drew were waiting in the hall, looking out of place and nervous. I didn't want to leave Danny, but we needed to find Natalie.

We started back toward the entrance, then I retraced the way to the Lady's reading room. I had an idea that even though the burrow under the park was big and sprawling, there weren't nearly as many people living there as there were in the House of Mayhem.

We found the room without much trouble and without seeing anyone. The fire was out and some of the wall lamps had been shut off.

At first, I didn't see her. The House of Misery didn't seem to be as big as the House of Mayhem, but it was just as convoluted, and if they'd taken her someplace else, I didn't know how we'd find her. But Natalie was there. She'd dragged her pillow under one of the low tables and sat staring into her birdcage. Her hair was messed up, the bows untied. She'd taken off the button boots and one sock.

I crouched next to her and went to pick her up, but she turned away, covering her face. When she raised her hands, I got a good look at her arm. A raw, oozing seam circled her wrist, red at the edges and nearly black at the center. Around it, the discoloration feathered out, spreading under the skin, working its way in the direction of her shoulder.

"Roz," I said in a low voice, trying to sound calm and conversational so that I wouldn't scare her. "Take the charm off the revenant, *now*."

Roswell came up behind me. "But what about the plan? Isn't the whole point to have it look real?"

"Take it off, now!"

"Okay," he said. "Sure. It's your show." There was a sharp ripping sound as he snapped the ribbon. Then he yelped and there was a heavy thump. "Oh, *Jesus*!"

I twisted around, but I already knew what I'd see. Roswell had dropped the revenant on the carpet, and there was nothing remotely human about it anymore. It was still moving, writhing on its back, but its skin was so gray it was nearly colorless. It squirmed over onto its hands and knees and raised its head to look at me. Its irises were a dirty yellow and so were its teeth.

From under the table, Natalie made a thin high-pitched noise, like a caught rabbit, and Roswell dove for the revenant. He threw his jacket over it and scooped it back up, keeping its face hidden, but Natalie was already working her way farther under the table, hiding her own face, trying to wedge herself into the corner.

"Natalie," I said, but she wouldn't look at me. "Natalie, it's okay. Come out from there." I didn't want to grab her, but it looked like I might have to.

Then Drew sat down next to me and took out a quarter.

"You like magic tricks, right, Nat?" He walked the quarter over his knuckles.

When she peered out between her fingers, he made the quarter dance along the edge of his hand and said, "I used to be your neighbor. Do you remember?"

She didn't answer, but after a second, she nodded.

I knelt on the floor and started working at the knot that fastened her to the chair. Roswell was trying to keep the revenant covered, but it didn't want to stay under his jacket.

When I got the ribbon loose, Drew leaned under the table, never looking away from Natalie, even when the revenant started to whine and struggle behind him. "We're going to take you home now, and you need to cover your eyes."

For a second, Natalie didn't move, but when he said it again, she dropped the bird and put her hands over her eyes. He picked her up, holding her close against his shoulder. He kept her turned away while Roswell unwrapped the squirming body, trying to keep it from clutching and pawing at him.

"This is bad," he whispered, knotting the ribbon around the revenant's waist, peeling its hands off every time it reached for him. "We're going to hell for sure. This is so bad."

"You haven't *begun* to appreciate how bad things can get," said a hoarse voice behind us.

Someone was standing in the doorway, so still and so backlit that at first I couldn't make out his face. His arms were folded over his chest and he was nothing but a shadow except for the flicker of his eyes.

"Forgive me being so bold as to say so, but we're in a world of trouble, aren't we?" He stepped into the room and I saw his face. It was the Cutter. He looked exactly like he had when he'd shown me out except that now he was wearing black gloves. They were heavy, with short steel claws sewn into the fingertips.

Natalie had her arms around Drew's neck, clutching at him, and I tried not to stagger as the Cutter moved toward me and the first clouds of iron seeped into the room.

"Would you care to explain what you are doing in the Lady's private quarters with two trespassers and a corpse?"

Roswell stood up, looking resolute and not half as scared as I felt. He was taller than the Cutter but young looking, without any of the qualities it took to be cruel. "What are *you* supposed to be, like some kind of boogeyman?"

The Cutter smiled. "I prefer to think of myself as a demon, personally. But it makes no difference in the greater scheme of things. I'm content to be called nightmare and monster and goblin, so long as they call me something."

I took another step back, trying to get away from the smell. "But that's not what the Lady wants—she doesn't like being named."

"The Lady has no *vision*. No *perspective*. She can't stand the idea of being anything but a god. She aches for a life that doesn't exist. We'll never be the race we were, so it's time to be something else."

I took a deep breath and felt it burn all the way down my throat. "What are you going to do?"

The Cutter watched my face. His expression was polite—mildly interested, even. Then he grinned, showing raw, swollen gums, and swung his fist into one of the bell jars on the mantel.

It shattered, spraying the room with slivers of glass. The sound was very loud.

Roswell jumped back, and Drew tried to shield Natalie, covering her face with his hand.

The Cutter kicked aside what was left of the broken jar and stepped over it. "This is not a negotiation. We are not bargaining. If you refuse to hand over that sweet little lamb, I'll systematically collect everyone you've ever cared about and start cutting pieces off them until you agree. Understand that I have no reservations about this."

I backed up, stumbling between armchairs and low tables, away from him.

He followed me. "You thought you could just come in here and trade us a child for a piece of worthless meat?" Behind him, the bell jar lay in pieces all over the floor. "We know that trick, cousin. We *invented* it."

331

"But you didn't recognize it when the Morrigan came for my mom. She left a revenant in her place and guess what? The Lady bought it. The Lady didn't catch her because she couldn't tell the difference—*you* couldn't tell the difference." I was almost shouting by the time he reached me.

He caught me by the front of my jacket, slamming me against the wall. Next to my head, a shadow box full of beetles fell and splintered on the floor. He twisted my collar, pinning me so that my back was against the wall.

Behind him, Roswell was a tall, indistinct shape, moving toward us.

The Cutter leaned toward me, resting his forehead against mine. "Fool me once," he whispered, "shame on you." He pressed the bridge of his nose against mine, his breath burning the back of my throat. His voice was rough and furious. "Fool me twice, and I will cut out your fucking throat."

"Hey," Roswell shouted, yanking at the Cutter's coat. "Hey, let go of him!"

The room was so murky now that I could barely focus. The only thing I was sure of were the Cutter's murderous black eyes.

He didn't look around. "Is that the trespasser talking, putting his hands all over me? You must be out of your mind."

"He's right," I muttered. "Stay out of this. He likes torture too much."

The Cutter laughed his slow, husky laugh. "Torture? No,
I just want to see the blood run, cousin. It's beautiful when
it catches the light."

He leaned close, laughing, and I smelled rust and under
that sickness, disease. His grin was a glowing slice of white,
floating in front of me like the moon. Then I blinked and
there was nothing but his breath against my face.

"Cousin," he said next to my ear. "Cousin, look at me."
He grabbed my jaw and wrenched my face close to his.
"*Look* at me. I'm going to brand you with my sigil, brand it
right over your heart, and you're going to meet my gaze like
a man. Then I'm going to break you, and you're going to
beg for mercy like a little boy."

He was so close that I could see the raw-meat texture of
his gums. I stared at his smile, wondering where Roswell
and Drew were, waiting for him to cut me. It was what he
wanted—pain, blood, the chance to make someone beg.

"We'll start with your face," he said. The knife was long
and sharp and strangely bright, like it belonged in his hand.
"Your smile needs improving."

In the rush of his breath, there was nothing but the smell,
the dizziness. The room was shrinking, squeezing in, and I
couldn't focus. I felt sick and almost weightless.

I was alone. Roswell, Drew were nowhere. There was

nothing but the wall at my back and the blade in front of me.

The Cutter adjusted his grip, turning the knife back and forth inches from my face. "Open wide," he whispered. I clenched my teeth and waited for the metallic taste, the pain that would blot out the world.

Then Roswell's hand swung into my field of vision, colliding with the side of the Cutter's face. There was a hiss and the smell of burning skin and he stumbled back. I didn't have the strength to catch myself as I slid down the wall onto the carpet. The revenant was sitting a few feet away from me. Her eyes were yellow and empty.

"Get the hell *off* him," shouted Roswell, standing between me and the Cutter. His voice sounded angry and impatient.

Then Drew was beside him, holding Natalie in one arm. His shoulders were set and his feet were apart, like he was expecting to get hit.

The Cutter sneered at me, baring his teeth, and for a second, he looked as scary and as nasty as anyone in the slag heap. There was a circle of puncture marks on one cheek that looked like a bite.

"Have it your own way," he said, starting for the door. "It doesn't matter. Stay and wait for the end. Honestly, I like it better that way—the horror, the screaming. You'll want to watch, of course," he said, glancing over his shoulder at

Drew. "Cuddle and croon to her all you want. She'll still be dead by morning."

Drew squeezed Natalie hard against his chest and she hid her face from the Cutter.

He cleared his throat and spat. Then he turned, kicking at the broken glass in the carpet, and walked out of the room. The door slammed shut behind him and a key turned in the lock. The sound was very loud.

Roswell stood over me, fists clenched. Then he opened his hand. He was breathing hard, looking furious. He was holding a bottle cap.

He put it back in his pocket and tried the door, making an attempt to force it with his shoulder. He kicked the handle and the hinges a few times but halfheartedly, then said the thing I already knew. "I can't. It's too heavy."

I stayed slumped against the wall. My vision was going and I could feel myself starting to slide sideways, tilting in the direction of the floor. At some point, I'd rested my hand in the broken shadow box and my palm was full of glass and pins and sharp, glossy fragments of crushed beetle.

Roswell crouched next to me and glanced up at Drew. "Hey, he's not looking too good. Think you can help me out here?"

Drew stood over us, still holding Natalie. "Just a sec. I don't want to put her down where there's glass. She's not wearing shoes." He sounded dazed.

Roswell was examining my hand, brushing off the loose debris, picking out slivers of embedded glass. He studied the blood that was welling up in the cut places, dark and sticky, almost purple.

"Looking good," he said, and I recognized all the old bravado and the cheerfulness for what it was, easy and fake. The voice he used when nothing was good at all.

It made me feel empty to remember how often he'd done this, sat next to me while I shivered and wheezed, telling me everything would be fine.

After a second, he spoke again, and for once, his voice was truthful. "Well, we're screwed *now*, I guess."

My hand stung as he removed the glass, but my breathing was better. "Danny's still out there. He could find Emma or my dad. He could still get help."

Roswell straightened up with a handful of beetle pieces and bloody glass, looking highly unconvinced. "Sure, maybe."

"Well, that's all we can hope for right now."

There was a scuffle out in the hall. Then the sound of a key in the lock and the door opened on Danny, looking rumpled and furious. The Cutter had him by the back of his jacket, lifting him up on his toes. There was a bruise darkening under one eye and his lip was bleeding.

The Cutter tossed him into the room and shut the door. Danny fell hard on the carpet and then picked himself up.

"Sorry," he said. "I tried, but she's not stupid."

Drew went to him, brushing him off in a vague, mechanical way, like he was dusting furniture. "Did it crap out? Was she mad? I knew we shouldn't have tried to move it—it must have shorted."

Danny shook his head, glaring down at the floor. "She made me try it."

Roswell stared at him. "But you were just supposed to show her what it does. How could she know what we were really here for?"

"Because it's a polygraph, goddamn it! She asked questions. What part of 'it works' did you not get?"

"Wait, she used it on *you*?" Roswell squeezed his eyes shut, then opened them again. He sighed and sank down on the couch while Danny paced the room and I tried to breathe as shallowly as possible.

"Sorry," he said again, glancing at me and covering his bleeding lip, searching around for something to blot it with. He grabbed a lacy runner off an end table and held it against his mouth. Then he sat down in one of the high-backed chairs and stared at the floor.

I took a seat on the sofa between Roswell and Drew. The revenant sat across from us on the edge of one of the velvet armchairs. Roswell leaned forward, watching her with a resigned look.

He sighed and turned to me. "We can't leave her."

She sat like a stuffed toy, propped against the arm of the

337

chair, not moving, not breathing. I considered her vacant eyes, dark yellow at the iris, a lighter yellow at the cornea. She was nothing like the blue girls, who whispered and laughed like anyone else. She was empty, and I wondered if it was my fault, if I'd done the raising wrong. If I'd broken her.

Finally, I shook my head. "I don't think it matters. She doesn't know where she is. She doesn't care what happens or who's around."

Roswell leaned forward, propping his elbows on his knees. "She can be destroyed, though, right?"

I recited the limited hazards the Morrigan had listed for the blue girls. "By cutting off her head or setting her on fire."

"And your friend with the claws—he looked like he'd cut her up just for fun."

I nodded.

"Then we can't leave her. I just don't know what we should *do* with her."

I closed my eyes and leaned my head back against the upholstery of the couch. "If we can get her out of here, I've got someone who'll take her."

I knew that the Morrigan and the House of Mayhem would take care of her. She was strange, maybe broken, but there was still a place for people like her, which was more than I could say for myself.

Drew sighed and leaned back too. Natalie was still holding him around the neck, hiding her face against his shoulder. "Get *her* out? We can't even get *ourselves* out."

And that was the truth. Being underground meant no convenient porches and no windows. The door was two feet thick and the hinges were on the outside.

We sat in silence, waiting for whatever came next.

The collar of my jacket kept brushing the raw gouges from the Cutter's claws, but I just sat on the couch and didn't try to adjust it. It didn't hurt that bad. The room was quiet and dim. I leaned forward with my elbows on my knees, thinking that sometimes this was just the way the game ended. Sometimes you did your best, and it all went straight to hell anyway.

CHAPTER 29

THE SEVENTH-YEAR SACRIFICE

It wasn't long before they came and got us, dragging us out of the dump hill and toward the graveyard in early-morning darkness.

They were tall bony men, seven of them, and all dressed like the Cutter, only none of them were covered in steel. One carried Natalie awkwardly under his arm. No one tried to take the revenant from Roswell.

The Cutter escorted me personally, staying uncomfortably close and wheezing into my ear. His breath rattled and caught, full of a deep, phlegmy glee.

"You're going to love this," he whispered. "She'll go into that crypt to get eaten, and then she's going to scream like blue murder. They always do."

"Bet you like that," I muttered, too breathless and hoarse to speak louder. "Bet you love watching kids get slaughtered."

"No, cousin. Oh, no. I'm going to watch your face."

On Welsh Street, the ground was still smoking. The church—what was left of it—stood crumpled and black, jutting at the sky.

The men shoved and dragged us, leading us into the cemetery toward the crypt. The air smelled like a new kind of smoke, dry and perfume-y like incense.

The Morrigan was already waiting for us in the unblessed corner of the cemetery with her pack of blue girls clustered behind her. All of them were soaked, and she was holding her doll. The rest of the House of Mayhem was fanned out around them. Carlina and Luther stood close together, hugging each other. Janice and the star girl were holding hands, and the blue girls all had little bundles of herbs tied with twine and burning gently.

When she saw me, the Morrigan's expression was grave. "What are you doing here? You ought to be home where it's safe."

I struggled in the Cutter's grip. "The Lady's going to kill Natalie. Please, can't you do anything to stop her?"

"Dearest," the Morrigan said, holding the doll against her chest. "This isn't what I would have chosen if I'd been given a choice, but there's no other way. Without blood, the whole town suffers." She glanced back over her shoulder, looking anxious.

The Lady stood in the shadow of the oak tree, wearing a long, dark cloak. The hood was up and it hid her face, but

I knew her by the embroidered train of her dress and the way the handful of house servants clustered around her.

The Morrigan turned back to me and opened her mouth like she had something else to say. Then she froze, staring past me at someone in the crowd.

It was Tate. She shoved through the crowd in her blue mechanic's jacket, looking absolutely furious, and pushed her way to where I stood, held motionless by the Cutter.

She gave him one cold, appraising look, then turned on me. "What the *hell*, Mackie! You told me you were going to take care of it!"

"I tried," I said, fully aware of how weak that sounded. How completely worthless. "Jesus, what are you *doing* here?"

"What do you think I'm doing? Emma said stay away from the graveyard, so I figured hey, it must be the place to be."

The Morrigan came scrambling over to us, careful to stay as far as possible from the Cutter. She stood in front of Tate, fidgeting and rustling in her burned party dress.

She was clutching her doll, but when she lifted her chin and spoke, she sounded patient and very adult. "You aren't supposed to be here. The understanding is that you choose not to see us when we do our darkest work."

Tate flinched back from the ravenous teeth but looked in no way dissuaded. "Yeah, well, I see just fine and I'm not going anywhere without my sister."

The Morrigan reached out, resting her hand on Tate's wrist. "This is aeons older than you or your family. Older than the town. Blood makes the sun shine and the crops grow. This is the truth of the world."

Tate stared down at her, then said in a soft, deadly voice that was almost a whisper, "Fuck the world. I just want my sister back."

"Enough." The Lady's voice echoed from across the stretch of unconsecrated ground. "Your sister is trifling, barely more than a pittance. This is not my concern, and if you continue to disrupt my affairs, I'll have no choice but to call for the man who sees to disruptions."

Tate glanced at me and for the first time, her expression was uneasy. She stared around the graveyard, like she was just now beginning to realize how many of them there actually were and how scary some of them looked.

When her gaze came back to me, the Cutter leaned in over my shoulder and held up a gloved hand, letting the claws drift lazily in front of my face, not touching, never touching, but letting Tate see how easily he could.

I watched as he flexed his fingers. "What do you want?"

He touched the side of my neck and the iron felt cold against my skin. "All I want is for you to stand here and watch the people you love be horribly mutilated. Is that too much to ask?"

I held very still, trying not to give him the satisfaction of seeing how much even a light touch hurt.

Beside me, Roswell and the twins were struggling to get free from the Cutter's bony men but without much luck. Tate had no one holding her, though.

"Let him go," she said, and she sounded hard and mean, like she was ready to destroy him.

The Cutter was so close I could feel him laughing against my ear. "You're a regular little firebrand, aren't you? Come and take him, then. I'm keen to see if you can."

His claws dug harder, harder. They broke the skin and I was breathing in spasms, trying not to make any noise, and everything happened very fast.

Tate bent and yanked the cuff of her jeans up, reaching for the top of her boot.

He let me go and stepped back, raising his hands like he was surrendering, letting her have me. Then he slammed his fist into the side of my head.

I hit the ground and for a second, all I could see was a shower of tiny lights. I lay in the mud and the ashes, trying to catch my breath. The ground was wet against my back, soaking through my coat. The Cutter crouched over me, resting his claws against my neck. His touch was so gentle it seemed indecent that it could possibly hurt that much. The mark of Roswell's bottle cap stood out dark on his cheek.

"Get off him," Tate said again. Her voice was very low.

The Cutter just laughed his low, rattling laugh. "No, precious, no. What's going to happen is this: I'm going to carve him up a little, and you're going to watch me, and that's how it will go because if you try to stop me, I'll cut a gully down his throat and the two of us can sit here in the dark and watch him bleed out."

The points dug hard into my neck and then I did yell, hoarse and aching, hating the sound of my voice. Suddenly, there was a flat, heavy thud and the claws were gone. I rolled sideways with a cold, searing pain racing up through the base of my skull.

The Cutter lay next to me. He had his hands raised, like he wanted to press them against his face, but the claws kept him from touching his own skin. There was a long burn down one cheek.

Around us, everyone stepped back. Tate stared out at them. She was holding something long and narrow, matte black in the light from the street. It was a crowbar.

The blue girls began to laugh in shrill, screeching howls as the Cutter scrambled to his feet. Clearly, the House of Mayhem had some uncharitable feelings toward him. They didn't care if he took a crowbar to the face. They were just here to bear witness to whatever happened. He glared around at them, then turned on Tate.

She looked small next to him. Young. His smile was wide and it promised murder and before that, pain. The most desperate desire of his life was that he wanted pain for everyone.

"Little girl," he said, and there was a lilt in his voice that sounded almost like regret. "Little girl, please put down your toy. You'll die if you don't."

She shook her head and adjusted her grip.

"Put it down, or I'll lay you open and leave your eyes for the crows." When he slashed at her, there was no warning. He raked at her arm, claws slicing through the shoulder of her jacket. Even when blood soaked through the canvas, she didn't back away.

Instead, she smiled. It was the same smile she'd given Alice in the parking lot. The smile that said, *I have fun when I break stuff.*

The Cutter was grinning back at her, like this was their moment. Like he didn't know that the surest way to piss her off was to draw blood.

She swung again, and this time the bar connected, slamming into his teeth. He fell, stumbling and slipping in the mud and the soot, blood dripping from his mouth and chin, seeping into the ground, smoking on the crowbar in Tate's hand. Already, his breath was grating out of him. He knelt between the headstones, shuddering and coughing.

Tate stood over him, holding the crowbar in both hands. She was still smiling, looking electrified and wild. Around us, the crowd was silent.

The Cutter didn't move. Blood was running from his mouth. He swiped an arm across his chin and glared up at her, looking savage.

"Attend to her," the Lady said, and her voice was shrill.

The Cutter struggled to his feet, spitting blood onto the muddy ground. Then he lunged.

Tate swung the crowbar hard, aiming for his hand, breaking off two of the claws. They flashed as they fell and the Cutter jerked back. She was moving away, already whipping around for another swing.

He caught her as she came toward him, opening a row of shallow slashes down the side of her neck, but she never flinched. There was just the Cutter and Tate and the bar. It was black in her hand and this time it hit him across the chest, knocking him back.

The Cutter staggered, then caught himself. He stood leaning forward slightly, and I thought for a second that he was going to throw himself at Tate, but he only raised a gloved hand and touched his forehead. The claws made a row of little welts where they brushed his skin.

"I stand down," he said. His voice was hoarse and ferocious, his breath coming in huge gasps.

"Really, sir," the Lady said from the dark. "I asked that

you remove this inconvenience and am quite mystified as to why you don't do it."

"I stand down," he said again, and this time he raised his head. The look he gave the Lady was murderous.

She spoke coldly from under her hood. "You do whatever I require, and at the moment, I require you to get rid of that girl."

He turned his back on her.

The Cutter faced Tate, who stood holding the crowbar, but he didn't make any attempt to challenge her. His expression was furious but rigidly controlled.

"You," he said. His voice sounded rough, and blood ran darkly off his chin. "Ill mannered as the devil, but you're clever enough with a blunt instrument. You and I, we could stand to go another round one day, don't you think?"

Tate didn't answer. She was staring past him, toward the Lady's corner of the cemetery, and looking more frightened than she had at any point during their confrontation. I followed her gaze and understood. One of the bony men had stepped out from behind the crypt with Natalie in his arms.

The Cutter gave Tate a jerky bow, then shoved past her, away from the cluster of rotting girls and out into the cemetery. The pair of broken claws lay on the ground at Tate's feet. He didn't look back.

"Enough of this." The Lady stepped forward, snatching Natalie from her handler and dragging her along toward the white crypt. "We're going in now, and we may be a while."

Tate lunged toward them, but two of the Cutter's men moved to intercept her. They caught her by the back of her jacket, almost lifting her off the ground. Her legs thrashed wildly, and she was screaming for Natalie in a voice that made my chest hurt.

I remembered what my mother had said when the Morrigan had found me, asked for my service and I'd agreed because I didn't want anything to happen to Emma. *Everything involves choice.*

I knew what she'd been trying to say—that you have to think about your options, weigh the consequences before you make decisions, but the advice was so worthless when it came to the things that mattered. This wasn't one of those times.

This was the endgame. The time when everything got quiet and there was only my fast, panicked breath and my heartbeat. There was only me. The one outside it, when everyone else had a place where they belonged.

"Wait," I said.

The Lady stopped with her back to me. "What do you mean by this, Mr. Doyle?" But she sounded like she was smiling.

"Let me go instead. It's the only real choice." It wasn't until I said it that I knew how true it was. "It's the only thing left to do."

The Lady turned and shoved Natalie into the crowd, almost throwing her at Tate, who jerked away from her bewildered guards and ran to catch her. Tate knelt on the ground, holding Natalie against her chest. It was the closest I'd ever seen her come to crying.

From the shadows, the Lady's voice was sweet and, under that, darkly excited. "Come along, Mr. Doyle."

Tate looked up at me, shaking her head, and I stared back at her, trying to make her see my conviction. *Just let me go.*

She squeezed her eyes shut and buried her face in Natalie's hair. The gesture made me more certain than ever that I was doing the right thing. The only thing. I turned to follow the Lady, who stood waiting on the stone step of the crypt.

As I came up to her, she pushed back her hood to show her face and I almost stopped breathing. She was badly changed from the woman I'd met in the reading room. Her eyes were bigger, blacker than the Morrigan's or any of the blue girls'. In the white of her face, they looked like lumps of soot, all deep shadow and no color.

I remembered Emma's story about going into the cave to be eaten. How if you went willingly, then death wasn't death, but transformation.

There are all kinds of things that can scare you every day. What if someone you know gets cancer? What if something happens to your sister or your friends or your parents? And

350

what if you get hit by a car crossing the street or the kids at school find out what an unnatural freak you are and what if you go too far out in the lake and the water is over your head and what if there's a fire or a war?

And you can lie awake at night and worry about these things because it's scary and unpredictable, but it's *real*. It's possible.

The Lady's deep, unblinking gaze was black and impossible.

She held out her hand, waiting for me, and I took it, letting her draw me away from my life, my friends, and toward the crypt.

"Wait," I said, feeling the word catch in my throat. "I just want to look."

Roswell and the twins were pinned against the churchyard fence, held there by the Cutter's men. Drew had the same blank expression the Corbetts usually wore, but Danny was watching me with a look like there was something sharp under his ribs and someone twisting. Roswell stood with his back against the fence, restrained by two men in black coats. He was still holding the revenant, watching me. Just watching.

Between the headstones, Tate crouched with her arms around Natalie. Her mouth was open like she wanted to say something, but what was there to say? Her sister was her family. The only right thing was to turn away from her, away from the whole shining world and toward the Lady.

For a second, though, I wasn't sure I'd be able to. Tate's eyes were on my face, and it was hard to give that up. To give up my life when it was finally starting.

The musicians and the blue girls stood quietly. This was what they'd come for, not out of pleasure or malice. They'd come to see their world renewed and that meant blood. It didn't matter that I was standing right in front of them. In all important ways, I was already dead.

"Come to me," the Lady called, her voice echoing to me from inside the crypt. The door was open now, a dark slash against the white stone, and I turned and followed her because it was the last, best thing to do.

In the entrance, I could smell wet dirt and cold stone. The floor was covered in a shallow layer of water, ground seepage or rain. I couldn't hear anything except the sound of my own heartbeat.

"You're bleeding," the Lady said from the shadows. "I can smell the copper and the salt."

In the dark, her face was ghostly, almost transparent. Her bones showed palely through her skin. When she raised her head to look at me, I could see her teeth and now they were just as cruel and as jagged as the Morrigan's.

She smiled and held out a hand. "Come closer and let me look at you."

I took another step, away from the ruined church and the circle of watchers, into the dark.

"I dreamed this," she said. "Dreamed of you for years, even before I knew you. But a dream is a poor substitute for the flesh."

We were inside the crypt now, out of sight of the churchyard. "How long have you been living off the blood of innocent people?"

She reached for my arm, pulling me close so she could whisper into my ear. "You ask me to calculate in years? You would be better served by gallons. Time is only the mythology of those who have not lived long enough to see every structure collapse, every condition fold back on itself. The people demonize us, and then a century later, they pray to us."

"Not in Gentry," I said. "It doesn't matter how much peace or prosperity you give them—they'll never worship you. Not like they did in your old home."

The Lady smiled, lips peeling back from her teeth. "Home? My home is wherever they know me. In Gentry, they make effigies to me, and you think it matters whether they burn them for spite or for love?"

"You're saying that it doesn't matter if they love you as long as they believe in you?"

The Lady nodded. "This is the natural order. Gods fall out of favor and become monsters. And sometimes they rise from the rank and file of the vanquished to become gods again."

"What about you?" I said, watching her starved face. Her eyes were impossibly dark, like time stretching back forever, and it was deeper and more complete than any famine or plague or war. It went on so long that it seemed to see inside me. "What are you?"

She smiled, reaching up to touch my face. "I am terror." Her hand was papery against my cheek, her skin getting thinner. "I draw strength from their fears and I feed on them."

"I thought you fed on the blood from their offerings."

She laughed, and it was a dry, moldy sound. "Darling, you are too delightful. I feed on the fact that they offer. I eat their devotion and their abasement. Now hold out your hand."

I let her take my wrist. She cradled my hand in both of hers, turning it like she was feeling for a pulse. Then, without warning, she sank her teeth in.

Pain surged up my arm and I gasped but didn't pull away. I took a shallow breath and then another. The force of her bite made huge white spots bloom in front of my eyes.

"I expected different," she whispered, scraping my hand with her teeth. "Since the day I first drank the blood of my own, I've been dreaming of it. The desperation, the surrender. Like a man they called Caury."

I nodded, trying to focus on breathing. My chest felt

tight. "You killed him," I whispered. "You used him for months, years, maybe, and then you killed him."

"The town was failing, sweet. We are bound to the people of Gentry, bound to help them, even when they wouldn't consider it a service. Even when the cost to them is great."

"Help them?" My voice sounded hoarse. "Yeah, you help them all right. Help their kids into coffins. Help them cover their houses in amulets. You think you're a god, but you're just a monster."

She shook her head. "You presume to name those who have no name. We are pandemonium and disaster. We are the dancing, gibbering horror of the world." She ran her tongue along my palm and when she raised her head, she was smiling. There was blood all over her teeth. "Look at you. You've been shunned, made an outcast, and still, you cling to life, to your *friends*. You love and keep them, even though they hate you." Her bite was hot. It burned all the way up my arm and my vision was blurring.

I breathed out, letting her drink, letting go of the guilt, the secrecy, the anxiety and the fear. With it came a flood of pictures and memories.

I thought of Tate, how my black eyes were okay with her. My strangeness was okay with her. And my friends were my friends, not by accident, but because they chose to be. They were all there, out in the graveyard—they'd helped me. Or tried to. My dad, trying so hard, so unbelievably hard, to always do the right thing.

And Emma. Emma laughing and smiling and crying, Emma twelve years old in her Easter dress with a flowery hat and fourteen, setting out tulips in the fall, asleep at her desk with her head on her arms, and helping me with homework, Emma with the hose, watering the vegetable garden. Emma, now, and for all my life.

I thought of her, and all of them, their faces and their voices, and all the ways I loved them and couldn't seem to let them love me back. I could feel the Lady's breath on the inside of my wrist, a hot, wet draft as she gnawed at me. The rhythm was slow and matched my heart. The pain in my hand was less electric now. It was fading, like the crypt was fading.

I reached out with my free hand, fumbling for something solid, finding her face and touching it. Her bones were sharp and wicked under her skin. The dark was pressing in. The Lady was strong and I was so tired.

"Do you know what I adore about people like you? Children might fear me, the town might demonize me, but at the core, their fear is uncomplicated. You have the complexity of hating what you are and where you come from. It's wonderful."

"Then take it," I whispered against the floor. "Take it away."

She let my wrist go, looming over me. She was pale and luminous in the dark, not a witch or a goddess, but something worse. Her skin was smooth now. Her hair was long and transparent like spiderwebs.

I rolled onto my back with my throbbing hand cradled against my chest.

Above me, the dark was alive with a riot of shapes, shadows and wings and nightmares. Something was swarming all around us, too much starved, timeless creature to live inside one body.

I closed my eyes, and her bite was painless now, pulling me straight down into the dark. I floated there, becoming not-myself. And still, I was the same person I'd always been. I was my earliest memories, cold and drifting, going farther from the pain, toward the pale moon, the rustle of leaves. The strange crib and the flapping curtains with their garden print. I was drifting farther and farther away, tumbling through dark, stale air, and then I landed.

I was slumped on a stone floor in an abandoned crypt, shivering in the dark while Gentry's Dirt Witch crouched over me, gnawing on my hand.

I took a long, rasping breath and started to laugh.

The Lady raised her mouth from my hand. "What is so devilishly amusing that you mock me?"

I smiled in the dark, feeling dazed and a little euphoric. "Everything."

She grabbed the front of my jacket and shook me. "Why are you laughing? What do you mean by laughing?"

But the question was so misguided, so pointless that I could only shake my head. I didn't need a reason.

None of the things she'd taken were gone. They washed over me in breakers, happy and scared and curious and hopeful and alive. They rose up and filled my chest until I felt like I was too full of it to breathe, I was so grateful.

This was love. All my life, I'd been so convinced I was beyond it, outside it, but this was love—had been all along—and now I knew it.

CHAPTER 30

THE TRUTH

The floor was wet under my head, and that was fine. It was exceptional. We were in a crypt, in a church graveyard, and the fact that I belonged there meant that I could belong anywhere.

The Lady crouched over me, clawing at my jacket, breathing into my face. "What is distracting you from our work, Mr. Doyle?"

My throat was dry and it hurt to talk. "I'm all of it . . . my whole life. All of this is me."

For a second, there was nothing but the sound of my blood as it spilled out of my hand, pattering on the stone.

"Then give me all of it." Her voice was harsh. Her fingers sank into my skin, pressing into the soft place at the base of my throat. "I want the fear, the terror in your eyes when you realize, fully and truly, that you're dying. I want your utter ruin, and I'll keep digging until I get it."

The paring knife was still in my pocket, wrapped in a dish towel. Her face was inches from mine, grinning down at me like a skull.

"I'm done with that," I said. "Done being food, done feeding you. I don't have anything you want."

She stuck her finger in one of the raw wounds at the side of my neck and I breathed out in a long sigh but didn't make a sound, even when she began to dig and tear at the burned place.

"Regret is one of the only true constants in life," she whispered. "Do you regret your bravado yet?" She dug deeper, ripping at my skin. "I can go all the way down. I can peel you open until you're fit to do nothing but scream."

I fumbled for the paring knife, sliding it out of the towel. "No. Not for you."

"You are so gloriously naive. How charming that you still think yourself to be strong."

I wasn't strong. I wasn't trying to be heroic or prove that I was brave, but her voice was arrogant and empty and it didn't scare me. The only thing that scared me now was how hard it was to focus, how numb my hands were. I tightened my grip on the knife, willing my fingers to work. Then, I yanked my hand out of my pocket and sank the blade in her shoulder up to the handle.

For a second, the Lady crouched over me, gaping like a

360

fish. Then she flailed away, falling backward. She landed hard, splashing around in the stagnant water.

I let myself slump toward the open door and the fresh air.

The first thing I saw was the sky, wide and spinning. It was still overcast, but the clouds were breaking up, showing patchy scatterings of stars. And then Tate was there, holding on to me, kissing me, and then I was just lying on the muddy ground, kissing her back.

There was a dark smear on the sleeve of her coat where I'd reached for her.

I grabbed her shoulder with my good hand and tried to sit up. She caught me as I overbalanced. I was light-headed and shivering, missing half my blood, but I was still whole. I was shaking and she just kept holding on to me.

As we sat in the mud, arms around each other, the Morrigan came trotting over to the steps of the crypt, where the Lady lay on her back, staring up into the marbled sky.

The Morrigan looked curiously at the paring knife. Her expression was almost scientific. "You've been injured," she said, bending down to examine the Lady's shoulder. "Will you heal? Does it hurt?"

"Ugly," the Lady whispered. "Monster and filth and traitor."

"No," said the Morrigan, stroking her forehead. "No, dearest, no. That's you."

All through the graveyard, the blue girls were whispering, giggling their weird, shrill giggles while the Lady coughed and squirmed, bleeding all over the stone.

The Morrigan knelt over her. She touched the handle of the paring knife, running her fingers over the place where it stuck out of the Lady's shoulder. In her other hand, she held one of the Cutter's broken claws. It smoked in her palm, giving off a rotten smell that made my stomach turn, but she didn't seem to notice. "You're terribly selfish, you know. I've loved you so long, and it was never dear or precious to you. I might as well have not loved you at all."

The Lady lay at her feet, looking up with black, horrified eyes. Her lips were a cold, deathly blue. "How dare you speak to me like that, you foul little beast?" Her voice was ragged.

The Morrigan smiled, showing all her jagged teeth. "You're nothing but an unsightly ghoul now, your man is gone, and I'll speak to you however I like."

"Insubordinate wretch—I should have you punished. I should have you whipped until you beg."

The Morrigan shook her head. "But you won't. There's no one here to do it."

She considered the claw in her hand. Then, with scary precision, she stuck it in the side of the Lady's neck. The point punched through the skin and then went in easily, sinking up to the Morrigan's fist. On the ground, the Lady clutched at her throat, shrieking up at the bare trees. The Morrigan straightened but left the claw where it was.

Around them, the pack of girls were creeping closer. The Lady's attendants didn't wait for the grinning crowd of maggots and teeth. They hurried out of the graveyard, away from where the Lady lay crumpled in the mud. Her cries were softer and more pitiful, and the Morrigan watched her with a strange expression, something close to satisfied. I wondered if this was what she'd been dreaming about, like the Lady dreamed of drinking blood.

But when she turned to face me, she didn't meet my gaze.

"I'm sorry," she said, looking at something on the ground. "I'm not the monster, I'm the good one. I'm love, you know." She was crying in little hitching sobs. "I'm the one who doesn't hold grudges. I'm supposed to be gracious."

She came shuffling over to where I sat, still shaking against Tate.

"Tell me you forgive me?"

Tate put her arms around me and I could feel her holding me up. I slumped sideways and rested my head against her shoulder. "For what?"

"For being so ugly and so wicked."

"I forgive you," I said, and the words felt pointless and

unnecessary. Her teeth didn't bother me much anymore and the only thing I had to forgive were the marks on Emma's arms.

The little pink princess came skipping across the grave-yard, flapping her star wand and leading Roswell by the hand.

The twins were right behind them. Drew was carrying Natalie, who slept with her head against his shoulder. The white dress was looking pretty dismal, fraying at the bottom and covered in mud. Her hair was snarled and stuck up in back like a fuzzy animal's. Danny was carrying the revenant, who didn't snuggle against his shoulder. It didn't do any-thing.

"You're losing blood," the Morrigan said, examining my hand.

I looked down at myself. The front of my jacket was dark and it was all over everything.

The Morrigan trotted away and came back again with Janice, who took a bottle out of her coat and offered it to me. It was one of the ones from the pharmacy room, brown glass, sealed with wax. "You'll need to drink this."

She put the bottle to her mouth and bit the seal. Then she peeled away the wax and held it out. I drank it in gulps. It tasted hot, and I felt breathless and light-headed but better. I felt unbelievably tired.

Janice was already opening another jar, scooping out a

lumpy paste and packing it into the cut on my hand. It burned for one excruciating second and then went numb.

I leaned harder against Tate, trying to stop my vision from blurring.

"What does this mean for Gentry?" I asked the Morrigan, glancing over at the Lady, who lay on the ground by the crypt.

The Morrigan sat down next to me. She cupped my hand in both of hers, then folded it closed.

"That the bad things will stop because I don't steal children and I don't burn churches."

"What does that mean for the town, though? Will the town stop being so good?"

The Morrigan shrugged and stood up, looking off toward the trees. "Has it ever been good in your lifetime?"

I shook my head. "Not really. Not since before I was born."

"Maybe it never was."

I nodded and looked out at all the headstones in the unconsecrated corner, marking the graves of the replacements who hadn't lasted and hadn't been revived by the Morrigan.

"Goodbye," she said.

When I didn't say it back, she rested her hand on the top of my head. The weight was strange and gentle. "I love you," she said. "And when I tell you goodbye, I don't mean forever or for long. Just that I'm going home now, and so are you."

She bent and picked up her doll, shaking some of the dirt off it and looking strangely adult. Then she crossed to the entrance to the crypt and stood over the Lady.

The fragile beauty was gone. Her face had turned a pale, chalky yellow and her veins showed black through her skin. Her eyes looked shocked and bloody.

"Ugly, sorry thing." The Morrigan shook her head.

She waved for the dead girls and they came in a whispering pack, lifting the Lady's body, dragging her away through the mud in the direction of Orchard and the slag heap.

It came to me in a weak, dreamy way that birds were singing somewhere. The light was changing, getting warmer. The sky was pale and the horizon was starting to glow red. It had been weeks since we'd seen a sunrise.

We didn't talk, just wound our way back through the headstones toward the street. Roswell and Danny tried once or twice to bicker over little things, but nothing took. Natalie still slept against Drew's shoulder.

I stumbled into Tate and was startled to find that she was real and solid. She put her arm around me. The pain in my hand was faint. The graveyard seemed almost transparent, like I was dreaming it and dreaming the six of us and the narrow, muddy path.

CHAPTER 31

DAYBREAK

On Concord Street, the porch light was still on, glowing in the weak dawn light. We climbed the front steps in a little huddle, like we were reluctant to be too far away from each other.

I tried the knob, but it was locked, and I had to lean against the porch railing for a second to stop the world from spinning. Then I pushed myself away and rang the bell.

When Emma opened the door, she took one look at me and threw herself into my arms. I was bloody, covered in mud. It was all over everything, drying on my coat, streaking her face and hands, and she didn't let go. She looked like she'd been crying for a year.

Inside, my dad was pacing the kitchen, raking his hands through his hair. My mom sat patiently at the table, clasping her hands on the tablecloth like she was waiting for him to stop.

When we gathered in the doorway, they both looked up.

My dad's expression was a mix of shock, confusion, and relief but mostly relief. My mom looked like she was about to pass out, and I was more aware than ever of how gory I was. Emma clutched my arm and beside me, Tate and the twins looked like something out of a war documentary. Roswell was the only one relatively unscathed. His expression was alert and quizzical, like he'd gotten there by accident.

My dad stood on the other side of the table, staring at me. At all of us. "Are you badly hurt? Do you need to go to the hospital?" His voice was husky and I smelled the sharp, rusty smell of anxiety.

I shook my head, leaning forward and bracing my good hand on the table. "Some of the blood's not mine."

He nodded and passed a hand over his eyes.

My mom was staring at Natalie, who was awake now, holding Drew around the neck and looking dazedly around the kitchen. My mom went to her, taking Natalie's face in her hands, staring into her eyes.

Then she let Natalie go and turned to me. "You did this? You took her back?"

I didn't answer. It hadn't been me. Or at least, not by myself.

"You went down there just to bring her back?"

I nodded. The next question was going to be, *Why did you do something so incredibly dangerous?* or, *What made an insane risk seem like a good idea?* And I didn't want to talk about that part. The reality of how indifferent I'd been to the world, how much I'd stopped caring in the weeks before meeting the Morrigan was just starting to sink in.

I opened my mouth to cut her off, but the truth must have been there on my face because she didn't wait for an answer. She crossed the kitchen and hugged me, wrapping her arms around my neck. "You came back," she whispered. "You could have disappeared forever, but you came back."

It felt weird to be standing in the kitchen, hugging her. She wasn't the kind of person who cried or hugged, but she didn't let go.

"It was a brave thing," she whispered, clutching the back of my jacket. "A very brave thing."

If I was honest with myself, I hadn't been particularly brave. I'd just done the dirty work and the desperate things and then closed my eyes and hoped for something to work out. That wasn't being brave. But it was nice to know that she thought so.

I went up to the bathroom and washed off the worst of the dirt and the blood. There were still claw marks all over my neck and down one side of my face, but the gash in my hand was already closing, the edges drawn together by the power of Janice's green paste. If it kept healing, it would be gone in another few hours.

In the mirror, my reflection looked white and exhausted, half dead, but my eyes were brown instead of black, and half dead was still more than barely alive.

Emma was waiting in the hall when I opened the door. Her shirt was streaked with dirt and the dark plummy smears of my blood. For a second, we just stood in the upstairs hallway, looking at each other. Her face was exhausted.

"What did she say to you?" she asked, draping my arm around her shoulders so that I was hugging her.

I pulled her against my chest and thought about what my mom had said, this thing that was so mysterious and so rare. "That she was glad I came back. She hadn't thought I'd come back."

"What she meant is that she loves you."

"I know."

Emma smiled. "I do too. But you knew that."

That made me smile too and I squeezed her so hard she yelped. "Always, crazy. Always."

CHAPTER 32

ONE OF US

Monday was as normal as it could be under the circumstances. Which is to say, pretty normal. The innate ability of Gentry was to let things go right back to the way they'd been.

In the cafeteria, people were more subdued than usual, and Alice had the same raw look that Tate had had the day of Natalie's funeral. People didn't avoid Alice the way they'd avoided Tate, but her usual circle of friends wasn't so friendly. I got the feeling that it was mostly by choice. She and Zoe clung to each other, like they could close the gap Jenna had left. Everyone else was outside it.

Jenna's funeral had been on Saturday. I hadn't gone, but for once, the idea didn't make me feel lonely or outside of things. I would go to the cemetery some time and stand in the unconsecrated corner and look at her grave because she was someone I'd known. She was part of the town and so was I.

As I watched, Tate came shoving her way toward me

371

through the lunch crowd. It was cold out but sunny, and the light from the windows played on her face. It lit up her hair in a way that no one else could see, but that didn't matter because I could see it, and I liked it.

"What are you looking at?" Roswell said, turning to follow my gaze.

The lights were buzzing and the sound didn't really bother me. It was just the sound of the school, the sound I heard when I was knocking around out in the world.

I smiled and could feel myself going red. "Tate."

Roswell nodded, looking very serious. "Well, as far as forgiving you goes, saving her sister's got to help, but you'll probably have to spend some time together if you actually want to date her."

When Tate reached us, I took hold of her hand and she let me, looking stern and ferocious, like she was trying not to smile.

After school, she walked me home. I'd never been very comfortable inviting people over, and it was kind of novel to ask her if she wanted to come in. She let me take her jacket, and then we started up the stairs to my room.

"Keep your door open," said Emma, leaning out of the family room. She was giving Janice lessons in seed germination, which seemed a little misguided, considering that the House of Mayhem had no natural light.

I hadn't heard anything from the Morrigan, but Janice had been over every day, just like always, and I was tempted to admit that maybe she and Emma truly were friends, no strings attached.

I raised my eyebrows at Emma. "Are you serious?"

She smiled. "No. But I'm channeling Dad, and if he finds out you took a girl upstairs unchaperoned, he'll flip."

Tate followed me up to my room. She looked around at the scattered homework assignments and the clothes. "You're way messier than I thought you'd be."

My bass was on the floor in its open case. I'd been playing all weekend, trying to capture the sound of my thoughts, the things I'd felt when I lay in the crypt, cold and dazed and smiling. Sometimes I even got close, but after my show with Rasputin, it seemed weird to play alone. I still liked the feeling of the strings under my fingers, the deep tones easing out of my headphones, but the bass was only one sound, and the stories would be better with a band.

I shrugged and went over to the bed. "There's a whole array of skills I do not have, bedroom organization being one of them."

"At least you're not a time waster," Tate said, raising her eyebrows and folding her arms over her chest. "Straight for the bed. Is this your way of saying I owe you a make-out session?"

I shook my head, leaning across the bed and pushing the window up.

After a second, Tate followed me out onto the roof. "I would have anyway. But not because I owe you."

We sat on the roof, looking out at the street, and I put my arm around her. "How is it, having Natalie back?"

Tate laughed, shaking her head. Then she stopped and took a deep breath. "It's wonderful, and it's scary. I never realized it, but I kind of got used to not having her. She changed, even in just a couple months."

I nodded, reminded eerily of my mother and of all the ways that life underground could change someone.

"It'll be okay," I told Tate, not because I thought Natalie would ever go back to exactly the same person she'd been before, but because whatever happened now, at least she would be herself.

Tate leaned over and kissed me. "You did good," she said. "I mean, I thought you were totally going to screw it up or else not even try."

"Because I was such a dick about it?"

She sighed and rested her head on my shoulder. "I just figured you'd do whatever it took not to get involved. I mean, it's what people do."

"I *did* try not to get involved."

"Maybe, but you came through in the end. When it counted."

There was a whole sprawling world underneath us, filled with ugly, vicious, beautiful people. The line between the two places was thin, hardly a separation, and both ran on pain and blood and fear and death and joy and music.

But for now, the sunset was enough.

I reached for Tate, feeling for the warmth of her hand, and linked my fingers through hers. The only thing that mattered was the weight of her head on my shoulder.

Our lives were limitless and unknowable, not perfect, but ours. This was life in Gentry.

This is just what we do.

ABOUT THE AUTHOR

Brenna Yovanoff once thought she wanted to grow up
to become an editor. Although it turns out she was
mistaken, she doesn't regret her days as a slush-pile
reader or the fact that she's memorised large stretches of
The Chicago Manual of Style. Her short fiction has
appeared in *Chiaroscuro* and *Strange Horizons*. She has an
MFA in creative writing from Colorado State University
and currently lives in Denver. *The Replacement* is
her first novel.